Arlene Colombe Hiquily

Memoirs of the Frog Prince

A Novel

Marion Boyars
New York • London

Published in the United States and Great Britain in 1989 by
Marion Boyars Publishers
26 East 33rd Street, New York, NY 10016
24 Lacy Road, London SW15 1NL

Distributed in the United States by Kampmann & Co., New York

Distributed in Canada by Book Center Inc., Montreal

Distributed in Australia by Wild and Woolley, Glebe, NSW

© Arlene Colombe Hiquily, 1989

All rights reserved.
No part of this publication may be reproduced, stored in a retrieval system or transmitted in any form or by any means, electronic, mechanical, photocopying, recording or otherwise except brief extracts for the purposes of review, without prior permission of the publishers.

Any paperback edition of this book whether published simultaneously with, or subsequent to, the casebound edition is sold subject to the condition that it shall not by way of trade be lent, resold, hired out or otherwise disposed of without the publishers' consent, in any form of binding or cover other than that in which it was published.

Library of Congress Cataloging-in-Publication Data
Hiquily, Arlene Colombe.
Memoirs of the frog prince.

I. Title.
PS3558.I58M4 1988 813'.54   88-6378

British Library Cataloguing in Publication Data
Hiquily, Arlene Colombe
Memoirs of the frog prince.

I. Title
813'.54[F]

ISBN 0-7145-2888-9

All characters in this book are fictitious and are not intended to represent any actual persons living or dead.

Permission to quote from *Zen Mind, Beginner's Mind* by Shunryu Suzuki is gratefully acknowledged to Zen Center, San Francisco.

Typeset by Printit-Now Ltd., Lloyds Bank Chambers, Upton upon Severn, Worcestershire WR8 0HW, ENGLAND

Printed and bound in Great Britain by
Biddles Ltd, Guildford and King's Lynn

There is no prince without the frog

When you are you, you see things as they are, and you become one with your surroundings. There is your true self . . . You have the practice of a frog. He is a good example of our practice – when a frog becomes a frog, Zen becomes Zen. When you understand a frog through and through, you attain enlightenment . . .

Zen Mind, Beginner's Mind
by Shunryu Suzuki

These poets are going to exist! When the infinite servitude of woman shall have ended, when she will be able to live by and for herself, then, man hitherto abominable – having given her freedom, she too will be a poet. Woman will discover the unknown. Will her world be different from ours? She will discover strange, unfathomable things, repulsive, delicious. We shall take them, we shall understand them.

Arthur Rimbaud

To Martin Breese, without whose
enthusiasm and hard work this book
might never have been published.

There are two versions of the Frog Prince. One is that when the princess dropped her golden ball into the pond, the frog offered to bring it up to her, if she would let him come and live with her. The princess agreed, but when the frog dived down and brought her the ball, she grabbed it and ran back to the palace alone. As she was sitting at the table eating with the king, her father, there was a knock on the palace door and the frog was brought in. The princess didn't want to see him, but after her father heard the frog's story, he said to her, "A promise is a promise."

So the frog came to live with her. He followed her all over, even sleeping on her satin sheets. One hot afternoon, while she was taking a nap, she felt the frog's slimy skin touching her and a terrible feeling of disgust took hold of her, so she seized the frog and threw it against the wall. At that moment, a magnificent prince stood before her – the frog skin lay on the floor, like a peeled fruit. The prince had been under an evil spell, and hitting the wall had released him. Then they were married and lived happily ever after.

. . . The other version is that when the frog brought up the golden ball, the princess was to give him a kiss. The same things happen. She runs to the palace. The frog arrives. The king listens to the frog's story and says, "A promise is a promise." The servants then bring the frog in on a golden platter and place him on a table before the princess. The princess closes her eyes so as not to see this awful monster when she puts her lips on its slimy skin. But lo and behold . . . on opening her eyes, she sees before her a handsome prince released from his spell. So they got married and lived happily ever after.

In one story it is by rejection the frog becomes a prince; in the other version it is love that turns the frog into a prince.

Once in a ladies' room, Adrienne had seen scribbled in lipstick on the bathroom wall . . . There's a Prince Charming out there somewhere – you just have to kiss a lot of frogs to find him . . .

ONE : SHADOW TRADER

And Adrienne remembered that once upon a time . . .

Arthur leaned over – pulled down the gold zipper on her dress and laughed feebly. She pushed him away as the plate of spaghetti with tomato sauce splattered over his pants hitting him in the groin like the explosion of a hand grenade.

– For God's sake Arthur, she cried – You're drunk out of your mind.

He just continued to laugh, pleased to be the center of attraction. They were having dinner with Hyacinth – a painter friend (she had changed her name from Daisy as that had been too common a flower). Adrienne got up and cleaned the spaghetti worms crawling on the floor.

– You're a mess, she sighed.

Was she always doomed to be cleaning up his behaviour at every social gathering? Luckily Hyacinth had given her a belated birthday gift of a pair of green tights. Arthur put them on – made a theatrical gesture of a clown sunning himself under a spotlight, dropped his tachiste painting trousers and slithered into the snaky tights. Then he hopped around on all fours croaking . . . That was one of the beginnings of the frog prince.

When she had first met him on an island in the Baleares, he had been drunk. Why had he seemed different then? What had she expected of him? To reform him, accept him as he was?

What had she wanted him to do or be for her? To dive down into a watery unconsciousness where she was afraid to go and bring up for her those wonderful buried treasures that she had lost somewhere; that only he could give to her, muddy but once cleaned full of grail light.

Now he hopped around the room and then sat down again eating out of her plate, picking up the spaghetti worms one by one and gulping them down like some expanding bull-frog. Her only wish was that he would suddenly disappear. Could she ever open up to this extravagant side where he would take her out of herself whirling into space with no vehicle but the sheer motion of his presence landing her on unknown worlds? But each time fear held her down. She couldn't leave with him. She saw herself shedding skin after skin, her chest filled with them – old snake skins hangered into infinity . . .

He held tightly onto her hand and began kissing her neck with a wet, slobbering tongue as if he were licking her for flies.

– I need you so honeypie, aren't you my little lovey dovey?

Again she made the gesture of pushing him away as if somewhere there must be a magic wand.

– Here we go again with that sentimental shit.

She just couldn't open up to his desperate need. Never than when he whined for love was he more repulsive to her. It was like a bad child who broke all his toys and at the same time kept screaming for affection. He had once said he needed to expose himself – there were iron bands around his heart and he couldn't break them unless he was drunk. She remembered her childhood hero. Heathcliff (later she found he might be very difficult for a woman to live with) in the book *Wuthering Heights*, the family doctor had said of Hindley, Cathy's drunken brother, that instead of drinking why didn't he just hit himself over the head with a hammer and knock himself out.

Wouldn't the result be the same?

How many times had she waited for him, in how many bars, in how many cafés, parties, at friends before she could safely go home and hide herself in the bed – before he decided what was his "last drink." He was an absolutist. If there was a drop left in any bottle, he would have to finish it like the Nordic god Thor, who drank and drank from the magic horn till he almost washed all the oceans off the face of the earth. If there was any drop in any bottle he would have to gulp it down. He was insatiable. It was as if he had been denied his mother's milk as a child and he could never forgive her or for that fact any woman. He always held onto his bottle and never drank from a glass if he could help it. Adrienne had made many faux pas in the beginning that now she didn't care about, of hiding extra whiskey, beer or wine bottles on top of the piano cords, in the oven, in the dirty laundry even among her Kotex pads; but he was uncanny in sniffing them out like a pig on a truffle hunt. He complained he was under an evil spell that only she could break. Would he ever become a complete man? Was she doomed to carry around inside her this unformed fetus sucking off of her? Every drunken spell only threw him back again into her protective womb.

He would literally burn himself up to reach oblivion. Before he had come to Paris, he worked on the docks of Antwerp. Once after drinking all night in a bar, he had gone home to his hotel room and passed out – a lighted cigaret in his hand. The cigaret had fallen onto the bed and the mattress began to smoulder. The neighbours saw the smoke coming out from under the door and called the firemen who had dragged him out by his singed hair and doused him with water, while he had been dreaming he was lying on an African plain under a blazing sun. He had burnt his passport in the room. Another identity gone.

After they had come back from the Baleares, they settled in Paris. One evening they had gone out drinking, which was rare for Adrienne as she didn't drink much. Arthur referred to her as a repressed alcoholic – they had both gotten incredibly drunk. She hardly remembered getting home and falling asleep fully dressed on the bed. She had a strange dream that she was lying face down in scorching sand and around her was a low hedge of blue and yellow irises giving off tremendous heat. She opened her eyes and to her horror saw at the edge of the mattress low flower-like flames. Arthur must have taken a cigaret before he had passed out as she didn't smoke. He was lying face down. She tried to move him but couldn't. She ran into the bathroom filled a basin with water and threw it over the flames and him. The flames dribbled out but he didn't move. She rolled his dead weight nearer the wall – with his wet hair he seemed more of a drowned man. She took towels to mop the water up – moved herself into a fetal position and passed out. An hour or hours later, Adrienne had no idea of the time, she felt her hand burning and woke to find spurts of flame shooting out in volcanic craters, erupting on the whole side of the mattress.

This time she pushed Arthur violently. He shook his head and like a sea creature coming up from the deep to daylight, he focused open the film from his eyes. Immediately he saw the fire and went into action. It was as if he were back in the army giving commands under stress. (He had been in Vietnam).

– Get up, he ordered.

– There's only one fucking way to deal with this. We've got to get the mattress outside. That fire's in there for good.

The mattress weighed a ton. They got it onto the floor.

– God damn it . . . move it! – he cried.

She couldn't. The flames rose higher as they tried to drag it along the floor, caught by air currents.

– I'll run outside and find someone, she screamed.

Luckily they lived on the ground floor. It was 5am, winter and still dark. She ran into the street. It seemed as if the few stars in the sky were burning also. An alley cat brushed by her feet. Then she saw a garbage truck across the way. There were two men piling up the garbage. Their breath was smoky. One man was black.

– Quick, quick – she cried out, – I need help – there's a fire!

The two men stared at her blankly. Then the black man grumbling, slowly followed her into the house. Arthur had pushed the now flaming mattress into the hallway but couldn't get it through the door. Together the black man and he slid the burning mattress into the street. Then the black man, still grumbling, went back to the garbage truck. There was no one else in the streets. It was a deserted city with the stars now fading away in an ash colored sky. The flames had died down in the mattress and smoke was drifting upward as in a bombed-out war site.

They rushed back home, locked the door, put some old boards on the springs, threw the covers with black holes over them and fell asleep. For weeks the house smelt of rancid smoke, part of the wood floor was burnt and the carpet scorched. There was an evil smell, that clung to the room, of dark forests and abandoned cellars. The plant over the bed had burns tattooed on its leaves like stamped cattle marks of possession. But for some reason she felt very guilty, as if she had let go. For the more he abandoned himself, the more she would have to be on watch – on guard. Her role was to become more and more conscious, spying on those interior fires that might ignite in secret.

They got another mattress at the flea market, but the old

mattress lay in the gutter for over a week, till it was shoved down to the end of the street. One day though, as she was crossing in front of it, an old lady passed by and poked it with her cane – blackened stuffing, soggy and pus-like oozed out.

– Isn't it terrible the things that happen, – and she sighed and shook her head, – people probably smoking in bed. I hope there were no children around.

But there were other dawns when he came home after an all night binge and he slept endlessly into the afternoon with the shutters closed, and especially the summer days when the muslin curtains flew into phantom forms and the room smelt of funeral parlors – the sickly sweet smell of alcohol that preserved his body and of mushrooms rotting in the ground – and wearily as she moved about on tiptoe in the next room wondering about all those infinite deaths he perpetrated to become as unconscious as possible – with his mouth half-open and his eyes turned inward and glossy as if to return to the breast. If it has been said that we are human because we have memory; it was with him to blot out memory, to finally black out in a no man's land of shadowy forms and when he at last woke up, she would have to recount to him like some ancient myth what impossible feat he had accomplished in his state of oblivion.

One time he had come home so drunk he could hardly stand, weaving back and forth till he made her seasick. He had grasped the table as he sat down and a glass ashtray had fallen on the floor and broken. He had leaned over to pick up a piece and cut his hand – blood spurted out. She bandaged his hand and got him into bed with his clothes still on and he passed out. The next morning he had no recollection of why his hand was bandaged, not even when she showed him a bloody handprint on the sheet.

Or there were other days when he couldn't stand to be

reminded of the horrors of the night, when he cursed her and all those motherfuckers in this no good world and refused to remember, becoming violent if she told him what he had done, or of the nightmares buried inside him. And on those gray days she felt full of ashes, as if she also shared his hangovers.

In the beginning of the story of the Frog Prince, it is said that the prince was laid under an evil spell and only the princess could release him, but it doesn't say for what reason the spell was laid on him. What was the guilt he was expiating? Was it that he was not completely ready to be human? Did he still want to hide himself in the old evolutionary marshes, put his head under the water and float beneath the green slimy mosses; did he refuse to take the responsibility for who he was? The fairy tale gives no explanation.

She saw all those shipwrecks he performed on himself as the waves finally drove him nearer shore. He carried along tree trunks, orange crates, old doors and bottles filled with imploring messages sent from desolate beaches, and sometimes he dragged great heads of seaweed onto the shore and then abandoned all these objects to rot – leaving her to try and salvage some of the wrecks and allow them to dry.

One stormy day they didn't get up, but stayed in bed with the shutters closed and listened to the heavy footfalls of rain sloshing in the courtyard mixed with heavy rumbles of thunder. He said great kegs of beer were being shoved around in the sky and when a flash of lightning hit the room – a barrel had split and the gold light of beer poured for a moment over him – she saw his wild hair and rough beard outlined in the amber light.

And it brought her back to her childhood, to the house in Long Island where she and her sister had lain in bed playing Monopoly while snakes of rain crawled over the porch windows and outside stood a giant cedar tree, behind which hid her demon lover waiting for her, sniffing behind the trunk. She could hear his feet shuffling through the wet grass and his hot smoky breath clouding the porch window; but only twigs and fir needles could be seen above his head as his fingertips tapped on the panes and the low wind of his voice beckoned to her. But she only hugged the covers closer over her, afraid of his summons that would take her out to some place from where she might never come back.

Sometimes Arthur looked in the mirror but he couldn't see his face. It was then he realized he might be a vampire, not one of those old fashioned kind that lived off blood, but a parasite living on alcohol, living off others. He did not know who he was – an outsider, a voyeur who watched life through a keyhole, that was why he couldn't be alone – when he was alone he ceased to exist. He had to people his solitude with images and characters like a television set that had to be before him night and day even if the scenes turned into nightmares – it was better than being alone. It was on these days, when the images seemed to unroll behind the shades of his eyes, that Adrienne wilted under the captured static of his stare. She felt dry as if a thin film of dust was settling in the corners of her heart and she became invisible because there was no one by to observe her. It was a landscape of mist, the days of a no man's land where there was no boundary to their world. An early twilight room of empty sucked-out bottles, ashtrays filled with mangled cigaret butts, dirty socks, stained underwear, splotches where wine had dried like blood, greasy plates with half chewed bones, the heavy odorous smell of sperm and over it all the leaden chloroform smell of alcohol. It was a barren land out of which emerged the shadow trader.

The shadow trader arrived at dusk. He slipped out from a

corner of the room with rolled up shadows under his arm like scrolls. He had all sizes of shadows, from babies to adults. He was always looking for the shadows of people who felt they no longer existed. He snapped up the shadows of people who sat motionless watching endless television, or those passive spectators in movie houses sitting up upright like Peruvian mummies. Suddenly he'd snap on his flashlight in the darkened halls so the spectator would think it was the usher as he registered the shadow on his scroll. Or in bars, he'd take the measure from behind people sitting on the bar stools, their frozen ice-cube-eyes slowly dripping into their glasses. He needed all these shadows to bury in the foundations of buildings. His was an ancient trade. In the early days, the shadow traders had hunted for new born babies or virgins – these bloody sacrifices strengthened the foundations of a new building – then with a change in customs they had gone in for roosters and cats, and now the shadow trader had to be happy with just shadows. He put them in the new structures of supermarkets, prisons, insane asylums, hospitals, schools etc. But there was only one catch – whoever's shadow was buried in the building would die at the structure's inauguration, so he had to sneak up unaware to trace the shadow on one of his shades. The shadow trader was a recurrent nightmare with Arthur. On days of bright sunlight he always tried to walk in the shade.

There were other days though, when a sense of power would come over him. Could he really be Superman or Batman and fly on membrane wings over building antennas as the advertised Kraft moon coated the windows with orange melted cheese; or would he only fall – his wings turn into an ordinary cloak, like the somnambulist that crawls slowly along the rooftop, his metallic eyes pried open guarding their precious luminous liquid – but wait – his mother's voice calls him – emptying his balanced eyes – and in a long leap he feels himself splashing over the pavement.

She knew why it was when he got drunk he always got beaten up, thrown down, cursed and spat on. It was because of the complete exposure of himself – all his defenses were down. He was so completely open, nobody could take it. His was a betrayal of the great animal law that says every beast must always at every moment be on guard and defend itself. The animal must hide in a hole, use mimicry, claws, growl, hold onto its territory. But he, he didn't care about holding on to anything – money, objects, all disappeared from his hands. All he wanted to do was drink and vibrate with love potions poured down the throat of humanity. He offended the great law that says everything must be preyed upon and eaten.

For we all take hostages inside ourselves to protect us from the brute and with the shock of suddenly being assaulted, using the innocent as a barrier; or if someone should surprise us in our untouched areas, we suffocate or attack the creature and cover the wounds with slabs of Kotex to make believe the blood is flowing in a monthly natural cycle while we are busy closing the doors, the windows and covering the womb and prick with rubber insulation. Nothing must come unexpected . . . the guest should telephone or write. Anything that comes unannounced we capture like game. The goldfish in its aquarium is reassuring, no pheasant flaps through a city window without being eaten. Even our grain is carefully stored in separate sacks in the cellar. Only indiscriminate mice gnaw at the bags, slowly sifting the bound grain into anonymous piles – where old women washing clothes in the basement steal a few grains for the birds and still remember to leave their left-over meat for the threatening starved cats locked outside – hiding in torn down deserted lots.

He had no sense of possession. Money, clothes, belongings, he scattered around him like worn-out carcasses. In all the places he had lived, he had left parts of himself trailing behind like old snake skins. Money that people counted in secret and hid in mattresses, shoes, cupboards, he threw away in his Eldorado of drinking – the dream of money changed into alchemical gold . . . on a terrace at sunset with the ruddy glow of alcohol gilded into a Midas palace of golden people holding golden liquid. He lived in a golden haze so completely abandoned that he depended on the complete stranger like a blind man in the metro to let him through the door.

He actually belonged to that body of *clochards* who accepted no commodities. She had once seen a *clochard* sitting on a bench in a square – a red and white lampshade on his head, his eyes burnt-out bulbs. He wore three coats, one on top of the other like a set of Russian dolls. At his feet stood a suitcase tied with rope and a parked baby carriage filled with empty bottles. He was reading last year's newspaper. Later, on a rainy day in the park, she had passed an old man on a bench sitting under a torn umbrella and in a tree nearby a few wet birds huddled under a large leaf.

Then there was an old woman who lived in the neighborhood who dragged a leash tied to an empty dog collar, but there was no dog attached. What was she waiting for? Waiting for her dead or lost dog to continue to give her at the curbstone the comforting sound of piss? And that drunken *clochard* asleep on torn newspapers over a warm pavement grille – his hand half-open, clenched in nailed agony – still grasping his invisible bottle that had long since rolled into the gutter.

But the most poignant scene was a little scenario she had come across in a deserted lot; a rusty frying pan filled with water, a yellow plastic basin with an empty sardine can in it, a broken mirror, a black crushed hat, one sock stuck in the mud, a few empty wine bottles and a soggy book, pages scattered around with the title *The Invisible Man*.

These were people who had no walls for their universe. When they sat on park benches or lay in the streets – they saw their walls opening into space. They belonged to the same race as the wandering saints who lived in caves or forests. What was the degree of their holiness? Was it their utter acceptance or unacceptance of life? But they still had one more step to make until the drunkard fell down screaming in the gutter with no final support – until he was finally beaten, humiliated, rejected, broken, cursed, ready for his crucifixion – could he finally come to terms. It was only at that ultimate moment that God the mother – not the father – could come down to him, pick him up and give him her breast of endless liquid to suck.

It was only by learning to integrate into the world that one learned to defend oneself and adapt that special mimicry that fitted one best. There were even flies that imitated bird shit to escape from being eaten. There was no animal in the kingdom which left itself completely open except for the servant – dog. The cat still had its claws of independence.

One night after a drunken scene, they were sitting on the bed, Arthur suddenly pulled out his upper plate of false teeth and held it in the palm of his hand. Adrienne had now been with him over two years but she had never known about this. His lip fell over his gum and he lisped . . .

– See, I'm no longer the handsome young man you thought I was – His gum was pink and protruding like a frog's – How do you like me now?

It was as if the business of age and corruption had prematurely begun their work. She remembered a picture of Artaud before his death – the lizard lips, all his teeth gone from too many shock treatments.

– I was in a fight when I was sixteen, the guy nailed me

against a fence and punched me six times in the mouth . . . some teeth fell out and the rest abscessed.

Adrienne tried to think about all the things she'd heard on teeth. The oddest things ran through her mind . . . A day before his death Rimbaud had dictated to his sister – "Maritime Co. Item . . . 1 tooth only . . . Item . . . 2 teeth."

Nietzche had gone crazy watching a dead donkey with wormy eyes, its yellowed teeth hanging from rotted gums and its mouth full of flies. Christ had bent down before a decaying donkey and praised its beautiful teeth. The women in the old ladies' home always put their false teeth in a glass of water before they went to bed. Poe had written in *Bernice* how the hero had carried around thirty-two small white teeth taken from the tomb – "All these teeth are ideas". The psychiatrist said a dream of falling teeth could mean loss of sexual energy, masturbation or a death wish. In a dream book, falling teeth indicated the death of a parent or a friend. "But Grandma, what beautiful teeth you have," cried Red Riding Hood to the wolf – "With the jawbone of an ass I can slay a thousand men and from the hollow place that was in the jaw, out came water". And Jason sowed the dragon's teeth and up sprang a crop of strong armed men. The Talmud said, "A tooth for a tooth," but "He," replied to turn the other cheek . . .

Suddenly it felt as if everything was illusion before her and she could imagine why monks sat in graveyards to meditate. How was it if one lifted the cover of flesh to see the tripe and the bowels, or of the unglorified pictures of cunt and prick dissected in a medical book. Could one go beyond illusion to find something? Like in the theater, to go behind the backdrop to the ribs of the stage – ladders, canvas, ropes, skeletons of scaffolding. The sense of unreality comes with the painted appearance of scenery, the sky, the clouds, the pines and the white swan being dragged along the stage on pulleys to the lamenting of trumpets and cymbals in the last act of *Lohengrin*. Is it finally the third act when the backdrop's hung and the curtains come down; or are there other sets helter skelter backstage – bits of painted sea, a crescent moon on a rope, a gray cardboard rock? After all is there anything behind the scene in a rightful natural order? And those orange cliffs – this seagull maybe pulled up by a string. Will it all peel off like old paint in an autumnal transformation to finally disappear and become a blank white page of winter?

– Now do you love me? – he whined and he drew her closer to kiss her with his pink sticky gums. He opened her blouse and started sucking on her nipple.

Then she realized what he was asking was not just love, or love me for myself – No he wanted to be loved for more than himself. He wanted a love that went behind all appearances, behind this Hollywood dream of perfect teeth, a straight nose, shiny angel hair. He wanted a love that embraced him whether he was covered with vomit, piss, or shit. A love that went right back to the cradle when the mother took the baby who had been sick over itself in her arms and crooned lovingly over him. There *were* people who loved each other with – piles, hernias, hanging breasts, flabby pricks, no teeth, who were bald, hunchbacked, cross-eyed . . . But what he was asking was to be swallowed whole – what he wanted was a total love that consumed one the closer one got to him. He was asking for an abandonment that no human person would ever be capable of giving him – to dissolve into someone. What he was really looking for was actually only to be realized in Christ, perhaps the only one who would be able to quench his terrible thirst.

That night she dreamed a dentist was drilling her tooth – pus oozed out . . .

– Look it's all black, disgusting – the dentist said.

Suddenly she was sitting on a bench in a train station. She saw a sign lit up by electric lights saying – 12 o'clock – BLACK IS BEAUTIFUL – then three black men came and sat down beside her. One was young with bushy hair, another wore sunglasses, an overcoat and a scarf, and the third had long hair and a beard.

– I'm so glad to have found you – she said. I thought we'd miss each other.

– No – they chorused – We've been waiting for you.

The man with the overcoat rose and came over to her. He took off his white silk scarf and put it around her neck. He smiled and then they all got up and went out through the gate onto the train, still staring at her . . . leaving the train door open.

In the morning she looked at Arthur. He was sleeping heavily. No signs that the teeth weren't his real teeth. He was the same, only there was some little door in the back of her mind she wanted to lock and forget about.

Arthur's dream of going out had to do with violent emotions. Drinking heavily in smoky jazz bars and dancing orgiastically till the sweat poured down his face, beating out heavy rhythms on the wooden bar, or punching someone so he could finally get beaten up. One night some friends brought him home with his eyelid cut open and his lip swollen, explaining he had fallen in the gutter and had been grazed by a car. In reality, he had been beaten up at a bar. He loved to sit in Arab cafés shuffling the sawdust – those Arabs who no longer believed in Mohammed but believed in Alcohol – who drank until their eyes had films of sand shadowing across their pupils, watching a crescent moon through the bar window shining on the steel skeletons of the new buildings which they had just finished cementing or lifting with iron cranes. Now their tired used hands, again new born, held foamy glasses and they shuffled the sawdust as if saved sand dunes were still pouring out of brittle hour-glass shoes. Or Arthur would stand in alleys, or sit on curbstones drinking with *clochards*. When he went out to drink, he never came home till he could find nobody left to drink with.

Adrienne's idea of going out was gentle. It would be in a sanatorium like in *The Magic Mountain* under a feather quilt watching the snowflakes fall behind glass panes as purple mist like silk wrapping paper covered the mountains; or stretched out on hot sand gazing at a blue-eyed sea with strong arms curled around her like a peaceful child with its father. If only he and she could meet inside a Rousseau painting lying down next to a silent lion, the full moon slipping into the darkened landscape; but there was still the red snake hanging above, watching them from a branch. One had to begin with the flesh turning its red key in the dark lock – trying to open forbidden doors.

Then some days there would be endless scenes – once he'd left her in a rage over what she couldn't remember except that he had been pretty drunk. Two days had passed and he still hadn't come back. She began to feel this need for him again. *He* was like her drug or drink; it was as if she was going through withdrawal symptoms when she couldn't be near him. Her tongue became dry, her heart began to beat faster, twitches shot up around her eyes and lips. Violent pains constricted her heart. She had a terrible desire to scream. She had to lie on the bed and stuff the end of the pillow in her mouth. She wanted to cry out his name . . . Every souvenir of him became magnified and full of his presence – a cigaret butt left forgotten on the table, a scorched hole in the tablecloth, an unwashed beer glass with a pale sea foam stain around the rim, a piece of matchstick he had used to clean his nails, a button on the floor fallen off his shirt – a slipper half sticking out from under the bed. It was almost enough to give her convulsions. She had to run out; find him.

She had a telephone number of a friend where he might be. She went into the neighborhood café. In the phone booth, was prophetically written in red – I AM A DRINKARD. She dialed the number – waited – Sorry wrong number. She tried another. There was no answer. Another combination . . . a busy signal. She tried again. A man's voice answered. Her heart began to beat so fast she could hardly speak, – Sorry, there's no one here by that name – Then again . . . You have the wrong number – and she saw herself as an antique plaster bust of a woman without arms, a wreath of white roses on her head, resting on a pedestal in a glassed phone booth – the receiver off the hook, hanging down by a black snake wire and a voice repeating . . . Wrong number . . . Wrong number . . . Wrong number . . .

At that moment an old man knocked on the door. He stammered,

– Can you tell me where Lot Street is?

– I never heard of it – she cried loudly, running out of the booth.

He came home that night very late. He was pale, blood over his eye, his coat torn. Their love-making was wild, passionate as they clung to one another on their bed raft that led out into an ocean where there were no landmarks to lead them to a stable port.

TWO :   DISSECTION

One afternoon, Arthur was sitting outside a café. It was an autumn day and leaves were falling onto the table . . . leaves the color of beer. He smiled. All his metaphors were now related to alcohol . . . a wine-red sunset. A little further up the street, he saw a pile of newspapers half covering an old *clochard*. He was lying by a large tree which had a crude heart carved on its bark and before him Arthur saw the chalked irregular heart in his class in med school . . .

. . . Professor Gunther drew a chalked imperfect heart on the blackboard. There was the human heart diagrammed and bound. He was sitting on a hard wooden bench in the back of the room. Label the left ventricle, let the blood run through the veins and arteries; but there's always a partition between the left and right side. Under his shirt, he felt his heart beating, even dripping blood like grains of sand. The Professor was probing into hearts, lifting the skin and squeezing the blood – heart and flower organs. He looked around the class. You could label the heart on the blackboard, but how about in the classroom? Roddy sitting next to him, he could bet, was thinking of the student nurse he was going to fuck tonight. He could see her naked with no face, then suddenly she became distorted as in a medical drawing of organs. How about it "Prof" Roddy with your red face and pudgy hands – get up in front of the class and show us the organs of a woman – her cunt, her breasts, her thighs but no face . . . what's the difference? Then he remembered Liza and went pale. She'd left him for Hank, his so-called best friend, the thing you always read about in books but never really happened to you. He clenched his fists; he had to get over her. There was that girl, Enid, who sat in the front row, she reminded him of her; but did he really want to know her and get caught up in all that shit again? The thought of Liza still made him want to puke.

Then he saw Professor Joris, his psychology teacher, with narrowed blue eyes under steel-rimmed glasses clipping the nerves of the unconscious, labelling the mind with its hundreds of rooms - some uninhabited, some empty with no windows or doors, and some rooms with holes in them where birds and bats flew in and out. And the hidden closets – unused attics with old memories buried in rotting trunks. His nerves were raw, on edge. This afternoon he was going to assist at his first dissection down in the basement. Before he'd only dissected frogs . . . there were the frogs swimming in an enormous aquarium – their eyes bulging behind the glass and he saw himself taking the net – which frog would it be? Silly as it seemed to others, it was always a painful choice. A few frogs seemed to know and hid under the stones all huddled together. One had its pale chest pressed against the glass, its throat throbbing. He closed his eyes and stuck the net blindly into the water. He heard a thrashing sound and there was a frog caught in the tiny netted shroud. He grasped the slimy frog under its webbed arms. He could hear the little heart going . . . pit a pat . . . pit a pat . . . Its froggy eyes looking (imploringly?) now that was going too far . . . white belly slightly swelled. He dumped it into a formaldehyde jar and closed the lid. The frog jumped up and down for a few seconds and fell backwards – its arms and legs quivering – then it was still, a jellied film forming over its aggie eyes. He waited, then lifted the limp frog out of the jar, laid it on its back on a wooden plank and stretched out the arms with its incredible five green fingers, pinning them down – a crucified frog – its fine curved lips in a slightly opened grimace. He took a pair of thin scissors and delicately slit the white skin from the throat to its belly. The greenish skin on the side was slightly freckled. Underneath the first skin, there was another fine plastic layer like a glass pane holding all the organs in place. He cut the transparent covering and there was the tiny heart still faintly throbbing, – intestines threaded like pink beads – all neatly laid out on the plank. Following the instructions, he gave it the Galvani treatment of electro-shock and the frog's legs suddenly convulsed like a child's mechanical toy left in disuse that has suddenly been touched. Soon the frog was only left in its bits and pieces . . .

"The frog is a Batrocien . . . the circulation is incomplete because the two bloods mix in the ventricle. The temperature lowers in winter and rises in the summer. The circulation follows the variations of the exterior atmosphere . . ."

He felt a poke on his arm. Roddy leaned his red face toward him.

– Hey look – and he showed a sketch of a headless woman being fucked by a headless man. Arthur handed the drawing back silently and looked down at his desk. Someone had cut an uneven heart in the wood. He remembered Liza had always worn a small gold heart around her neck. There was a stir. The class was over. It was raining and the gray windows were dripping. Suddenly he thought of his nightmare of the night before. He had seen himself in a coffin filled with old newspapers, his body disintegrating and the juices running through the coffin sudsing over the floor. He really was in a state about this dissection. It brought him back to the time he'd been about nine. When his father owned a bar in the country just before they'd moved to Atlantic City. It had been a fall day and he'd gone for a walk. The road was deserted. The weather was bad, it had started to pour and a whopping storm had blown up. He had stopped by an old cemetery when a flash of lightning struck a tree by a gravestone. The gravestone broke in half, the earth turned over and out stood something like a thigh bone. In that split second he'd thought – that was once a human being – a man, a woman, a child. It came to him those bones moldering in the graveyard could happen to everyone – his mother, father, himself. It was his first realization of death. He ran home in the pouring rain. When he got back, he had developed a high fever and was very sick for a week. It was then he had decided to be a doctor. Yes he'd cure people – keep them from dying as long a possible. Now he saw just how little a doctor could do.

Jesus, he'd better get hold of himself. He got up. There was no one in the classroom. On the blackboard the heart had been half erased. He walked downstairs to the lunchroom. He saw Enid talking to a few girls. She looked pale but perhaps that was his imagination. He looked over the crowded tables and saw Roddy chewing vigorously on his food. No fucking thing bothered him. He wouldn't have any doubts even if he was biting into an arm. He went to get his tray of food and squeezed next to him.

– Remember, when you cut up the corpse, it's only a piece of meat, Roddy joked.

Arthur felt queasy.

Roddy continued – Shut your mind, don't think what you're doing. It's just a rotting piece of flesh.

Could you go in and cut up some man or woman without thinking about them? He got up, left his food and went into the study room. Somehow he felt something would be decided today. Would he ever have the guts to be a doctor – to be objective, or whatever the hell that meant?

The large clock over the blackboard ticked loudly. It was one o'clock. Time to go. He went into the hall. The class was beginning to assemble. Professor Gunther had gone to get the medical instruments and flashlights. The stairs to the basement had no light.

– Here we go to someone's funeral. Roddy jeered. Guess if it's a man or woman's insides spread on the table. No one laughed.

Professor Gunther came into the hall holding a flickering flashlight, distributing the others. The light was very orange, lighting the shiny instruments into inquisition weapons. They filed down the worn stone steps, Ku-Klux Klan shadows hooding the damp walls. When they got to the basement, a sickening smell of formaldehyde filled the air. Indistinctly he could make out two forms lying on cement slabs. Careful, he told himself. remember when you are dead you no longer belong to the kingdom of flesh. Now he could see the first corpse. It was an old man.

Professor Gunther was saying – Just in case you're interested, this man – and he patted the corpse familiarly on the chest – was found dead in the street – according to the autopsy, he had choked on his own vomit – which is very common with alcoholics who pass out and don't expectorate.

The corpse was greenish. The pale eyes with brown flecks, open-staring nowhere, the throat had been cut open and the red tube of his oesophagus exposed . . . a tag tied around his wrist. Here was a package all ready to be shipped out. Enid was in the back. Her thin aquiline nose quivering, her hands clasped together. Professor Gunther had turned to the next slab. It was a middle-aged woman. Her breasts were long and flabby. The hair between her legs – worn like a used rug – the mouth open and the dyed hair black at the roots. Her stomach had already been opened and purple intestines lay exposed.

– This was a prostitute who died in a hotel – people with no relatives, no one to claim them, or with no known identity can be used for dissection purposes – continued Professor Gunther. Suddenly Arthur covered his mouth with his hand, he felt he wanted to puke. The Professor turned toward him motioning to one of the students to take over and took him by the arm.

– Go outside, my boy (Enid was watching) lots of people get sick. Don't worry you'll get used to it.

He ran upstairs and out into the street. He went into a bar, took a few drinks and went home.

When he came to his class the next day, he found a note saying Professor Gunther wanted to see him in his office.

– Step in . . . step in, my boy. Sit down. Now tell me is anything bothering you? Your academic work except for English hasn't been up to par and you've been coming to classes at very irregular hours. I've been talking your case over with Dean Garner and we've decided it would be better if you took some time off to adjust yourself. Are you sure medicine is the field you're interested in? We've checked up on your aptitude test and of course my boy, it takes all types to make this world. You may have, let us say, more the subjective temperament. You did quite well in literature. Think over what I am saying and let me know your decision. Professor Gunther smiled encouragingly and patted him on the back.

So this was the tactful admission of how he was typed. He went to the locker room, took out his few belongings, there was still a half bottle of scotch, and walked out. There was the end of one dream. Finished with Liza, school. Enid was out. It was then he had signed up for Vietnam and what he had been through made the dissection seem like a picnic . . .

Everything focused again when the waiter tapped him on the shoulder.

A small crescent moon had risen timidly in the sky.

The *clochard* got up from under his old newspapers, picked up an empty wine bottle and walked away . . .

THREE :   ISLAND

Adrienne was at home cleaning up. There were times when her spirit craved the paintings of Vermeer – white lace tablecloths, fruit that looked as if it had been polished, cupboards neatly arranged with china, women big with child smiling like the Mona Lisa at their interior mystery with their transparent skin, sewing tiny silk caps by a fireplace where every trace of ash had been scrubbed as it fell and the late sun dripping like molten butter on the silver trays. She longed to iron, scrub, sew, to take away this awful passivity she had in this life with him – the stained rugs and curtains, the dirty handprints on the wall, and this odor of alcohol that hung over everything. She looked at the photo on the mantelpiece: there they were in bathing suits on the beach, the water in back of them. He was holding her around the waist, together on the Balearic Island in their first days of meeting . . .

But in its few tourist years, the Balearic Island had changed its gray monkish landscape to a worldly scene of imported labels on garments sewn with fancy button hotels. The old trimmings of pine had brightened into an artificial green and even the silken water seemed dyed a brighter blue as if to keep the venerable white foam far distant. But in the mornings before the prop men and waiters woke, dawn was hung with catarrh and the breath of rotted vegetation. Then from inhaling tourist smoke and car exhaust, the island paled – cancerous cells of new houses multiplied in uneven rhythms and plaster columns grafted to the land. Still, though, like the false hope held by dying patients, there were again unbelievable days of peace when the island's blue sea eyes looked inward calm and limpid.

... and she saw again Arthur's eyes, magnified behind his mask of glass, swimming towards her in the translucent sea. She had been playing with a yellow beach ball in the water, but as she swam after it the waves always pushed the ball farther out. Then Arthur had come toward her, browned like a figurehead fallen off a ship – his trunk thrust ahead against the waves, but as to his feet there was no telling if they were webbed, a fish tail or ended in snake skins – they sank behind him. His trunk was propelled forward by an underwater motion. He glided through the small waves with amazing speed and with a few strokes caught the yellow ball. What was her surprise to see green webbed fins behind him, till she realised he was wearing flippers.

– I'll give you the ball – he smiled lifting his mask – If you invite me home.

She laughed – Sure, just give me the ball and I'll put you up.

He threw her the ball. She caught it, wading out of the water, waved and walked along the beach to the house. She thought of Rod. He had been gone now over six months. He had left her after five years to go back to the States and then had found someone else. She thought of the last time she had heard from him. He had arranged to call her from a friend's house. She remembered looking out the window at the blue sky, waiting for waves of sound to phone through. She wondered how he'd find his family, his childhood? Would it be lying lightly after so many years like autumn leaves, or had his childhood gone underground and hardened and would he have to dig it up with a rusty shovel from some cellar or backyard? His call was an hour late. There was his voice thin . . . far away . . . She couldn't follow . . . How are you . . . fine . . . Having more downs than ups. I've been eating so much I have a large gut ... I found an old friend ... I'll stay awhile ... That was all. A formal American voice. Maybe it really wasn't Rod on the phone, but the robot who was asked to stay home and take messages while the master went out.

– You sound so far away ... distant – she murmured.

– I'll write next week – he replied and hung up. But he never did. He had once said that love also included betrayal. It was a death, but with no resurrection.

Yes – betrayal had come in a great storm sweeping the leaves from their tree, leaving the branches bare and birds no longer nested for fear of cats. Under that once – green tree, they had kissed years ago in a foaming sunrise of hysterical screaming birds. But since then the tree had been abandoned, its branches hung with confetti and torn strips of posters. It was now a manmade tampered landscape – as unnatural as are certain chosen trees beaten by Japanese gardeners with corrective iron bars dwarfing the sensitive trunk; until little by little their secret raptures with no leaves to hide their nudity were pressed inside the mold of more forceful arms, and hugged against anonymous trunks where these same stunted gestures repeated in miniature faithful copies.

As she dug her toes in the wet sand, she recalled her dream of the night before. She and Rod were walking along a canal. He had just told her he was going to marry the "other" girl. A red wool child's cap hugged his head and his mouth was round and flayed. And she had said after all these years what about me? He took her arm and led her into a hallway of abandoned toys. Then, suddenly remembering his coming wedding, she took a new green bill out of her shiny black purse. After, the dream switched to her childhood home in New York. There was a knock on the door and a troop of people with a dark gypsy woman pushed into the house bringing a black iron coffin. She tried to get them out, but they went into her bedroom. Then they tried to push the coffin into a closet, the kitchen, and then the hall. The cover of the coffin had the same lid as Rod's typewriter. Rod wrote ineffectual sentimental poems. Finally the troop picked up the coffin and went into the bedroom and tried to lay it on her bed.

– It must stay here twelve hours – they said.

– No, no – she cried – Take it out.

It seemed the gypsy woman was celebrating mass for a daughter who had died a year ago. But the group claimed that there was a man's body in the coffin. Finally they decided to take it out of the house. When they got to the door, the gypsy woman stared at her and the coffin turned into an empty unzipped guitar case (Rod played the guitar). They left. But what had happened to the body? She began looking anxiously all over the house – under the bed, in the closets, but there was no corpse. Suddenly on a table, she saw a tiny pressed heart, the color of dried blood – packaged in cellophane paper. She picked it up and threw it on a shelf. It must be a souvenir she thought, and then began to arrange the house . . .

She felt very light as she walked back, her feet leaving footprints that were quickly washed away by the water: as if a great weight had fallen off of her and she saw those misty blue-green eyes staring at her behind the glass mask.

The next afternoon Arthur had found out where she lived. She had been staying on the island since Rod had left her. She'd saved up some money from English lessons she'd been giving in Paris. Sometimes though it was very lonely. Her house was the last one on the Cape, high up overlooking the sea. It was small and white with green shutters. In the back was a rocky garden planted with dried-out cardboard cactus. She was sitting on the veranda in a wicker chair reading when he arrived. His long hair was combed back – damp from the sea, his reddish beard filled with shiny sand particles. She always seemed to remember him wearing a green velvet jacket with gold buttons over trunks and bare legs. Later she realized he had on a used green corduroy vest with copper buttons – the material filled with cigaret burns which later she had mended. He was carrying a bottle of cheap Spanish cognac. He sat down at her feet, opened the bottle and took a swig.

– Here I am.

– I guess you are – she said quietly. And she looked into his large greenish eyes. She drew back quickly, afraid of being submerged in them. The yellow beach ball was next to her. He took it and bounced it up and down a few times. She had an orange towel wrapped around her: she had just washed her long sun-bleached hair with buckets of well water. Her feet were bare. He put his hand on her ankle. She felt a tingling sensation and suddenly decided she wouldn't play it coy. She looked at him – his breath was coming faster, his eyes half-closed, his cheeks flushed. She could smell the alcohol and also a heavy musky odor. He drew her head down to him. She felt his salty tongue explore the border of her lips then gently move inside more profoundly. She felt as if her backbone had turned to jelly and there was nothing left to hold her up.

– Let's go inside – she said.

She got up adjusting the towel. Still sitting down, he watched her, as she closed the shutters. They went into the house. It was cool and shadowy. The stone floor was bare except for a small straw rug. The room was simple. Only some dried flowers, shells and a basin and pitcher on a small table, and an Indian cushion on the floor. The white-sheeted bed looked ghostly. He took off his green jacket, slipped out of his trunks and dumped them on the floor. He sat naked on the bed holding the cognac bottle over his sex, then picked the bottle up to take long swallows. She sat next to him. He opened the orange towel. Buttered sunlight melted over their bodies through the slats. He pushed her gently down on the bed, his hands stroking her breasts till the points were hard, sucking around them with pink lizard lips. His hands then moving down to her cunt, his fingers combing her hair – bits of sand pressing into her ass as he lay on top of her – sweat pouring from his chest. He penetrated her in long thrusting motions, backwards and forward like long waves hitting the shore and moving away again. Once in a while a cormorant screeched and the sound of surf hit the rocks below. She smelled alcohol, seaweed and the spicy odor of sperm. She kept going on and on. She felt lifted higher and higher as his waves raged into a tempest and with the alcohol he kept going on and on as if it preserved him inside her with this image of a ship enclosed in a bottle that would never be released, would never sail out to any ocean but rest caught in its glass womb. She went on and on till she suddenly crashed and foam came pouring out of her – splattered into a thousand drops: but still his long lunging movement went on churning inside the bottle like some great storm had blown up – and again she burst and at that moment it was as if the glass had broken into hundreds of pieces, the ship thrown up on the beach, and he came in long gasps of Ahhhhhhhh . . . into . . . Ommmmmm . . . as he lay exhausted on top of her, shipwrecked against her shore. They lay naked and sweaty against one another and he told her he hadn't made love in a long time. He leaned over the bed, took another shot of cognac and they fell asleep in each others' arms.

When they woke it was late afternoon and they went for a walk along the pine trees near the beach. That afternoon stayed with her as one of her most vivid souvenirs. She remembered a young girl sitting under a fig tree embroidering colored flowers on a black kerchief: around her salmon-dusted sheep nibbled dry grass among broken bottles and stones. One of the sheep – sick, lowered its head under the sparse shade of a pine tree, the bell around its neck clanking against the bark. A sickly sweet breath came out of its mouth and threads of flies were knitting knots on its dusty wool.

They walked to a cluster of pine trees. In the middle was a deep sand pit. They climbed down. There was a strong scent of rosemary and thyme. They lay down in the sand: the grains sticking to their damp bodies. Their love making was hidden, she felt like a ripe melon opening and bursting from its skin. Nobody could see them except for a lonely seagull swooning in the sky and sentinel pine trees that gave out warnings with their antenna needles to the guardia green lizards scaling the edge of the hole who stared at them with second degree eyes.

All this sea, sky, void was like honey to her being – with an infinite tenderness she met him in a closing lid of horizon.

When they climbed out of the pit, a swollen orange moon was rising over the sea. The sky was violet and green dripping into the sea in a newly dyed batik print. An old woman with a straw hat and a salt-stained dress carried a bamboo fishing cane – her floating hook line seemed to drag the goldfish moon along with her. They walked to a native café on the beach where old ladies in black shawls and men in patched blue pants sat in rows, their back to the sea, facing a small television screen watching spacemen land on the Sea of Tranquility, while the orange moon rose higher and higher over the pines.

From that time on he just kept staying with her. They never even talked about it. In the beginning, he had a little money. Now he was into photography which he did sporadically. It didn't seem to bother him that she paid for everything since money meant nothing to him. And she – she was in that euphoric state and because nothing cost much on the island:

she just let everything slide by, happy to be with him. Soon she'd have to go back to Paris to begin her English lessons again ...

The tourists followed the trade route from Katmandu, to Goa, to Ibiza searching for drugs and spices to keep their flesh from rotting. First, they went looking for gurus and dipped their hankerchiefs into the Ganges and worshipped those saints who had gone mad lusting after God, like other men do over women or money. They sat in the lotus position and beggars came and left them rice. The guru said there were three things never to look at without preparation – the sun, the soul and the pupil of an eye. The hippies sat on the beach looking at the naked sun that left a golden flower on the retina.

But the herded tourists sat and watched the sea with color television eyes framing the world into desired projections and carrying suitcases of portable travel posters.

On the island, they'd built a new hotel over a natural well, but so many thousands of gallons of water were pumped up that the water level lowered at the other end of the island and the roots of the pine trees died out. The dead trees were cut up and what was left of the dark forest fell into chairs and tables. A cup of blood dropped in the moss, stained the leaves into a murdered autumn and searchers looking for mushrooms found small bones stacked like walnuts. Leaves echoing like stone rang in a petrified forest and the ring of the cup stamped in the log flashed its burial on a stump of age. The arc of an axe had split the crutched inner core. What was inside the dark heart? A fearful corner filled with day.

Tourists sat in their anonymous hotel rooms writing postcards home or swimming in the lobby pool painted turquoise blue; while outside, the patched dungaree sea looked faded from too many rinsings. The full moon lit up the hundred hotel windows and what was left of its force silvered the tops of pine trees. At night in a house on the cliff, each window lightened and darkened as somebody walked through the rooms with a candle.

Down in the woods, German couples fucked on the ground as if the pines were their bedroom furniture . . . cars and motorcycles grazed on dirt roads, radios blasted loudspeakered by the wind – plucked white chicken feathers sudsed over the sand and colored balls and umbrellas bloomed in artificial gardens. New porcelain toilet bowls hived against trees. In the once secluded pine forest, streamers of toilet paper buzzed with flies. The early community of Essenes, with their cult of purity, were only allowed to shit once a day after sunset – each with his own private shovel burying his turds, animal-like in the hot sands.

Where she lived was so high up that the cormorants built their nests in the cliffs. She could look out over the sea to a natural sphinx-like stone with an enigmatic face. Phoenician pirates had once worshipped this landmark on full moon nights; now the new moon made crescent horns over the sphinx's inscrutable Coca Cola smile. Nearby passed the TANIT, the tourist boat, named after a Phoenician sea goddess. The boat took the tourists between the two islands. The women sat in the bow, their hair blowing, breasts thrust forward like cut-off stumps of bronzen antiquity – figureheads piled like booty, helter-skelter.

In the old days when pirates were sighted in the distance, a woman would stand on top of the cliffs and signal this danger to the people below – if she lifted up a white slip, the pirates were coming over the foam, a yellow one if still far out under the sun, and her rose slip was a waving of blood in the nearby arena of water. But when the ship landed, the women gathered the swollen material around their bellies and flaunted themselves as harbors already occupied.

Now by the low cliffs, generations of old ladies came down to bathe at sunset still wearing layers of petticoats. They left the white and yellow flounces spread out in caps of foam and waded through the dyed sunset sea in flamingo ruffled slips cackling as the water lapped their wrinkled yellow toes.

She remembered Gary who used to go out on bad drinking and drug binges. They had found him on the TANIT in a corner behind the ropes. His wrists slashed and LAST TRIP written in blood on the opened palm of his left hand.

Then there was Grant who lived in an old Arab tower, the walls inside painted with sunflowers. Grant was an Australian who had been to India and gotten into yoga. Often on moonlit nights, he'd sit in front of the tower in the lotus position trying to lower and raise the moon with hypnotic passes of his hands. He also had a meditation exercise with which to draw the sun down and light it up inside himself. In his right hand he held a picture of the sun, and then, staring at this image till it shone like a ball of fire, could swallow the paper and become illuminated.

He lived with a junkie, Mike, who was always spaced-out on some drug. Mike had tried everything – even swallowed morning glory seeds and vomited up night glory flowers – crawled up the vines and held onto two white clouds till he fell in blue space onto the sand, while a naked girl poured water over herself from a child's pail and a flute bird whistled – in the background of a number seventeen tarot card. Or Mike stayed endlessly in bed after a shot – the sheet covering his face in the final grace – flies settling on the stained yellow spots. It was only at night that he drifted outside and sat down by the mulberry tree next to the silver well . . . his pale-fixed face uplifted to the stars.

On the island grew a hallucinatory herb, estromonium, from which the old native ladies used to brew a bitter tea out of its dark green leaves, soothing for gas and stomach cramps. They sat on their verandas in embroidered kerchiefs, rocking back and forth in wicker chairs, sipping the bitter green tea and farting in the late summer days – their filmy eyes spaced-out, watching hippies embrace on pine needles. Mike went on a trip with estromonium. He had gotten up to go through a door in the wall – only there was no door.

Larry, an American, lived in an old mill. He was the Don Quixote of planetary charts drawing conjunctions of moons and suns, trying to find out what was a good day to see his girl friend Rosie whose planet was all fucked up. Rosie lived in a cave – the floor lined with seaweed where she meditated naked to each rising and setting sun. Rosie ate only brown rice and chocolate and broke out with tiny red boils which Larry explained was because her sun was in exile. When Larry, after a favourable horoscope, wanted to move in with her, she refused.

– One hermit to a cave, she said.

In the winter most of the tourists left the island. Only the Fonda was opened and there wasn't much to do. An American called Cowboy Tom used to get drunk with the priest. One night when the wind had been howling for days banging the doors and shutters, making everybody on edge – Cowboy Tom pulled out a pistol and made the priest kneel at his feet.

– You bastard . . . admit I'm God here, screamed Tom, till they jumped him and cooled him out.

The cold winds swept in from the sea and the pine trees along the coast crouched down permanently hunchbacked. The heat went out of the sand like a short circuited electric blanket that gave no more luxurious comfort. The land became a closed parlor of souvenirs. The new hotel was deserted – gulls built nests on the window ledges, seaweed piled up on the beach, great waves swept over the red veranda tiles and green lizards crawled along the afternoon terraces.

In those days there was only sea, sand and the sleeping form of the dark sphinx stone where expectation embraced the distant horizon waiting for impossible sea serpents to rise . . .

Every evening at sunset, she and Arthur watched an old beachcomber walk along the deserted beach carrying a shipwrecked door on his back and humming a monotonous song. His pale blue eyes drained into the sea. He was an opening into no recognizable world. Then they would walk to the Fonda. On the way, stood a burnt black station wagon – in the back the doors were wide open, in front the steering wheel and windows gone. Sometimes on dark nights a fiery outline of a body sat in the driver's seat where some man had long ago burned to death. Or on clear windy nights orange dust rose from the road, but on windless days often tiny *tourbillons* of dust spun along the road, tumbleweed ghosts coughed into balls that rolled along the sand and then hid in a bush.

Next to her house on the Cape, Catalina, or Granny as the tourists called her, rented out her large stone house. In the old animal stalls she had rebuilt small rooms. She had sold all the animals except for one pig which she was fattening up on tourist garbage. Odile, a French girl, rented the room next to the pig pen. Every morning Odile took her shower, throwing pails of well water over her naked brown body and standing in the sun to dry off. The near-sighted pig would stand up against the gate with his shit-covered hooves, gaping and squealing at her. Granny's son, Antonio – a little simple minded – would climb up on a ladder when she bathed and pretend to paint the wall. One day he leaned over so far, he fell and broke his leg. Since he had nothing to do, he'd hobble out to the fields with the pig and crawl around on all fours, both of them grunting and squealing – the pig rolling in the dirt like a fat pink baby.

If anyone saw Antonio, he'd say the pig had escaped and he was bringing it home. Antonio didn't wear any shoes, his soles were thick as leather; but imitating, the tourists, he took to wearing shoes and suffered from corns and blisters.

In another of the reconstructed stalls was a French gay, Raphael, whose long hair was dyed henna after a trip to Morocco. He often sat under one of Granny's fig trees – covered with bright silk shawls, yellow egret feathers in his hair and little jingling bells on his ankles playing the guitar. One day Granny had caught him clawing at her figs with his bony spangled fingers and she'd chased him over the rocky ground with her pointed black umbrella – Raphael trailing his feathers and shawls like some exotic bird ready to take-off.

At the end of the beach where there were mounds of seaweed, the hippies bathed naked. The *Guardia* were always spying on them with binoculars. Naked couples lay face-down in the sand with white shell asses slowly turning pink under the blushing sun. On Sunday, the Spanish men strolled above, along the cliffs, their hands in their pockets, searching the beach with seagull eyes for floundering naked girls stranded on the sand – nude girls crouching in the sand like pale foreign sphinxes with inscrutable smiles.

In the pine woods an old man in black with a stubble beard and no teeth used to sit against a tree, jacking off . . . waiting for naked German girls to ride by on bicycles.

At the end of the day, farmers brought their donkeys to the beach and they rolled on their backs, their legs up, dry shampooing their hides in the sand. Some campers living on the beach had bought a young donkey that loved to roll around on dry pine needles. They used the donkey to get provisions in town, but at the end of the summer the donkey got colic and one night braying and hee-hawing, let out terrible green shit farts and dropped dead. The campers just left the donkey's body on the beach and the sweet decaying flesh drew swarms of green-bottle flies. At the same time a baby whale got stranded on the other side of the cove, its skeleton ribs looking like a ship-wrecked hulk. The heavy odor of decay spread over the island in a festering bandage.

Going into town, they passed the carpenter's shop with a great mulberry tree in the yard. The falling purple berries splattered the wood, staining the edges of the boards. All day long there was a foghorn buzzing from the electric saw cutting into the pine boards – boards for fishing boats, furniture and coffins. One afternoon she remembered there had been a funeral. The men were busy finishing the wood coffin to put the body in. The church bells rang. A black horse pulled the gilded glass hearse through its last view of town. The priest walked beside the veiled widow with her little girl holding a limp doll. Her husband had drowned in a storm out fishing, and his body washed up on the shore a week later was almost unrecognizable. Men in tight Sunday suits straggled behind the hearse, dropping out as they reached the Fonda to quickly gulp down a cognac, then followed the ringing hooves on the lime road to the cemetery – wiping their eyes and mouths on their shrunken sleeves.

Now that it was summer on the island, burials were quick. The corpse brought flies into the house. In the 30's burials were late . . . flies and maggots entered through the bullet holes, but now the bones had dried out, covered over with sand and pine needles. Lately some campers high on an acid trip had manicured with red nail polish some skulls in the common grave and had painted on one of them "ALAS POOR YORICK I LOVED HIM WELL".

She thought of the day they had gone for a long walk on the beach before he had been afraid of the shadow trader. They were wearing only bathing suits and they trailed barefoot along the wet sand. He carried a picnic basket over his shoulder filled with beer and cold chicken. As they walked along the beach, she saw a plastic doll's head with its glass eyes half buried in the sand. What could she divine from this sign? In front of her was the doll's left arm pointing towards the sea; then a pink rubber glove with three ripped fingers and, on a rock, the remains of a torn fishing net and always plastic oil bottles. She stubbed her toe against an empty bottle of tranquilizers, (to relax the day) and a comb broken in two. Then coming toward them was the crazy toothless man singing his monotonous song, carrying the door on his back. His eyes were so blue they matched the sky behind him. It was as if he had blue holes in his head. The man lifted his fingers to his mouth and made a sign of puffing at something. Arthur reached into the basket and gave him a cigaret. The old man took out an orange rope lighter and lit the cigaret, staring at her. He then waved and went on – a door opening into a blue void.

They came to a hollow in the sand. There was no one about. The sea was as flat as a mold of lime Jello. He buried the bottles in the wet sand. They took off their bathing suits and plunged into the lukewarm water. The salt pained her eyes. He grabbed her and in the shallow water pinned her down on the wet sand and made love to her, small ripples of water licking over them. She was now in a completely liquid world – in the warm water there was no inside, no outside. It was back in the womb again. They lay curled around one another like pulsing octopuses. He got up. She lay there a few more minutes abandoned to the sway of the water. He dug out a few bottles of beer and they ate the chicken with bits of sand in it grinding under their teeth. Neither of them spoke. She avoided his eyes or she felt she'd be sucked in. They wrapped up in towels, lay under a pine tree and fell asleep to the hypnotizing hum of the cicadas.

When they woke up, the sun was setting. She noticed lots of cuttle fish backbones laying over the beach. She told him they could make money picking them up for canaries to sharpen their beaks on. They started back. In the distance a dead sheep was floating on the water – golden under the sun. Its legs were tied with a cord so the sheep wouldn't graze too far. It had probably fallen off a cliff. She passed the same doll's head and arm. The only person they came across was a young guy in a gym suit who ran out of the pine forest, flexed his knees three times before the sea, then lifted himself off the ground like a ball and bounced back into the woods – a gold chain of light swinging off his stop-watch. When they got to the Arab tower, Mike was walking along the beach hugging his arms around his black salt-stained jacket, trembling, always cold after his fix. He took his walks at night.

They lay on the beach watching the moon rise. It was the night of the full moon and on this night the fishermen were out hunting the giant manta ray which rose to the surface attracted to the full moon light. Four fishing boats swayed on the molten sea hooked up with extra spotlights on the bows. The fishermen sat like movie prop men arranging a scenario. Strange ghost-like shapes waved on the surface of the water. In this illusion of stagelight the manta rays danced against a backdrop of nets ready to be raised by theatrical deception. Suddenly a rope drew up the curtain net and in it they saw a manta ray – its fleshy white wings flapping wildly like a fallen angel.

Before reaching their place, they passed Granny's stone house. She was sitting by the window, her face yellowed by a petrol lamp. She was leaning over a table. They could see her head, partly bald from always wearing a straw hat, and her thin rat-tail braid. Granny was trying to put assorted coupons together, cut out of Spanish soap powder boxes. The prize of the contest was an ancient gold doubloon. Granny saw them and motioned to her.

– Come by tomorrow. You can pick the mulberries from my tree, but put on an old dress. The berries stain.

The next morning, she had gotten up early. Arthur was still sleeping. He always slept late. She had a letter to mail about her job in Paris. The local post office was only opened for two hours a day and, on top of this, the woman who distributed the mail could hardly read; she put the letters in alphabetical order but the catch was that sometimes it was under the first name as well as the last. The tourists stood in line waiting for the post office to open. Tourists greasy with Nivea cream melting under a sauna sun. Ahead of her some Germans were sending home little green lizards. She could hear their tiny claws scratching on the inside of the cardboard boxes. As she looked in the post window, she could see bundles of unclaimed letters under a bench. She wondered how many letters had never reached her. After mailing the letter, she walked slowly back.

She passed three women with long dusty dresses collecting the fallen almonds. One woman, a black patch over her eye, tapped the branches with a long forked stick. The falling almonds hit the ground in streams of piddling rain. Rythmically they peeled the green husks which lay about like heaps of lizard skins, dropping the warm brown nuts into large wicker baskets. The morning was already very hot. A group of goats huddled under a fig tree were scratching their noses on the bark. They hobbled against the trunk with their tied legs trying to nibble the fig leaves that shaded their yellow sun-dial eyes. She felt exhilarated as she walked back. It was like being drunk. Her whole skin tingled. She saw Arthur as she had left him, lying naked on the white sheet curled up in the fetal position. His reddish hair, dyed by the sun, covering his face. She thought of his body tasting of salt.

Arthur was dreaming he was painting an immense wall which was standing by the sea. He was painting it green. There was only this wall, one dimensional, no ceiling. He was naked, dipping his paint brush into a sea of green paint. As he painted, the water rose higher and higher till he was completely covered with green . . . He awoke drenched in sweat. It brought back the memory of Maurice, the house painter he'd met at a café when he'd first been to Paris. At that time he'd been broke, looking for a job. He saw Maurice's face shiny, cracked around the eyes as if he'd been covered with old varnish. Maurice had started talking to him and then bought him drinks. He said he was a house painter but on his days off went to the Louvre. Delacroix was his favourite.

– Ah, those women, he'd sigh – on harem cushions.

The sleeves of Maurice's white coat were covered with spots of paint like little abstract paintings. He said he'd had the coat for over fifteen years and each spot told a story of the apartment he'd painted.

– See – he pointed out – this blue spot was for an invalid who wanted to feel he was in the sky . . . this gray one was for a woman who stayed in bed hoping he'd jump in with her, only she had a black mustache and smelled of sour milk. When he'd heard Arthur was broke, he'd gotten him a job house painting. Arthur remembered in one place he'd painted nude women on the walls before covering them over, and in another place he'd gotten drunk and spent a night on the floor, in the morning his hair had been green from the paint.

Once Maurice had invited him home. He lived with his mother who was blind in one eye. There was a parrot standing on a bar in a cage. Maurice had gone up to it and said bonjour, but the parrot had just stared at him with its wicked eyes.

– That's life – Maurice had sighed – No answer, not even from a damn parrot. And Maurice told him he'd started painting posters but not getting any work he'd done walls. Then he'd showed him a cardboard file. He took out some carefully wrapped papers and placed them under a lamp with his warped fingers, the paint ingrained in the skin like warts. He'd held up a luminous yellow paper, – look this is the first wall color I ever painted over fifteen years ago for a honeymoon couple. They were so nervous they left the choice to me, and here's a gray for a pastor. I tried to make it like a mist. He'd only shown him a few papers like a miser who gets his greatest kicks from looking at his stuff privately.

Then he'd pulled out a brilliant pink piece of paper and he caressed it.

– See this – he said – holding the paper like it was the wing of a butterfly – ten years ago when my father died, I took my mother to Dieppe . . . it was in August and one twilight as I was walking along the harbor, a shade of pink like the landing of a thousand flamingoes colored the water. It was as if the whole sea had been dyed rose. I felt blinded, the world in rose colored glasses. After, I forgot about the color, but a very rich couple wanted their apartment in different shades of pink and in the salon I painted this sunset mauve . . . Arthur remembered Maurice's face cracking under the yellow light – Just think, if lava came pouring down and a thousand years later they dug up the rooms, it would be like Pompeii – he'd lifted his arms excitedly above his head (he'd put on a clean white jacket in his honor) and for a moment it was as if a summer sheet had been placed over an aging chair that the owner had left behind. Not long after this Maurice had died of a heart attack. What had happened to his pink apartment?

Later he'd been on the streets and then gone to live with a black American painter, Aldos Solomen, and his black buddy, Jackson, who played the drums and Christ what great drunks they had had together . . .

At that moment Adrienne walked in.

— I ran into Tony, he's giving a full-moon party at his house tonight. Tony, an American, had lived on the Island for years. Adrienne knew him when she'd been with Rod. His house on the Cape was near hers. A whole group of people were camping there. It was a traditional stone house with white-washed walls, small windows to keep the house cool, red tile floors and a long veranda. Inside the style was Indian — with beads hanging from the wall, Buddha incense burners, cushions, shawls and dried flowers and thistles stuck out of water jars. In front of the veranda large pieces of driftwood sprawled as if the ark had finally hit dry land.

Tony was as white as a frog's belly. He considered it unhealthy to get sunburned and practically never left home. He had had a monkey, Harry, who only drank wine but actually one day trying to get water from the well, fell in and drowned. Tony was too lazy to fish him out so everyone drank wine, cooked in wine and washed in wine till someone dragged Harry out and cleaned the well . . .

That night of the party the moon was full, bluish — shining on the rocky, pitted surfaces of the ground in a moonscape television scene. Arthur and she walked slowly in spacemen gestures through the artificial atmosphere. Every once in awhile, a cactus appeared standing by like a prickly moon creature. She had worn a turquoise dress with gold beads, her long hair sticky, bleached very blonde by the sun. She thought she looked like a photo negative. He had on a white shirt unbuttoned to the waist, an Indian scarf tied around his neck and a torn pair of jeans. Before they got to the house there was a smell of hash mixed with the scent of rosemary. Candles flickered on the walls of the veranda reflecting on large green wine bottles. Girls with long hennaed hair and light flowered dresses mothed around the flames. Most of the guys wore patched jeans, sleeveless tee shirts and beads – their hair long and lank from the sea water. As they came up, they could hear . . .

– I was so stoned in Kabul, I couldn't get off that fucking bed for three days . . .

In a corner sat Sam, an American who had just come to Europe still in search of a myth – his eyes anxious, doe-like were filled with greenness from grazing so long on lost reservations of plenty. His friend George, stood in the middle of the room on the white woven line of an Indian rug. It was as if all traffic had stopped, no one around him on a parallel of his own degree . . . posing for an identity picture he was afraid to send home.

The whole crowd was there. Gary with drugged eyes – glassy, owl-like, reminded her of those trays of glass eyes in a taxidermist shop in St. Michel – eyes to fit the socket of every beast. Gary lay on a cushion, his pale hands folded over his chest. It was a month later when he cut his wrists on the TANIT. Odile, with frizzy hair and a green sari, was darting her pink tongue back and forth, reptilian, searching for her prey for the evening. Raphael trailed behind her. He had more feathers and bells than ever and fluttered hysterically around the room. Grant came in, his blonde hair and copper skin glistening with astral light. Mike by his side in a dark coat and ghostly white skin was a fungus growth crawling up from a dark cellar. Someone handed Arthur a joint. A group in yoga positions were passing a pipe around. Rosie sat in the middle of the floor next to George who, still unmoving, now posed as a cigar store Indian. She had on a sheer blouse showing her plump breasts. A few red boils searing one cheek. She was throwing coins for I Ching reading. Larry watched her with horoscope eyes taking in his lines of conjunction. She waved to them.

– Hey, come on over and have a reading.

Arthur had gotten No. 64, before completion. She vaguely remembered the lines:

> *There is drinking of wine*
> *In good company. No guilt.*
> *But if he gets his head wet.*
> *He loses his way.*

It hadn't meant much to her then.

A guy was lying on the floor in the throes of an acid trip – staring upwards, hitting his bare feet back and forth on the stone floor.

– I've got it, he screamed, I've got the secret . . . the ceiling is really the floor . . . That's it . . . God damn it . . . It's the secret.

No one paid any attention to him except Julius, a pusher, who sat watching him and drumming his fingers on a little wood table. Julius always made her skin creep. He was a crack, a door shadow against the light in his tight brown jacket, attracted to the smell of bad luck and to those people whose characters had begun to rot like garbage. He had a peculiar swift glide of folded and hidden beetle wings no longer able to fly. A slime of oiliness ingratiated his personality. Bernie, his side-kick, completely fucked-up, sat blankly next to him. Rumor had it that Bernie had been in the C.I.A. and they'd doped him up to keep him from talking after he'd dropped out. Bernie's eyes looked like scratched out mirrors.

A guy in a bathing suit was playing drums on the veranda under the full orange moon and someone in a straw hat near a cactus strummed a guitar – a scene out of a grade B movie. By a low wall a few goats stirred, shaking their bells. Once in a while a glassy eye caught a reflection from the moon.

Arthur drank glass after glass of wine. He'd found a pair of green flippers and was hopping around on the rubber fins till he slipped and gave up. A girl in a shiny dress got up and danced to the moon, swaying her arms back and forth. Tony, whiter than anyone except Mike, was expounding.

– When I went on the last acid trip, I smelled so bad that tiny Geisha girls swam out of the well, jumped down my mouth – scrubbed and washed inside me, getting smaller and smaller rinsing out my blood vessels, scouring my intestines then leaving by my ass hole, and fuck it if they didn't turn into hairy monkeys . . .

Sam interrupted him.

– I'm gonna take a girl to Afghanistan. When I get there I'll trade her in for a camel.

Odile watched him her pink tongue darting in and out.

– I'll cross the desert with the camel and shove hash in plastic sacks down the camel's throat . . . just pick up the "shit" when I hit the border and I got it made.

George looked sceptical.

– It's better to do like Gurdjieff. Paint birds yellow and sell them as canaries. We just have to get the hell out in the rainy season.

A few androgynous couples were embracing on the veranda. With the unisex clothes and hair, they could have been Platonic twins looking for their other half.

Interrupting everyone was Phil. He considered himself a full-bred iconoclast – the real image breaker. Anyone's belief in drugs, food, love, politics, no matter what, he was systematically against and always argued the opposite side. He was the Socratic thorn of every party.

Rosie called out,

– Hey, let's go swimming.

Phil interrogated,

– Why should we go swimming?

But there were a lot of enthusiastic responses.

– Yeh, in the cove by Moby Dick.

– Okay – Arthur called out – If we can take some wine – and lifted up a bottle triumphantly.

The moon spiced the landscape with a crystalline layer of salt. They filed down a pathway in the cliffs. The whale, now a skeleton, lay a ghostly shipwreck by the rocks. They undressed and jumped into the brilliant water of moonlight and trails of phosphorescent cigaret butts. Arthur took off his pants but rolled in with his white shirt making him look like a manta ray. He turned over and blew jets of water from his mouth, bits of phosphor floated around him in a trail of sparklers. He swam back and forth churning the water disappearing under a bath of bubbles. He went down into prehistoric layers and came up with seaweed in his hair, finally rolling out onto the beach, a strange creature carried from another dimension, bloated, white jacketed, passed out on the sand. Suddenly Larry, his head in the stars cried out.

– Look up in the sky.

A reddish disc was sailing slowly across the sky.

– It's a U.F.O. – a voice yelled.

The reddish wheel whirled above them. Then in a few moments it got brighter as if sending out rays and sailed blinking back and forth till it disappeared behind a small mountain. What it was she was never sure. Maybe Ezekiel's wheel. They all flung themselves on the sand – naked wet creatures having left their masquerade and camouflage of illusions on the beach. The whale skeleton bleaching under the acid moon traced shadow bars on the sand.

The day before they were supposed to go back to Paris, it was understood they would be going together, they went and sat in a café in the square. She saw Arthur with his glass of beer meditating on the foam. A middle-aged American couple walked by. Both were heavy. The woman wore a tight peasant blouse and a dirndl skirt, the man had leather Tyrolean pants and a camera strapped to his shoulders. They looked as if they'd made a recent trip to Switzerland and, as the church bells chimed, stepped out of a distorted childhood cuckoo clock. The man shaded his eyes and looked at the Spanish hills with the cord roads tying the red rocks too tight . . . following his camera image of billboard horizons to plateaux of green mossed tables, waiting for the knotted turns to be untied on delivery. In back of them three old ladies in black leaned against a white-washed wall by a window of pink plastic geraniums. The local birds, clothes-pinned to the telephone wires, flew into musical notes as the chimes arpeggioed them into the air. The bells stampeded the sheep in a ravine below feeding on dry grass – suddenly running blindly in a fire panic, kicking up trains of smoke from their tinder hooves.

The man stopped to take a picture of a bullfighter poster on a wall. The matador had just thrown his red cloak over the bull's horn. The bull pawed the ground, a banderillas sticking in its back, its tongue out – foaming from its nostrils. In a second, almost as if he'd been shot, the man grabbed his chest . . . blood oozed out of his mouth dripping down his chin. He keeled over on his face. Convulsions shook his body. The woman screamed. The man doubled up and was still. The café owner rushed out with two waiters, one waving a white towel. They turned the man over. His eyes were open, the pupils rolled back in the white sockets. The camera had broken and the film exposed, stretched over his arm like a discarded snake skin.

– Está muerto, . . . Dead, – the café owner announced to his English clients.

The woman kept on screaming. They lifted the man up, his Tyrolean pants flopping on top where a button had snapped, and carried him into the café. When they got inside they looked puzzled. There were only chairs and tables except for a billiard table where two men were playing. The owner made a sign and the two men, holding their cues, stopped, pointing them upward as if in a last military salute. They lifted the man carefully up onto the table, his limp hand hitting a ball. Blood was still trickling from his lips. The waiter took his towel and spread it over the man's face. The cloth turned red on the bottom. The owner pulled a white tablecloth from a drawer and covered the body. Only the dusty shoes stuck out on the green table. They had watched the scene through the window. Arthur reached over and picked up the exposed film, looked at its empty surface and dropped it.

The doctor arrived with his leather satchel. A little boy ran into the church and came out with the priest who was busy adjusting his dusty black robe.

– The doctor and the priest are just a little too late – he said ironically, – Maybe life is just a game . . . The man a dead ball . . . gone like a hole in one . . .

She saw summer–white sheets covering the furniture. Death had been covered up when she was a child. Nobody ever died, they just passed away . . . Death is shush, shush . . . hush,

hush . . . it was obscene. Cover it up. She remembered she'd once worked in the office of some oil company. She'd been a file clerk for a while. One of the secretaries had died of a heart attack. She'd fallen over her typewriter in the middle of an unfinished letter . . . We have just discovered a new oil dep . . .

The girl was laid out in a funeral home and all the employees gave money for a wreath of flowers. She'd gone with the company to the funeral home. There was a large wreath of roses by the coffin – TO OUR REGRETTED CO-WORKER – but on her chest, above her crossed hands was her typewriter with the unfinished letter still in it. The company had decided she'd died in the line of duty and she'd gotten her weapon with her. The girl's name had been Sylvia Blotter. Adrienne had made a poem to her:

>*Sylvia Blotter is dead,*
>*She has been sopped up into eternity.*
>*Only carbon copies filed away,*
>*Never to be done another day . . .*

Arthur remarked that maybe the man should be buried with the billiard table.

That last evening was melancholy. A strong wind began to blow. They walked slowly back to the house. Tumbleweed balls rolled along the road. At the top of the cliffs they could see white caps churning around in heavy suds. The shutters banged back and forth all night . . .

FOUR :   A FUCKED UP WORLD

They found a small apartment in Paris behind the old section of Montparnasse and settled in together. Arthur fixed up the tiny bathroom as a darkroom and time and again developed photos he took of the neighborhood; then he'd forget about it for awhile. She was back to teaching English. They were living on her money, just scraping by.

One early evening in June, they were sitting outside a café by the house near the market. The sky was turning from rose to violet with a crescent moon sticking through like the horn of a unicorn. The fat Spanish woman, her cart filled with waxed cherries, stood in her usual place, her black cat brushing its pink tongue along the inky fur. In back of her were stalls of fruit and vegetables – bunches of watercress next to red beets, cauliflowers piled in rows looked from the distance like old Roman plaster heads wreathed in green leaves – tomatoes and potatoes balanced in precise atomic diagrams.

The local prostitute, her dyed hair the color of Roquefort, slouched against the *triperie* window hugging a large leather handbag. In the window, a calf's head with plastic roses on its ears, stuck out its sand paper tongue lecherously. The old flower woman was putting aluminum paper on the stems of the violets. When she thought no one was looking, she took out a cheap violet perfume and sprayed it over the flowers. The odor floated through the market as if the violet sky was also pouring out scent. The herb man, in a crushed black hat, usually drunk, watched carefully for customers behind the window of a café. His cart was a small kitchen garden of parsley, thyme, rosemary, laurel and garlic. When a young girl bought something, he'd suddenly pull a white mouse out of his sleeve and as she screamed at the trembling red-eyed creature he'd laugh and laugh.

Across the street, decorating the bakery shop, stood a mosaic woman on a pillar in the form of a baguette. Her breasts were white and doughy and her hair the color of toast. People walked out of the bakery holding their baguettes like magic wands, waving them in the warm night. They stepped out with faces that were too-baked, glazed, stale, crumbling, doughy, or in a series of cookie moulds with the same head like a little boy bandit in a stocking mask.

Old men were standing at the zinc bar staring with dreamy eyes at the porno movies down the street – a billboard of red-light nipples flashing on and off. Two old ladies came in for their apéritif. They lived in their house. One had tight gray curls, the other a bun. They came over and shook hands with them.

– Good night – said one very proud of her English – You good? – and they went to the counter.

Arthur called out for another beer. He was in a high mood. Facing them was the run down Hotel des Meuses. True to its name, in a niche above the door stood three stone muses with their arms wound gracefully about each others' waists. A pigeon sat at their feet preening its feathers. A taxi passed with two nuns wearing white owlish head-dresses followed by a crane dragging a wrecked car. A billboard of Black Lion Shoe Polish catching the last rays of light, polished up the Black Lion. A middle-aged man in a gray suit with sunglasses walked into the café. He had only one arm; his empty sleeve had its cuff carefully placed in his suit pocket.

Arthur turned to her,

– By the way . . . Did I ever tell you about my hallucination? And I don't mean on acid. He took a swallow of beer and licked his lips. – A while back the American Center used to give jam sessions all night long. Jackson was playing drums with some guys, anyone who could get up and jam. I'd been on a steady high for two days, no sleep . . . It must have been about 6 am, the sun just hitting the windows, when I saw this old guy with white hair sitting next to the piano. He looked like that guy in the film of *Dr Mabuse* with the three black stripes on his head. Suddenly I noticed his left arm, there was a piece of wood coming out of his sleeve and attached to it was a silver hook like Long John Silver. I couldn't take my eyes off it (he took a long drink of beer). Well believe it or not, he got up and sat down at the piano. The back of the piano was facing me, so I couldn't see his hands. The music was real weird, it gave me goose pimples. Now how the hell could that guy be playing with one fucking hand? So I got up and went to the piano . . . and if I wasn't a son of a bitch . . . he was playing with two ordinary hands . . . no sign of a hook. You can believe it baby, I stopped drinking for a week.

. . . But often Arthur would go out on his own, wanting to be just with the boys drinking. One evening he ended up in a café in Montparnasse with a few buddies. It was late and he was really flying. Where he was sitting he could see himself in the mirror, one mirror aligned to the other and so he saw his image repeated on and on in the endless succession of faces in Tibetan mandalas and he thought of a Charles Adams cartoon where face after face repeated in a barber shop until suddenly a monkey's head popped up. As he watched himself, it seemed just his head hung in a silver space, balloon-faced, his neck only a thin string to hold it down. He pushed his chin into his neck so as not to take off, or explode into a thousand different pieces of rubber skin – but the balloon swelled larger and larger like a carnival mask about to rise.

At that moment an old *clochard* passed by holding out a dirty felt hat, making a sweeping bow. Arthur grabbed him by the arm.

– Hey, sit down buddy . . . and have a drink.

The *clochard* looked a bit puzzled, but sat down like someone who is not sure he has been invited to dinner on that day and leaves his coat on.

– Waiter bring my friend a drink – shouted Arthur imperiously. The waiter, with a white, not-too-clean napkin over his arm, walked dignifiedly over.

– I'm sorry but we cannot serve this – and he hesitated – man.

– The hell you can't – Arthur yelled, banging his fist on the table and throwing half a glass of beer into the *clochard's* lap.

The waiter forcefully seized Arthur's arm and pulled him into the street. Arthur's friends dragged him by the other arm.

– Let's get him out of here – one called.

The *clochard*, realizing that tonight was not the night he was expected, took off.

When Arthur stood outside the café, he again saw his face reflected in corridor after corridor of mirror. Nearby was a pile of bricks. He took one before his friends could react and threw it against the mirror. He saw himself split into pieces – bits of a mouth – eyes going in all directions . . . Once he'd read a baby elephant had escaped from a traveling circus in a city and every time it saw a reflection of itself, it lunged toward it. Finally it broke a plate glass window in a shop. The way they got the elephant back was to show it an adult elephant and it went docilely back to the circus. Because when a baby elephant is alone in a strange place it looks for its mother. What was he looking for?

The waiter came out with a busboy. There was a general free-for-all and Arthur got beaten up in the face before he managed to escape and fling himself on a bench across the way. He mused . . . so there's a void in the mirror. They've splashed the last can of paint against the walls and an old left-over custard pie. Reflection of nobody sitting in a café chair . . . The last glass cleared off the table . . . the last word spoken. An empty aquarium bubbling and bubbling . . . Ask the waiter – poets with silver trays to serve us the left overs. The night club turns off perspective. The saxophone arm runs out of the picture. A quick squeak of the rat's tail . . . red ketchup light spreads over raw flesh . . . Lovers hide in corners, change color and disappear into the background like anxious chameleons. Just think, in bed they get lost looking for one another . . . Beasts come up through the sink drain, their warm sticky breath clouds the mirror . . . It isn't a blue hand dripping liquid blue from an ancient galaxy, but a small red hand caught sticky with jam against the cupboard door . . . Hands, signposts to cross foreign borders . . .

He never knew how he managed to get home and fall on the bed. Adrienne was waiting at home. She was prepared, like Florence Nightingale at the front, with a sponge to wash off the blood and as she nursed him he screamed,

– Those motherfuckers . . . motherfuckers – till he passed out.

She sat in a chair watching him – his mouth open, snoring heavily, his face swollen and red. And she saw herself in the mirror as an old woman with a white veil over her gray hair. She was mixing flour and water to make dough. She patted the mixture into a round ball, put it in a bowl and covered it with gauze. Then she just sat and waited for the dough to rise; but it didn't rise and she realized that it never would because she'd forgotten the fermenting yeast . . .

That night Arthur kept thrashing around in the bed muttering,

– Come on baby . . . Come on – turning over and hugging the pillow to him. When he woke up, one eye was half closed, his lip swollen. – Oh, my God – he moaned, sweat pouring down his forehead – what a dream, don't know if it's as good, but I fucked my mother last night. I seem to remember Caesar dreamed he fucked his mother and he took over ... was it Rome? Anyway, after I fucked my mother, I went in a boat over the water to some island where there was a letter waiting for me from her, and inside the envelope was a cut-up frog with pieces of seaweed. The frog's head was pressed as if a car had run over it and a dried leg scratched me on the finger ... I always dug my ma. I remember once when I was about thirteen ... my dad was still into drink ... I heard my mother crying in her room. I peeked through the keyhole and there was my father – drunk, stark naked, tearing off her slip. One of the straps broke and her heavy tit was sticking out. The old man must have heard me, cause he came out and gave me a terrific beating ... cursing me up the line. All I could do was stare at his hairy balls ... Jesus, what a life ... Get me some beer honey, I can't stand it ...

His hangover was an unusually bad one and he needed to drink beer to get over it. He stayed in bed nursing it along. He was bored, so he dragged out all the old American newspapers, printed in Paris, which she'd saved for the fireplace, or to line the garbage can and he started reading the headlines ...

– It's sure a fucked-up world. It's no damn good – he complained reading the headlines ...

– How's this one ...

THE SLOT MACHINE CAME TO A BAD END

The man said he thought that the machine was short-changing him so he took out his revolver and shot it dead. "That'll teach you. You'll never cheat anyone again."

– Now isn't that something? Arthur commented – What would he have done if the machine had shot him back? What the hell we need is machines with more initiative.

She could see he was getting very high.

– Well, well and how about this . . .

A FUTURE U.S. BOMB WILL DESTROY MEN BUT NOT HOUSES

This leads to economy. When we take over, we move right into the house. No waste of money to start rebuilding. Just shovel people out. This is a clean way to kill.

– Ab – so – lut - ly right – he exalted – Get rid of the whole human race, then we can have nice clean buildings and cities, with no one to dirty anything up. He picked up a bottle of beer and took a long gulp.

– And what have we here . . .?

A MILLION PEOPLE HAVE DIED OF STARVATION IN BIAFRA

30 tons of bibles were sent to the remaining population. There will be 24,000 more waiting. 35,000 on the way from the sea and 10,500 translated into native dialects.

– Now isn't that just fine? I wonder how they cooked the bibles. Tell me Adrienne, do you think they'd be better fried, boiled, stewed or grilled? Which would be most tasty, maybe barbecued, or maybe they sent the bibles for its wonderful recipe of how to feed all these people on three fish . . .?

– Here's another corker . . .

KEEP AMERICA CLEAN

The air is so polluted . . . Ever think what would happen if thoughts like farts dumped in the atmosphere . . . Everyone's beautiful and loving ideas flying around . . . I suppose in one minute the whole fucking world would drop dead . . . or . . .

POLLUTION IS SO GREAT ON ITALIAN BEACHES

The ban on swimming was rejected and everyone was advised to get polio, tetanus, typhoid, cholera and smallpox shots before bathing.

– That's all we need, to be vaccinated for every damn disease before we walk in the street . . . I'll write to the government to take measures – and he opened another bottle of beer to emphasize the gesture.

AN ACCIDENT ON AN ATOMIC BASE AND THE WHOLE WORLD COULD BLOW UP

– I guess I don't need any comment on that one.

EICHMANN SAYS HE'S ONLY A COG IN THE MACHINE

THE PILOT MAJOR CLAUDE EATHERLY, WHO SAYS HE'S GUILTY OF THROWING THE BOMB OVER HIROSHIMA, IS DECLARED INSANE

– That's right brother, push a button and you could blow up the world. They sure shut up Eatherly's mouth. What the hell if you kill a few hundred thousand people. It's normal. It's in the game. If you feel bad about it – go and get fucked – take a few tranquilizers and go to bed . . .

WITHOUT A NAME, COUNTRY, OR PAPERS, A MAN TRIES TO PROVE HE EXISTS

– My dear Professor Gunther could have always used this guy for his dissections – then there would have been a noble reason for him to have existed. Wow, here's a beauty . . .

DINOSAUR FOOTPRINTS HAVE BEEN DISCOVERED ON CONEY ISLAND

SKIPPY, A HORSE, 3 YEARS OLD, HAS BEEN EATEN BY BEINGS FROM ANOTHER PLANET. UFO OBJECT FOUND BESIDE HORSE

A SWAMI IN INDIA BROKE A 40 YEAR VOW OF SILENCE TO SAVE COWS FROM BEING EATEN BY THE STARVING POPULATION . . .

At that moment the door bell rang. Adrienne opened the door.

It was Jackson, his black musician friend who played drums in his sober moments. He was Arthur's best drinking buddy. Oh, God, now she was really in for it. Jackson always carried his bottle of wine with him in a leather sack slung over his shoulder.

– You're just in time – Arthur beamed happily – Adrienne baby, we need some more to drink.

– You've had enough – she pouted in a sulky voice.

– Come on now, is that a way to treat a friend?

She knew she couldn't resist or there'd be a terrible scene; so without saying any more, she went out for new supplies. When she got back, they were both installed on the bed in nests of newspapers. Jackson had taken off his large black felt hat, his leather jacket, and was swinging a pair of colored beads around his fingers. Jackson was right in the act.

– What everyone needs is to fuck more . . . there'd be less wars.

– Right on there brother – Arthur joined in – and no assassinations either . . . Here's a killer headline . . .

DO IT YOURSELF. ACT OUT ATOMIC BOMB EXPLOSIONS. SMALL SCALE MODEL WITH HARMLESS CHEMICALS

– Now isn't that a good idea? I think we should order one for all our friends, and it's a marvelous toy for the kids.

Jackson waved his hand.

– Man, you know what I was thinking today? This ain't a world for dwarfs. Suppose they has to phone, they can't reach that fucking phone in the booth, or if they has to climb up into them buses – they damn well has to be carried . . . How come we ain't got nothing out there for them? Arthur followed along.

– Yeh, well how about the giants, they can't get into the

booths either, or the buses, or maybe sit on the john. I keep saying we got a lop-sided world.

Somehow Adrienne really had to agree with them. Was being drunk a way for them to adjust to all the bullshit – the so called normal behaviour?

– Oh, my God – Arthur suddenly cried, his eyes flashing on a headline –

– You really can't beat this one – as he waved the paper . . .

AN ENTERTAINER WHO HOLDS WORLD RECORD FOR STAGE CRUCIFIXION WAS DENIED ENTRANCE TO JERUSALEM

– Well, well, it says crucifixion is not allowed in Jerusalem . . . I wonder why they didn't think of that two thousand years ago – and he threw the bunch of papers on the floor.

– You listen here Arthur, I got a humdinger. Did you know about this here dude who wanna be Superman?

– Me . . . I always wanted to be a Superman. When I was a kid, I'd open an umbrella and jump off a high spot into the sand . . .

– Well, anyway there's this here dude who wanna play Superman but he gone out too far. He wear a skin-tight blue outfit with the S on the back of his red cape, the high boots and the whole trip . . . and at night, it was in California . . . he'd jump on them bungalows waking up the folks. But what was so weird was he wear a cop's suit over the Superman deal and he went hid in a phone booth. So first he make it out as a cop, and then this baby strip to the Superman job and fly at them motherfuckers walking by. (Adrienne suddenly thought meaninglessly does anyone know where Lot street is?) This dude though get so uptight that he don't know his ass from his elbow – if he is Superman or a cop, and he really get spaced out. But the game sure must've started to drag cause he weren't seen flying off no rooftops no more or jerking out of phone booths. No one see him around for a month, so the cops break into his pad. The joint's empty, neat as a pin. It was a hot fucking day, so one of the cops go to the kitchen thinking maybe there's some beer in the fridge, well he opens the door and what was there . . . oh, man, . . . this here dude frozen stiff decked out in his Superman trip . . . his blue knees stuck under his chin . . . he'd goddamn tied ropes around his self and then must've shut the door . . . his fucking hand froze solid to the rope . . .

Musing, they both took another drink.

FIVE :   IN EXILE

Jackson always called Arthur "wild man" and he looked the part, sitting in bed, his hair sticking out at the side like helmets of Celtic bird's wings and his heavy reddish beard. Arthur was usually cold with liver chills after too much drinking, huddled with covers around him like bearskin. But at the same time there was something comic, a little cockeyed about him – an illustration of Asterix with his flushed face and waving arms. She remembered from her literature class how the Celts were supposed to have poetic imagination, romantic fervour, and rapid changes of mood. All this made the Celts less able to cope with the rude more practical tribes.

His charm was his irresoluteness and changing chameleon moods. Arthur had often said that in the end the Celts had talked away their heritage. Adrienne with her Jewish background had been nourished on the idea brought down from generations of Jewish mothers – "an eye for an eye." Her mother's opinion was that no man would ever be good enough for her daughter. All men were bastards, You, Adrienne – her mother proclaimed – came of royal background, every one of the men in the family had been rabbis. Her mother had traced the family tree – their heritage she said was as good as the royal family. Only a prince or a king could be good enough for her daughter. Hadn't she any pride? But Adrienne saw herself as the wandering Jew in exile.

– Go a little faster – said the wandering Jew to Christ on his way to Golgotha. And Christ had replied,

– Yes, I shall go ahead, but you will wait for me.

What had her family of Jews been doing for centuries but waiting? She, after a long time, had come to some strange idea that she must come toward Christ. Wasn't He the last crowning glory, maybe only He would finally be her prince – her king? Why had the Jews been kept pure but to give birth to this magnificent rose without thorns? The thorns had been put on by human hands.

And what did the wandering Jew mean? Go a little faster. The Semitic idea of time was not the same as the Celtic. Loyalty to someone was the length of time you were with them; like her mother who said I gave you all the years of my life. I sacrificed myself. Where is your gratitude? What was this idea of reward they wanted – the eternal admonition to husbands and children? But in Arthur, in his Celtic appreciation, in the space of moments, whole worlds would crumble and be built again from entirely new material.

Her worlds were always built over and over again from the same ruins.

How many times had Babylon been destroyed and rebuilt with the same bricks? The Celts hid in forests where there were no signs and made no graven images. They never even transcribed words, only spoke them. Their time was moon time. She thought of Arthur who could sleep all day and only become alive at night. But in spite of this, the Semitic complex was that every Jewish boy had to be a Messiah and every girl the mother of one.

But Arthur had his point of vulnerability, his "Achilles' ear," Adrienne called it. It was the awakening in the morning with a hangover and the shakes. It was the guilt, the nightmares accumulated, and at that moment her reproaches of – You did this . . . or you did that to me – could drive him crazy. Then she could get to him, he was weak. It was the same principle her mother used.

– Do you remember what you did to me fifteen years ago? I'll never forget it. Every insult was counted up, stored away for use on a future day of judgement, to be brought out with a roar of trumpets and scored on a golden blackboard to be added and subtracted for a final result in the account book of angelic dividends.

His was a mind of blank pages written on and erased again and again, soaked in a weathered litmus solution. He was always amazed when she brought up some violence or injustice he had committed, even a few days ago. He had so completely changed into someone else. He was always going through a metamorphosis that, however, was never complete, like a tadpole which might have webbed feet then these would drop off to develop back into a tail or fin. There was no catching him, or making him face up to anything. He slipped completely through her fingers. What the Jew could do was to forgive, but forget he couldn't. This was the thorn in his side. She knew though if she were to survive, she must learn to do both . . .

. . . She remembered when she had finally told her parents she had – bought her ticket to Damascus – Her father had stood up in his undershirt and her mother shook her head under a black-veiled hat. Relations crowded into the living room holding sunglass hands over their eyes . . .

A violent wind blew the ancestral photos off the wall; they lay on the floor staring at her with reproachful eyes. Words flew around the room like locusts.

– You are a deserter of the Holy Temple – its walls will fall down and crush you . . . Our daughter worshipper of a living God . . . You are cursed.

Her mother slapped her and her father pulled out a hypodermic needle and stuck it in his hairy chest; then pushed the needle into her mother's swollen thigh and poured the blood into Elijah's golden cup.

– Drink this – he ordered – blood is thicker than water or wine.

She took the offered cup of ancestral blood and threw it against the wall . . . a flash of lightning lit the room. The walls went red as the seven great plagues stormed in the window . . . Frogs . . . Flies . . . Lice . . . Boils crawled over their flesh. Hail iced the room. Locusts ate their clothes – the rugs, the curtains, and left them naked in a skeletal room . . . and Darkness fell like a hangman's hood. Then the blood multiplied – coagulating into a thick red sea, choking them as curses rose bubbling in their throats. She was drowning in this sea of warm red blood – till she reached a window and smashed the glass. Another flash of lightning lit the room in a holocaust of fire. Showers of sparks burned her eyes and in a blind fall, she dropped unconscious on a sandy road – a long way yet to go . . .

Then they called out the apprentice angel . . . the one who would come to sprinkle lamb's blood on the Egyptian's door. He was to slaughter at the Butcher of the Golden Calf, a sacrificial lamb and put this sign of blood on the heathen's door. The sacrificial lamb lay bleating on a wooden plank – his eyes turned inward like a battered doll. Hooked on the wall unredeemed meat hung down, dyeing the butcher's hands and aprons a bloody red. But he, the angel, immaculate in a blood-proof smock of shining white – hiding the hunchback of his folded wings – lifted a silver knife cutting the lamb dumb with only the gurgling blood on the sawdust floor.

Swiftly the angel with transparent fingers touched the blood seven times and hopefully it congealed, pulsing in an ebb and flow . . . petal after petal of jellied blood, he molded and enfolded, as a feather falling from his wing turned to stem, and blood grew inward and outward toward a fleshed red rose.

And he opened the breast of the still warm lamb cupping out the swollen heart, inserting the new made flesh. Ah, then the silent heads of calves, coquettish in their wax-wreathed roses, began to bellow and moan; tears running down their glazed blue eyes. Slowly the other sober carcasses hanging transfixed from golden hooks, trembled and shook like menial caged beasts when an unbelievable earthquake opens their wire door and a fissure gapes in a mad hole dragging the familiar landscape screaming down into chaos.

After, there was a stunned silence – where meat became meat again and the darker heavy velvet of blood hanging in the antechamber, waited for the Jack Spratt of dark and light devoured in a reconciliation of sun with the charcoal of the cock's burnt cry attending each bloody sacrifice to re-open again the carnival curtain.

And Adrienne saw herself and Arthur walking through the meat markets at Les Halles one early dawn. And how many bloody dawns had he held between his arms? The red sun spilling over crucified meat and two black bulls bleeding beside the sky, while he swayed and held her against his thigh . . . his lips slightly wet, eyes opaque that covered lost rainbows and his damp skin shivering over her with lust. And in that dawn some gay, alone at a café table, held a bunch of roses in his pale ringed hands, tearing effeminately petal by petal and in a sing song voice . . . He loves me . . . a little . . . not at all . . . passionately . . . Petal by petal till only the thorned stems, discarded yarrow sticks, settled on the table and the petals lay scattered in drops of blood.

Back she went to the Passover service at home . . . and she was spilling drops of wine on the white linen tablecloth. Her father was reading the service.

– "And the Lord spake unto Moses. Go unto Pharoah, and say

unto him, Thus saith the Lord, let my people go, that they may serve me. And if thou refuse to let them go, behold, I will smite all thy borders with frogs . . ."

And for each plague, she had dipped her pinky in the wine glass scooping a drop out and spilling it on the tablecloth – the seven plagues God had sent to the Egyptians . . . Frogs . . . Flies . . . Lice . . . Boils . . . Hail . . . Locusts . . . Darkness . . . and death to the firstborn. The wine dotted the cloth like a newly-placed bandage.

In the middle of the table was the burnt lamb bone of sacrifice and the apple, honey and cinnamon symbols of the building mortar. Then her father had handed her sister and her the bitter herb of horseradish, and honey on a piece of matzo for them to eat – the bitter and the sweet of life that must be accepted equally. She took a hard boiled egg and dipped it in salt water. She was hazy about the egg. Was that death to the new born? Then Elijah's gold cup was put on the table and filled with wine and an empty chair placed in front of it. This was the night the prophet came to sit with each Jewish family. Once a strong wind had flung the window open, the wine trembling in tiny red sea waves, and a bat had flown in through the window – almost a miracle as it was in New York City. Her mother had screamed throwing her arms over her head and her father had rushed around the room with a broom. The bat was amazingly tiny, its comic book wings fluttered around the room in circles the broom threw down Elijah's wine – bleeding over the cloth. She had screamed to let it alone, but luckily the bat had flown out the window over the rooftops.

But she was in exile.

She had not found her holy land.

Each year they re-lived their exile – wandering Jews trying to find their way back. For a long time she had been trying to figure it all out . . . Is life really only a fountain? She had gone on a heavy occult trip – Blavatsky, Levy, alchemists, Tibetan books, the Tarot etc. The whole bit. She had lit candles and incense, wore flowing robes, ate no meat, only rice and nuts or just fruit, nothing really helped except for Rudolf Steiner, who had said man had lost his spiritual blueprint and only by re-tracing Christ could he make a foundation.

With her heritage she had lost her way. In the Cabala it is stated that the trouble with this world was that part of God was exiled from God (his feminine side). Nothing down here was in its right place and the only way to fix it all up was to find out the proper name and place of each thing. Things were masquerading under a false identity, but the catch was to figure what the real proper name was – a sort of Scrabble game. And her family had been reliving this exile as long as she could remember hoping to get back to some sort of promised land. But it seemed the whole human race had been kicked out of paradise and here was everyone trying to arrange all the spare parts, to find the right piece in this fucked-up puzzle – even all the couples were trying to get it together, to find out who went with whom. But now they could no longer go two by two into the ark and shut the door and portholes and wait till the green leaf appeared. Each went one by one like a tourist passing through a foreign land with no roots. There was no jumping into the alchemical crucible to be turned into gold, or joined together in the Great Work to become King and Queen . . .

In the dining room in her old home in New York City, there had been a Chinese lacquered cabinet. On one side of the river stood a mandarin and on the other a lady, but there was no bridge between them. It had always upset her. She had a real thing about couples. When she went to a restaurant, she always arranged everything in couples – salt and pepper, oil and vinegar, knife and fork. A goldfish or a bird alone made her anxious. Arthur said it was her ancient heredity of two by two. It was true. The Jews had two candles every Friday night, two angels of peace walked back with each person from temple; and in the old days in Palestine when the new moon was expected, two men were sent to the shores of the Mediterranean where the horizon was clear, to watch for this new moon. As soon as two people were reported to have seen it, the beginning of the month was announced.

SIX : YOU WILL LOSE SOMETHING

She had come to Europe catching the virus of Paris injected by Rimbaud, Miller, Fitzgerald etc. Just before she left, her father had died of a heart attack. Her mother, according to the Jewish custom, had covered all the mirrors with white sheets. What was the reason? To keep the dead from seeing themselves again, or to hide the mirrors because the dead were still around and might see themselves? She didn't know. Anyhow, they'd covered every mirror in the house. One day, trying to put on her make-up, she had pulled out her compact mirror in the bathroom and had slipped and the mirror broke into slivers . . . frozen pieces of ice from the Snow Queen. In a little drawer in the bathroom were all her father's toilet articles – a half squeezed toothpaste, a toothbrush with worn stubble, a shaving brush and lavender shaving cream in a broken box, the razor with a few grey hairs stuck in it and corn plasters. She saw his bare toes with the bent yellow nails and the thick ridged Life Saver corn from his rubbed shoes. She had to close the drawer or she felt she'd be sick.

All the sheet ghosts hung on the wall, slight breezes stirring them as if some horrible pregnant form was moving under them. Once she had picked up the edge of a sheet . . . Would her father be there? All she saw was a silver hole with her frightened blue eyes.

Towards the end, he had been gasping for air, trying to open the windows, tearing at his chest, till all the buttons snapped off his pajama tops. It was summer and the air conditioning was on.

– Open the windows for God's sake – he cried.

But her mother was firm.

– No, no, all that outside air is too hot and humid. It's bad for you.

In the last years of his life, her father had been a travelling salesman. Before that, he'd been his own boss in a cocktail glass company that made imports from Belgium. He had even named a cocktail glass after her. The Adrienne glass. It had a tall thin stem and the top part was curved like a crescent moon.

During the depression, the company had gone bankrupt and he had become a dress salesman, working for someone else. It had been a real blow to him and he had never been the same. From a jolly, easy going man, he became anxious and withdrawn. Once he had even taken to playing the horses – newspapers and calculation sheets strewn all over the living room. Sometimes in the afternoon, he'd lie down on the sofa, his socks full of holes, unshaven, the blinds drawn and her mother screaming. She always remembered the word MONEY.

Besides covering all the mirrors, they had also taken down all the photos of her father. She had found them face down in a drawer. There was one of her mother and her father and his mother taken in Atlantic City. Her father was posing in a Homburg hat and a swanky overcoat with a cigar in his hand. Her mother stood by him in a cloche hat with a veil and a pair of sables. In the center her grandmother, in one of those boardwalk carriages, sat upright in an enormous fur coat. It was winter and in back of them was the sea with the whipped cream surf and a few seagulls on the crest like cake decorations. The picture was yellow and curdled and, in spite of the weather, like the end of a hot afternoon. She remembered that Arthur's father had a bar in Atlantic City. She'd have to ask him where it was.

Once in a fight with her father over some guy, she had run away to Atlantic City for a weekend. She must have been about sixteen. It had been late fall. She had walked along the almost deserted boardwalk. The sand was covered with dried seaweed and half-buried cans and bottles. The sky and the sea were a dirty tattle-tale gray and the waves sudsed and churned in a giant unending washing machine. The seagulls cawing seemed to be crying – Nevermore . . . Nevermore . . . She had spent the night in a little hotel off the boardwalk. In her room everything was damp – the walls, the sheets, even her clothes. All night long outside, the waves roared like wild animals.

The next day she took a walk on the boardwalk. Along the sand, horses were galloping with bare chested riders – centaurs knitted close to the horseflesh in a Gauguin painting. Auctioneers in open air shops shouted their wares over loads of watches, sugar, dishes . . . One dollar . . . do I hear more? . . . Who'll make it two? . . . bludebludeblu . . . Sold to the lady in the red coat and his hammer came down with finality. An old lady in a red coat came over to get a set of dishes.

In a glass case, a mechanical wax gypsy gave out fortune tickets. She sat mummy-like in a red bandana and large gold ear-rings. She had put a coin in the slot. The gypsy turned her head, moving it up and down, the black glass eyes staring into space. Her manicured hands with a flashing green ring pointed to a Jack of Diamonds. Out came a pale green paper . . . you will meet a stranger who will change your life . . . But beware. You will take a long trip. You will lose something, but you will find it again . . . Your lucky number is twenty-seven . . . She had kept the paper a long time till it fell apart. That afternoon she went home. She wouldn't really leave home for good till she went to Paris.

Her mother had a mania for covering everything. In the summer when they went to Long Island, the city apartment became a ghost with the mirrors, chairs, sofa, beds covered. Even the toilet seat had a cover. Both sex and death were to be covered over. A slit or a protuberance was obscene – the Victorian hangover of hiding piano legs as male pricks. Her mother had given her definite rules to live by. A man must respect a woman. He must pay for her. She is entitled to a decent life – wall to wall carpeting, terry cloth toilet seats, matching sets of dishes, silverware, crystal, naturally all the modern conveniences. And as for the fur coat, that was a definite status symbol for a nice woman. How about minks Adrienne thought, they were really a royal society, outdoing humans. They were born with fur on their back and they didn't have to force themselves to open their legs for it . . . Then every night there was the cry . . . Close the windows, the curtains. Don't let any drafts in . . . keep everything foreign out.

Luckily her mother had never come to Europe to visit her. She had now been gone thirteen years. She had no two plates alike. The toilet seat was cracked (she was lucky not to have a Turkish toilet). The small rug on the floor didn't hit the walls and was spotted with wine and grease. She used mustard glasses. The window was cracked and drafts came in constantly. As for a fur coat, she had an old sheepskin she'd found in the flea market, and on top of all this she was supporting a guy. She thought of her poor father, what would he have said? He always predicted she'd find some kind of hippie with a beard and not a pot to piss in, as he put it.

But her father was dead. She saw the funeral. Her father laid out in the pink quilted coffin in the funeral parlor, powdered, spruced up, his bloated hands crossed on his chest, dressed in his best pin-striped suit and tie, even with socks and shoes. Her mother had wanted him to have his horn-rimmed glasses, but her aunt had discouraged that – glasses over closed eyelids to see what? Somehow Adrienne could never make any connection between this dummy and her father.

They buried him in the cemetery among her mother's hysteria and the rabbi's speech . . . Upright citizen . . . What a fine man, good father and provider . . . She couldn't see the connection. As they lowered the coffin, the rabbi threw three broken pieces of pottery on top of the lid. They made a hollow ringing sound as they hit the lead coffin. Three pieces for the vanity of all things – vanity of the eyes, vanity of the nose, vanity of the mouth . . .

She saw her father sitting in his favorite old gold velvet chair, biting his nails, chewing on his soggy cigar before the television set. He used to give her money to go to the corner drugstore to buy Anthony and Cleopatra cigars. She remembered the cigar box with Cleopatra lying half-naked on a gold couch and Anthony in a leopard skin lying at her feet with a palm tree behind them. Was there a snake nearby? Then she and her sister would get a gold cigar ring to put on their fingers.

Sometimes, regretting he had two daughters and no son, he'd take her to a ball game. He spoke little, maybe because her mother talked a lot. On Sunday he'd take her and her sister to a Chinese restaurant on Broadway. It was upstairs and she could see the people below hurrying by. Inside there was an odor of fried pork and incense. They'd go to Loew's double feature. He was very sentimental when someone got hurt. She could hear his little jerky sobs in the dark and got very embarrassed and pretended not to look at him, poking her younger sister who'd get mad and poke her back . . .

What was the link between this rubbery form and him? He

was a man who felt he had been a failure. As a business man he wasn't much good. He couldn't make any deals that were not completely straight and anyone could get credit out of him. He never broke his word when he gave it. A promise for him was a promise. Never could she remember when he said he'd do something that he didn't do it – a soda, a movie, a walk, the most simple things – if he said it he did it. But in the end, he just sat in his gold velvet chair looking at television – or looking through it, already somewhere else.

What would he have thought of Arthur . . .?

After the funeral, all the relatives arrived for a spread with herring, lox, pickles, chicken liver, potato salad, a turkey and Manischevetz wine. One aunt brought her mother a box of chocolate mint wafers. Her mother had taken the wafers ungraciously and waved them in the air . . .

– When your husband, Sydney, died, if you remember, I brought you a turkey . . . and this is what she gives me . . .

Adrienne was depressed as she heard the sympathetic moans, gravy dripping down their chins, their fat lips puckering like chicken asses. Her father was really lucky to be out of all this. Schlepping his suitcases full of dresses to out of town hotels and hanging around the lobby or sitting alone in his hotel room in one horse towns, looking at television, enveloped in his constant cigar smoke. The tears had started down her cheeks. She ran out of the room and flung herself on her bed. Her only image was of his cigar stubs crushed in the dirt around the giant snake plant . . . A little butterfly had flown in through the window . . .

SEVEN : BUTTERFLY

When she was about seven, a white butterfly had flown into her room in New York City. She had finally caught it by one of its wings. The free wing fluttered wildly as she pressed it onto her desk. Quickly she took a pin and stuck it into the fuzzy stomach. The brown body curled up and the pale wings panted and sprinkled the desk with a spray of fine powder. She watched as the pinned butterfly struggled . . . opening and closing its now torn wings like a white floured mouth. She took a glass jar and put it over the butterfly. Gradually it relaxed, the wings quieted and stayed open. There was a picture on the wall from which she'd taken the glass, put the butterfly under it, and hung it back on the wall – pressed into one dimension.

Soon after this, she had gone to camp. One morning she had gotten up early. The counsellor and the other girls were asleep – slipping into her camp uniform and taking her butterfly net she went outside. The sun was just rising and a violet mist hung over the wet grass. A few butterflies floated unfaithfully from flower to flower. Underneath a leaf there was a white cocoon.

She wondered where butterflies slept at night.

Before her on a rose thistle, a large yellow and black butterfly – a Tiger Swallowtail – was about to take off. It spurted into the air like a tiny flame. Quickly she threw her net over it catching the butterfly in flight and put it in a glass jar with a cotton dabbed with formaldehyde. She now knew what to do and was starting a collection.

Another afternoon when the bunk was supposed to take a nap, she went back into the fields. Framed against the blue sky flew a clear white butterfly. She ran after it with her net when suddenly her ankle twisted and she fell on a sharp stone. The blood stained a patch of daisies pink. Holding on to her leg, she stumbled back to the bunk with a bad cut. She still had this scar on her knee shaped like a red mouth. The next day she had to rest. It hurt a lot. All the children had gone out to play. Painfully she got out of bed and took her collection of butterflies with her. She hobbled to the daisy patch where she had fallen. One daisy was still pink from her blood. She opened her box of butterflies and took out a Swallowtail, a Monarch, a Cabbage Moth and all the rest of them and placed them on the daisies . . . opening their wings back and forth, puffing out her cheeks and blowing on them. The butterflies flew into the air like small kites and then down again for lack of wind. She had seen a little boy who had attatched a string to a butterfly and it had stayed up in the air like a kite. Some of the butterflies disappeared among the flowers. The Swallowtail's yellow wing tore. She remembered falling on the grass, tearing out clumps of weeds with her clenched hands, and crying and moaning.

– It hurts . . . it hurts.

Her counsellor found her there.

– It hurts . . . it hurts – she kept repeating.

The counsellor had patted her on the head.

– I know your leg hurts, dear, but it will be healed soon.

But of course that wasn't what she had meant . . .

Now there was a new phenomenon – the factory butterfly.

It was a city butterfly, no longer white but gray. It was a form of mimicry that had adapted to the modern dirty buildings. No more white butterflies would fly in the city. They would now all be gray.

However, the butterfly had become a symbol to her and it went back to Chris . . . She saw the dance hall where she had first met him. She was seventeen. The boys were standing outside the door watching the girls gliding up the stairs. The dance hall was packed with the limited amount of standard equipment of – eyes, nose, mouth arranged in unending variety. It was her first dance. Everyone was standing about in casual attitudes with the platonic hope of finding the ideal, but never conscious on the surface. Slowly everyone resignedly shifted from the capital key to the small everyday letter, making the most of what was present. There was the fear of rebuttal, the exposure of the self past the stated time limit . . . too highly focused, blurred, the shattering of the picture by the lack of poise. The boys with fisherman eyes weighed their bait, watching the movements and allusions of the coy fish, to the fish already scarred having been fished up before . . . the muddy water aroused and stirred. In the end there were still all the unsatisfied longings trying to project an ideal mask on the living flesh.

She hadn't been around too much as she had just gotten over a bad case of acne. Now only a few scars showed, heavily covered over with make-up . . . She was just starting to bloom. She would never be a real beauty as her face had too many hard Slavic planes and at that time she was very self-conscious. But later people would say she had a regal look when she entered a room with a more poised and cool behavior. Chris had seen her. She had no experience except for the usual necking and petting, though already most of her friends had had affairs. She was even afraid to tell them how naive she really was. It was as if she was in a vacuum, or sitting in some ante-chamber waiting for something to happen.

Chris had come over and asked her to dance; she felt flattered. He was about twenty, very sure of himself. There was a certain feline air about him with his yellow eyes and supple build. He danced pressing her very hard against him. She could feel his penis swelling over her thigh. He bought her drinks and spent the evening with her. When he took her home, they necked but she wouldn't go any further. After that they went out a few times – still she pushed him off. Finally he said either they went all the way or it was over. He knew she was a virgin but that seemed to appeal to him. But it wasn't his ultimatum that decided her. It was that she had had enough of blind dates, going to bars . . . drinking too much, listening to their dull jokes, their sweaty hands trying to feel you up. No, now with him, it was curiosity. She had to know what it was all about.

He lived in a boarding house in the sixties. She remembered the worn red carpet on the stairs that led to his room on the top floor, and the metallic sound of the key in the lock as he opened the door. The window was half-open, it was an afternoon in the spring, and the lace curtains blew slightly in the breeze. He had gotten undressed quickly, throwing his clothes on the end of the bed, and taken down the faded chintz bedspread. She took off her black bra and panties, bought specially for the occasion, folded her white blouse and skirt on a chair. He leaned over her. She saw his penis rising. He lay on top of her, spreading her legs apart. She saw patches of sunlight filter onto the rug. He began to rub her clitoris, put two fingers in his mouth – wet them and began again. He leaned over to a small night table, took some vaseline and rubbed it over the tip of his penis and slowly pushed it inside her. At that moment a grayish butterfly had flown into the room. It landed on the dresser, flickering its wings. He pushed harder down inside her. She winced.

– It hurts.

– I know – he said, soothingly – but it'll soon be okay.

He pushed harder and harder. She clenched her fists. Suddenly he gave a shudder and fell heavily on top of her. She could feel something wet and sticky on the inside of her thighs. He got up. She could see blood on the sheets. He went into the bathroom. There was the sound of running water.

She lay there and watched the butterfly open and close its wings. It flew over to the lace curtain, fluttered a second there and flew out the window.

This time there would be no outside scar for anyone to see . . .

EIGHT : WAX DOLL

One night when they were in bed, Arthur was sipping beer, looking at a photo magazine and Adrienne was reading . . . it was a quiet night, he hadn't drunk much that day, she asked him – it suddenly came to her – where was his father's bar in Atlantic City? It had been a long time since Arthur had thought of home. He could at that moment smell the sea and he felt a pain across his chest and he knew it was because of Liza. He turned over and put the magazine down.

– Oh, somewhere at the end of the Boardwalk . . . I think I'll take a little snooze . . . and he closed his eyes thinking of her again . . .

– Yeh, Liza was sure a good name for her. People used to call her "Mona" Liza. She had long auburn hair parted in the middle and he could see her hazel eyes . . . the one on the left had a slight cast in it, as if she was overlooking you to some distant mountain. She even had the damn enigmatic smile like she had some great secret, only it never came out. And was she passive. She never suggested anything. She'd always agree with what ever plans he made. Guys always dug her. He remembered it had made him both proud and jealous. She could sit for hours without talking . . . fucking rare for a woman . . . and just nod her head, staring into space. You could pin any archetypal billboard on her you wanted. Some people said she was light, others saw her dark, or she reminded them of their mother or their sister . . . but she was a chick who sure could drink. One of the few he'd met. They got together every weekend – drinking at his old man's bar. She loved mint alcohol. He could see her slowly sipping the drink with her long thin fingers curled around the frosted glass . . . the green reflecting and shading her eyes in a mask. On the wall he could see the starfish and the sea horse he'd found as a kid on the beach. Cloudy glass balls to hold up nets, hung above with lights in them and made the bar into an underwater cave. The more she drank the more enigmatic her smile got. She just sat there like some beautiful doll, but he remembered how soused he'd get and argue with everyone, the old man giving him dirty looks – he'd kicked drink after his bad heart attack.

At that time, he'd been going to school and also had a part time job selling water beds in a store on the Boardwalk. He had the key to the store and sometimes late at night, they'd sneak into the place and make it on one of the water beds . . . their nude bodies sloshing around on this womb of water and outside the breakers moaning and screaming . . . she was even passive in fucking, laying there like some fantastic wax doll . . . her eyes open . . . until she came . . . then she shook all over for one moment like she'd been wound up and then run down . . .

But in the end she'd made it with his best friend, Hank, and then fell in love with him. He had to give her credit – it was Hank who had first chased her. But he'd done everything to get her back . . . crawled on his hands and knees . . . practically kissed her feet and once even cried. The memory made him wince. Then one night he saw it was no use. He hit her . . . catching her over the eye. She never defended herself. Slowly he saw the black and blue grow around her eye, as if her face was a painting that was beginning to rot away in the corner because of a leak in the ceiling . . . soaking and darkening the area. That was it. And when she'd finally married Hank, he didn't give a damn, but he'd never make an ass of himself again for any woman . . . and that's how he'd fucking gotten himself into Vietnam . . .

NINE :   ACROSS THE CHINA SEA

He'd crossed the China Sea in a troop ship. He remembered those nights like black silky pajamas with orange dragons of flaming comets that would black out and fade into dotted rice-grain stars . . . The boat had arrived at Saigon at sunset, followed by a school of porpoises. Much later he was sent to Phoem-Yen, the village of red leaves. There one day, standing outside a shop, he'd met a girl with parchment skin – her name was Golden Flower. She'd taken him to eat in a cantine . . . A rotating fan hung in the middle of the room like in old movies on the East. The fan blew strands of her black hair across her eyes. They sat at a wooden table with cherry blossoms. She'd ordered soup for the two of them in one large bowl. The soup was light green with some sort of seaweed and on the bottom he could see a cooked coral starfish. Golden Flower took her chopsticks like a fishing rod and dipped them into the bowl, nipping off a bit of the star point. She handed him the piece. He had hesitated . . . then swallowed the orange point . . . it burned inside him like a trail of holiday sparklers . . . some white cherry blossoms fell into the soup, and at that moment he had seen the crystal ball he'd had as a child, swirling with snowflakes and suddenly remembered here it was summer, but back home it was already winter . . .

Later he had gone A.W.O.L. and had spent a week in a Vietnamese whorehouse. His special girl was only sixteen . . . very tiny but beautifully formed. She was already a woman, not comparable to an American girl of the same age. She'd taught him a lot about fucking. He realized now he was pretty lazy when it came to making it, and the drinking didn't help much. Flower of Joy, her American name, came to him when she was through with her clients. Quite a few G.I's were hiding out there also. They played cards, drank and fucked . . .

While he'd been in Vietnam, he'd mysteriously developed a group of warts on his left hand. Flower of Joy told him the way to get rid of them was to rub the warts on the back of a frog, then when someone touched the frog, he'd catch the warts. He thought, you always had to put your trip on someone else; there had to be some scapegoat to get rid of it.

But the M.P.'s were checking up and they all got caught. He'd felt bad about not seeing Flower of Joy again – luckily they'd only gotten a week in the guardhouse and after he'd been put in the tank division.

He thought back to the day when nothing much was happening, they'd filled the tank with beer, plastic sacks of ice and had driven to a secluded beach. They fixed a canvas tent over the tank, took off their clothes – lying naked in the sand, drinking beer. He had had to shit and had walked over to a clump of trees. Nearby was a small pond. Nothing better than to wipe your ass with dry leaves. After he'd walked to the pond and sat on a stump . . . It was so calm you wouldn't think there was a war around . . . the slow hum of insects and a few bird calls . . . when suddenly a small frog had jumped on his knee, its yellow eyes staring at him. He could feel its heart beat on his knee . . . No, brother, I'm not going to dissect you . . . It didn't move, when he remembered Flower of Joy's advice about warts. With a quick movement he grabbed the frog and rubbed his warts over its slimy back . . . he let go, the frog leaped from his hand into the still green water . . . plop . . . and it was gone with a few ripples by a lotus pad.

Whether it was coincidence or not, about two weeks later, all the warts except one disappeared. He wondered if someone had found the frog and taken his warts, or had the frog given them to another frog?

Contrary to what he'd expected, the violence in the tank division was certainly not as bad as hand to hand combat. Here you were covered up like a robot, though the whole thing could be blown up of course. He'd seen the ordinary horrors, but a buddy of his, Leo, had told him about a super-nightmare. He couldn't get it out of his mind . . .

Leo had described the bombing of a Pagoda called the Pleasure Gardens . . . His troop had thrown hand grenades into the courtyard . . . When the smoke and explosions had cleared away, they'd walked into the bloody mess . . . heads had rolled off bodies . . . arms, legs swam separated in the royal pool . . . blooming, as Leo had put it, with brain flowers and gut leaves floating on the red water . . . Then the soldiers had marched into the eunuchs' quarters, the bodyguards of the royal concubines, and they'd grabbed the poor devils and chopped off their pricks . . . their balls had already been sliced off, and hung the bloody pricks on a cherry tree . . . the pricks still dripping . . . dyeing the petals red . . . After that they went for the girls hugging and holding on each to each other . . . Leo said every girl had a different colored robe . . . screeching and waving their large sleeves like crazed birds . . . and ten guys lined up for one girl . . . making bets to see how many times he could fuck her and who'd make the highest score like holes in a pin ball machine . . . Leo said he'd backed out . . . He just couldn't make it . . .

After, they hit the priest's park . . . but an old monk had beat them to it and had poured a can of gasoline over himself and lighted a match . . . He exploded in the center like some mad comet going out in space . . . flames petaling in sizzling fireworks as he fried in his own grease. . . and behind him was this fucking twenty foot Buddha . . . smiling . . .

And he remembered when the war was over they had a big commemorative service for the dead. Bands were playing. Generals, covered with medals flashing under a hot sun, made speeches, "That our dead shall not have died in vain". Speeches that sounded as if they were on tape coming from the inside of their uniforms – wound up, turned on and off. Flowers galore were spread over fresh graves that were only marked with crosses, row on row. But it was not the fresh flowers covered with ribbons and cellophane carefully placed on the mounds for the anniversary of their death, but the later faded flowers three days old . . . red and orange petals decaying like bits of flesh with the black flies buzzing crazily in the sun . . . only then could someone speak of coming resurrection . . .

There was only one guy who'd missed it all – an American G.I. who'd hidden in a Vietnamese woman's cellar for five years. When they caught him, the war was already over. He was white as a mushroom. He said he only went out at night to look at the "television" stars. Once in awhile he'd fuck the woman, who wasn't so young, when she came down to the cellar with his food. And day after day, he'd sat in that hole staring at spiders spinning their webs, checking out how many flies would fall into the trap – he had a score card he'd kept for five years – marking it as he watched the flies struggle . . . their buzzing like the coming end of a burnt-out bulb. That score card of flies was all he had seen of the war.

Everything was cool in the army if you knew the difference between black, white and yellow. The "gooks" were yellow – the bad guy. You were fighting for liberty etc . . . The crap began with the guys who suddenly couldn't distinguish the color line anymore, who saw the "gooks" as someone human with a wife, kids etc. These were the ones who broke down –

had to be sent to mental hospitals – watched – weren't normal. They were confused over who was the bad guy and who was the hero. Then, after being in the bombers, it was certainly less horrifying than a dissection. No corpse around – "Clean bombs" . . . no screams, no unpleasant smells . . . no bodies rotting, only some smoke in the distance. You could even believe people didn't exist, but just went up in smoke like a stick of incense. It was hitting toy cities and figures when you used to be sick in bed, playing soldiers on the covers . . . a clean swap of your legs under the sheets and the soldiers scattered all over.

But sometimes, when the smoke cleared, it was like a flashback of an old horror movie. A hand was seen waving with no fingers, or a head was found half a mile away from the body, or a kid with a dog next to it lay charcoaled in relief. It was *The Last Days of Pompeii* – ashes preserved in a man-made violence.

At night in the bunks, a lot of guys screamed in their sleep. In the morning no one remembered. How much did one need – to forget, to black-out, to drink down, wipe out, space out, "tabula rasa" – Blow the mind up . . . dynamite it at the fucking roots that grew like jungle rot.

But at night the dead were legion. They crawled out of fresh graves . . . or swamps or plains, mounds, sand, mud . . . Some came crawling out with no arms or legs, just trunks rolling like rubber balls, others were just skeletons already eaten away with hanging flesh like torn dishrags . . . and the smell of rotting flesh got into the mouths, throats, noses. Green-bottle flies were so heavily clustered on corpses that they took the place of skin.

Some bodies that came out of the grave at night weren't even sure they had their own arms, legs, heads or trunks.

And the dead were legion at night and came and stared at the sleeping men . . . quietly disappearing in the early light like over-exposed film . . .

Arthur gave a shudder and woke from his reverie. He turned around. The light was still on. The clock showed 4. Adrienne had fallen asleep with her book beside her. He looked at her. She had two heavily marked lines on her forehead, as if she was always trying to grasp something she couldn't get hold of. Her lips were slightly parted, her broad nose breathing heavily. She looked defenseless. He leaned over and put his arms around her. She stirred slightly; a tiny moan escaped from her lips.

She must be dreaming . . .

TEN :   FOREIGNER

One afternoon Adrienne realized there was no toilet paper in the house and she'd have to go to the store. It was a hot day. She threw on an Indian blouse, a pair of old jeans and tied her long hair back with a rubber band into a pony tail. As she put on her sandals, she noticed her feet weren't too clean.

Walking down the street, she had the sensation someone was staring at her. She turned around. A tall, thin man in a dark suit with a slight smile showing a gold tooth, was certainly staring at her. She ignored him. At the corner, a little old man was giving out papers . . . MME ZOUMA READS YOUR PALM . . . TAROT CARDS . . . COFFEE GROUNDS ETC . . . in little blue and yellow tickets . . . too small for toilet paper.

She went into the hardware store. When she came out, he was standing waiting for her.

— Pardon me — he said apologetically to her as she stood there with the unwrapped rose toilet paper.

— I know its not polite, but I find you so sympathetic . . . would you like to have a drink with me?

She stared at him hostilely.

— I'm an industrialist.

What a shame Adrienne thought, he could have been an acrobat, a magician or a lion tamer.

He smiled. His eyes were dark, oily black olives and his gold tooth shone in the light.

– You remind me, I hope you won't be offended, of my dead wife.

For a moment that checked her. This was really a new twist.

– Just leave me alone . . . go away, she snapped.

He heard her accent. He recoiled.

– Ah, so you're a foreigner. Why don't you go back to where you came from.

He leaned forward. She could smell his heavy breath, then he moved backward, a bit like a marionette that has lost a string, and shuffled away. A young Indian girl passed. She had long black hair and a turquoise sari bare on one shoulder. A diamond inserted in her left nostril glittered in the sunlight and a red ladybird spot sat in the middle of her forehead.

Going back to the house, she thought about the episode. That was it. She was a foreigner, not only the foreigner, but on top of it, a wandering Jew in exile. She had utterly rejected this man, was he just another panhandler, or had he been sincere? Whatever it was, her first reaction had been to reject him. She rushed home. She had to go to the bathroom.

Adrienne wasn't feeling too hot that night and had gone to bed early. Arthur went off on his rounds. About four in the morning, she heard a racket at the door. Then she heard Arthur come in. He walked into the bedroom, but not alone – with some guy. Arthur's hair was disheveled. He was in a rosy good humor.

– Look I've brought a friend home.

She sat up dignifiedly in the bed, glad for once she'd put on a shirt.

– This is Robert, he said proudly.

She saw a blondish man with a rather long nose and pale blue eyes very close together. Immediately she didn't trust him. Arthur had his arm familiarly around Robert's shoulder.

– He's got no place to sleep tonight, he spent all his money but he's taking the plane for Canada tomorrow morning. I didn't want him to sleep in the park.

– Where did you meet him? snorted Adrienne.

– He's my good friend, and Arthur hugged Robert closer.

– He bought me drinks at the Snowflake.

– Why didn't you also bring a few *clochards* with him, said Adrienne sarcastically. But it fell on deaf ears.

– If he's taking a plane, I don't see why he couldn't manage a hotel room.

Robert held his hands imploringly together. He was quite drunk.

– Don't let me disturb you both, rather than disturb you, really, I'd rather sleep on a hotel . . . I mean a park bench . . .

– Like hell you would, muttered Adrienne under her breath as she threw her robe over her.

– Good night to both of you, she called out as she slammed the door and crawled onto the daybed in the living room.

They looked at each other surprised. She got into the bed in a vile mood when about five minutes later, Arthur stumbled in.

– I'm lonely, he complained.

– Really, but you have such a nice friend.

– I know, but I think he wanted to make it with me.

– That's nice . . . Why didn't you?

– Oh, come on. You know I can't make that scene. I tried it once, but nothing happened so I gave it up – and he fell on top of her.

– Oh, Jesus, she cried.

He giggled and put his hand between her legs, then he sighed.

– I don't think I am up to it tonight – and turned over, instantly asleep.

She lay pasted next to him in the small bed listening to the snores that came from the two rooms. She hoped Robert didn't have crabs or lice. Then, crushed in a corner, she finally fell asleep. She was awakened by the door to the apartment quietly closing. It was the softness of the noise that intrigued her. She disentangled herself. Had the guy snuck out because he'd taken something? They didn't have much, a radio, a record player, no jewelry, she'd sold the bit she'd had. She went into the room. The bed was completely topsy turvy – and then she saw why. He had peed on the bed. The sheets were soaked through to the mattress. She tore everything off. It was luck Arthur didn't come in at that moment – he would have seen Medusa snakes trembling from her head – her fury such that, just by looking at her, he would have been turned to stone. But luckily he continued to snore. She washed the mattress with chlorine, put a thick towel over the wet part – settled on the side in a blanket and fell asleep.

She dreamed her mother had died.

– Put her body under my mattress – she said to the attendant and went out. When she came home, she couldn't see her mother's body, but she noticed the form bulging under one side between the mattress and the springs. She lay down on the bed over the lump, resolved to sleep on it. In the night (still in the dream) she woke up to a terrible smell. The body was giving off a rotten odor. Again she went back to sleep and again waking up (in the dream) she realized the body was putrifying. She hadn't been afraid of sleeping over her mother's body, only disgusted. Suddenly she realized she'd need another bed. In the room were lots of glass doors with beds behind them, but nothing pleased her.

– I must bury my mother right away – she said to someone . . .

– All right – an indistinct form said – we'll bury her on Sunday. And she woke up with a start.

Arthur came in. When she explained about his friend, she could see he felt very sheepish.

– I guess I was drunker than I thought – he said feebly – He seemed like such a nice guy and I felt sorry for him.

She had to be honest, did she like to play the Jewish martyr in these situations and didn't she automatically reject all those who didn't belong to the élite?

While Arthur loved all the disinherited, pouring out undiscriminating kindness on everyone. What destroyed the barriers of blood kinship better than wine?

She thought it had all begun with Noah, who made wine and then had gotten drunk one afternoon and fallen asleep naked in his tent, and his son, Ham, had the impudence to peek in at him and see his respectable father dead drunk, naked on the bed; but his father had caught him looking and cursed him and all his descendants and poor Ham, he had been the begetter of all the blacks, Indians, underdogs – these races, the early missionaries had considered as animals, including women who were also without souls . . . according to Noah's curse on Ham. Then Christ had come along and made wine a sacrament. What did he use it for but to break down the blood ties of kinship, nationality . . .

Everyman was a brother at the bar, where a Jew could drink with a goy. But what had happened was that after the wine had broken the blood barrier it became a curse. It was no longer used as a sacrament and turned men back again into pigs without discrimination who ate pearls with their shit. Water seemed to turn to piss not to wine and she remembered some passage from Rudolf Steiner that it was the early

Dionysian worship of wine that broke down the principles of blood and race and also disconnected man's ties from the spiritual world so he could develop his inner ego to become free and have his own personal liberty, but man has gone too far down into his ego and now needs to re-discover the spiritual mansion with which the barrier of alcohol has closed the door.

ELEVEN :   LIQUID TRIP

She thought about all the spilling of liquid that seemed to go on with her arrival in Paris . . . She walked along the *quai* gorged with bookstalls, barges sailing flags of laundry – street cleaners with fresh twig brooms. She'd been ecstatic her first week there. Screens of words attached to her eyes by Miller, especially that little toilet where he'd had a revelation of the rooftops of Paris. Here she wasn't a tourist. She was on a pilgrimage – each cobblestone had an imprint of some venerable foot like the Gaumont Theater of stars in Hollywood. All of it made her giddy, when suddenly one afternoon walking, she had had to pee something terrible. Her small hotel off St. Germain had a stand-up Turkish toilet, so she knew what to expect. There was a café on the corner of the Beaux Arts. She went in and not knowing much French said hesitatingly "toilet". A waiter behind the bar, hiding a cigaret behind his hand, a puff of smoke escaping from his lips, pointed nonchalantly to the back of the café.

It was very dimly lit in the back. She groped till she found a door. She looked inside for a light but couldn't see one, so she closed the door. It was pitch black. She walked to what she thought was the middle of the floor, the hole was generally there, and lowered her jeans but being in such a hurry she even wet the back of her pants – the pee splashing on her feet. She reached out for paper, usually there were cut up newspapers, but there was only a phone book. Since it didn't seem to be cut up, she'd have to tear out the pages. She got up and opened the door, but what was her horror to see it was a phone booth. The pee was already beginning to flood the booth and drip out into the corridor. She ran out of the café in a panic and even years later never went back . . . "Wrong number" . . . "Wrong number" . . . there had been a creation myth where the first woman had peed and peed – making all the oceans of the world.

Her early days in Paris she had called her "liquid" trip. She was constantly spilling things, as if she'd been bottled up and finally it was all fizzing out. There had been that afternoon at the Tuileries writing letters home. The children were playing with colored sailboats and the goldfish in the pond were snapping for bread a little boy was timidly throwing in. She had just bought a bottle of ink to fill her pen. The ink was by her feet poised on the white marble tiles. She dipped her pen into the ink, the bottle slipped and turned over, the ink dripping on the marble in a Rorschach test blob. It looked like the map of France. She saw an African worker with a pail and a broom of twigs sweeping away some leaves. She ran up to him and pointed to the ink. He looked puzzled, but she motioned for the pail and brush and he reluctantly handed them to her.

Filling the pail with water from the basin, she swept the marble covered with the dyed-blue ink. A crowd of curious children watched her, their mouths half open like goldfish. Finally, when she felt she could do no better, she brought back the pail and the broom now blue like Disney twigs. The African was standing with his hands crossed, motionless – a Nubian statue among all the pale classic sculptures. For the next year or two when she went to the Tuileries, she saw the ink stain like a black and blue bruise on the marble, till the seasons healed and washed it away.

The other spilling had been Arthur's. They had gone to the

Montparnasse Cemetery looking for Baudelaire's tomb. Arthur had brought a bottle of wine with him to make a toast. In the distance an old lady was scrubbing, perhaps her husband's tomb – throwing away the dead flowers and sweeping away dead leaves with a cloth – as if her husband might suddenly appear, sitting by the side of his tomb in bedroom slippers, reading his paper, smoking his cigar – so she could still impatiently reprimand him for throwing his ashes disrespectfully on his grave and not into an ashtray . . .

They wandered around the graves till they came across the statue of Baudelaire lying down, the head against the cemetery wall. On his chest someone had laid an offering of two purple wax roses. The statue lay bound in a carved stone shroud – a fantastic tadpole, the hands in fins metamorphosing into a strange aquatic creature caught in layer after layer of gray seaweed cauls . . . suffocating . . . drowning. Above him hung a gargoyle with huge outspread wings, its face masked by a leprous growth of black fungus, the hands cupped under its chin – meditating. Arthur made a move forward and tripped on a broken flower pot. The wine bottle slipped out of his hand and spilt over the statue like blood bubbling up from the bound body. Quickly they ran down the path – turning they could see the wine spreading over the whole statue.

– Okay – Arthur breathed heavily when they got outside the gate . . . Fuck that scene . . . let's go to see Jimmy Morrison's grave. After all he was our modern poet . . . "the bright boy".

They went to Père Lachaise where he was buried. The cemetery guide gave them a disgusted look and pointed out the grave. There was no marker on top. It was anonymous except for two guys sitting on the side smoking. One was strumming a guitar. The other was cross-eyed and it was hard to say what direction his eyes were looking in. They were smoking a joint. Arthur and she stood watching them. The cross-eyed guy handed Arthur the joint. He took a few puffs, she hadn't wanted any, and handed it back. No one said anything. The grave was strewn with cigaret butts, a rose just about to wilt, a plug from a bath tub, some broken guitar strings and a few pieces of a broken record . . . the vanity of the eyes, nose, mouth, maybe.

There were slogans all over the plot . . . BURN YOURSELF UP . . . PULL ALL THE PLUGS OUT . . . LET THE TAPS RUN . . . HASH WASN'T GOOD FOR YOU . . . JIM IS NOT DEAD – HE IS DWELLING IN THE STARS . . . The guy continued to pluck at the guitar. A small faded picture of Morrison in a plastic cover stood at the head of the grave – a slight smile on the lips. The sun was shining. In the distance, a funeral was just finishing. Some well-dressed men and women were standing by while an enormous wreath of bright red roses was placed on the grave. On a gold ribbon she could barely make out the words *"A NOTRE PERE"*.

Behind them gray smoke was coming out of the large crematorium chimney. She had started to shiver, pulling on Arthur's arm for them to leave. As they walked back through the graves, the low wailing sound of the guitar seemed to come up out of the ground. After that time there was no more spilling, in the same way, except in that later dried out pond.

TWELVE :   CAROUSEL

They went up to Pigalle one evening. There was a fair on. Booths were lined up on the boulevard like tiny rooms in a dollhouse. Along the way was a carousel.

– Oh, let's take a ride – Adrienne said gleefully.

– Okay – Arthur replied a bit condescendingly – but I'm going to get a bottle of beer first.

He went into a café, to the bar, and came out with a bottle.

– Here's a great one for me – Arthur called out, sitting on a giant green frog with bulging yellow eyes.

– I'll take the swan – and Adrienne got inside a plaster swan; its long neck moving gracefully up and down – I always remember those swans at camp, they looked like they were ice skating. Adrienne waved to him as she leaned back.

The carousel music floated out into the night, colored lights turning round them like circular ribbons. An Algerian, with bushy hair and a checked suit, held up a wooden stick with rings. Arthur leaned over but missed the ring. They bobbed around and around always returning to the same place.

The silky lights maypoled around them. A boy and girl threw confetti over them. Arthur's hair was a pointilliste painting. He held his beer bottle in one hand over the frog's yellow eye and with the other hand he tried again for the ring. This time he caught it and threw it to her. She held out her hands. The gold ring hit the swan's neck and rolled into a crack in the wooden floor. She felt cheated. They floated on . . . the speed slowly coming down like the efforts of a swimmer in a slow motion dream gliding to shore. Adrienne's eye focused on a shooting gallery. In front of it stood a little girl with yellow pigtails in a white dress, a man, certainly her father, was proudly leaning over her. He had just shot a bull's-eye and was handing her a doll in an organdy dress. The doll had yellow hair, and was almost the same size as the little girl. It was as if he was handing her a twin.

When the carousel stopped, Arthur hopped off the frog patted its head and Adrienne climbed reluctantly out of her swan. They walked along the booths. She stopped. There in a glass case, almost a replica of the one in Atlantic City, was a gypsy fortune teller, except in large letters – *LA VOYANTE*. She had a gold turban and on her shoulder was a raven – a crystal ball sparkled with spots of colored light. Adrienne put in a coin. The head moved from side to side, gold ear-rings jangling. She touched the crystal ball with her waxy hands. A little yellow paper fell out . . . Beware of being too confidential with strangers. Watch your possessions . . . Your lucky color is white . . . Arthur didn't want his fortune. In a booth, a real fortune teller was doing the Tarot cards. An old lady with dyed red hair and sunglasses watched the table. Adrienne could see the Tower. Farther down in a strip-tease show, they could make out the top of a heavy woman in a pink slip loosening a strap suggestively to uncover her marshmallow flesh.

They stopped before a large tank filled with steaming water – a sign said *L'AQUARIUM HUMAIN*. A huge snake with greenish iridescent skin was swimming in a circular motion. A young girl in a gold sequin bathing suit and short black hair with bangs had her arm around the snake's neck – its red tongue darted back and forth. They glided around the tank like some crazy dream of a childhood fairy tale. At moments it seemed she was a mermaid when the snake's tail slipped between her legs and only her gold torso showed above the water.

During the intermission, the girl climbed out of the smoking water, gold drops fell off of her sequin suit. In her hand she held out a wicker basket. A man in sunglasses threw a coin but it missed the basket and fell in the tank. She turned quickly and like a great goldfish dived into the water. The snake was now curled up in a corner, its head knotted in its coils of shiny rope. The girl came up clutching a silver coin.

A revolving wheel of fortune stopped at number 27. A man received a box of sugar and a bottle of wine. Seven large dolls in rainbow dresses were lined up on the counter, their glass eyes staring into space. Pink cotton candy foamed over magenta clouds.

They went into a café. A three-piece black jazz group was playing – a piano and trumpet player and a drummer. The trumpet player, an old man with thick white hair and a beard, had deep creased furrows in his face. His head could have been a miniature landscape in a Southern cotton field. He blew hesitatingly. Once he even became angry, taking the horn out of his mouth and shaking it, as if it was impossible to communicate to the audience what he was hearing – this music that was inside him from some distant country. His yellow eyeballs turned upward behind half-closed lids. He was back listening to the rumbling walls of Jericho and though the danger was imminent, he could not get the danger across to the audience – that holy blasting of trumpets that seemed to ring inside his ears only came out as a pitiful cry.

Arthur ordered beer after beer . . . He tapped on the table with the ashtray in time to the music. Two couples walked in and sat down. They were young, not more than sixteen. One of the girls was very pretty. She had red hair which fell in short curls around her neck. She was wearing a blouse with embroidered flowers at the throat. They were all in high spirits. The boy with the red-haired girl took a bottle of carbonated water and squirted it in her face. The drops splashed dewy over her pink complexion. Arthur turned to Adrienne.

– How can he insult such a nice young girl?

– But Arthur, they're only kidding.

– Kidding my ass . . . he's not kidding. I'd like to go over and hit that young punk in the face. He doesn't know how to respect a nice young girl.

– Arthur please, leave them alone . . . let's go.

He turned, putting his face closer to hers – You know what, you're jealous . . . you with your fucking woman's bullshit. You don't even stick up for your own sisters.

– Oh God, here we go again.

She saw the young redhead laughing and the boy pushing away her hand as she tried to pull his hair. She saw herself at sixteen, skinny, pimples, awkward, not yet the swan. Was she jealous? No, it only made her nostalgic; a girl who grew immediately into a rose without passing by the road of thorns.

She managed to get him out and into a waiting taxi. He fell against the seat, his eyes closed and she thought of the red wig she had found at the flea market. When she'd come home with it in the late afternoon. Arthur was still asleep. She had pinned up her long blonde hair, tucked it under the wig and made up her face with gold sparkles under her eyes. She stared at herself in the mirror. She looked like one of those groupies that hang around jazz musicians. When she heard him stirring, she walked into the room. His reaction was not what she had expected. He recoiled from her – fear in his eyes, turning white . . .

– Okay, so I am not Goldilocks, I'm the Medusa – and she'd

shaken the red curls. He'd cried out for her to take that fucking thing off. He looked sick, but he would never tell her why. Had he been in love with a red-head?

They finally got home. He sat on the bed.

— Where's the beer? he demanded.

— There's no beer. Remember, I don't hide it anymore. He pulled her arm.

— Come on, cut out the bullshit and get me some beer.

— But it's two o'clock in the morning . . .

His eyes were glassy. He continued his monologue on beer, speaking to her, but he was also hearing voices from another place.

It was the hour of the beasts that go down to drink at the water-hole at night after the scorching day and drink and drink until their bellies can hold no more. If she gave him one bottle of beer, he'd want another . . . there was no end — his craving would continue until he passed out.

— You were jealous of that red-head . . . I should've punched the bastard.

Then she saw the sign in his eyes. He was gone — crossed the border. The pupils were no longer focused on her but fastened on a mirage . . . an oasis where the water-hole was filled with beer and all he had to do was jump in and drown himself in its golden liquid until forgetfulness covered him completely. Suddenly the murmur of his words stopped, his head fell back. He was out. She took a lighted cigaret out of his limp hand and crushed it in a cactus plant.

She turned the lights off, lit a small lamp and sat in the armchair by the window. A slight breeze came in through the crack in the pane. She heard a mumbling sound. She turned toward the bed. He was on his side punching the pillow, his eyes closed.

— Who the hell do you think you are? A princess . . . You

think you're better than anybody else – and he punched the pillow with his fist – Don't tell me what to do – You're just a motherfucker . . . I'll show you . . . He punched the pillow again and then lay quiet, a heavy raucous rumble coming up from his chest. He had been hitting the bed as if she had been there beside him.

She remembered reading in an occult book . . . that things are experienced as they are when one sees the bottom of a lake through clear and untroubled water . . . And she saw that August day at camp, when they had all gone canoeing on a mountain lake. The thin music counsellor, John Stone, was ahead alone, leading them in his canoe. Suddenly, losing his balance, his arms waved orchestrally in the air making a frantic gesture as if to grasp some invisible lead stick as he fell into the water.

The canoe turned over – he splashed a few times and sank. The sun had been very red over the mountains that day, bleeding into the water. In the distance two swans were dyed rose. John's floating oars crossed caught in the cusp of water lilies, then slowly drifted apart like ex voto crutches. The water was so clear that he could be seen lying quietly on the bottom . . . a little distorted from above like a concave mirror and as they dragged him up – the roped stems of water lilies bound his mouth – half-open in a crescent smile.

She felt herself whirling around and around on the carousel, the swan raising its wings and flying away with her, and other swans on the lake like ice skaters gliding on the glassy waters, their white serpent necks stretching out . . . hissing – their wings flapping, their feathers soft as sleep – and she was twirling away in a bandage of cloud . . . then she was dropped down . . . down . . . drowning in the gauze of a bright wound.

What if they were to find her floating in the tall reeds – her fingers webbed, her eyes dumb with beaks of horror . . . abyssed into too much whiteness before her time . . .

THIRTEEN :   FROG SWALLOWER

Adrienne looked into the courtyard. There was a beam of sunlight shooting in a shiny dagger across the gray cobblestones. Arthur was yawning, in a placid mood.

– Let's take a walk to Montparnasse – Adrienne suggested.

– Okay, we'll go to a café.

On the way down, they passed a fountain with four green bronze nymphs holding up a filigree crown. A trickle of water flowed from a spout in the middle.

– See that – Adrienne pointed – you won't believe it, maybe an Englishman by the name of Wallace – think it was in the twenties – had these fountains built all over Paris cause he couldn't get a glass of water . . . There used to be a tin cup attached with a chain . . . guess it's gone.

– Yeh – grumbled Arthur – Why didn't he the hell make them with wine?

By the Edgar Quinet square, a crowd was standing around watching something. They made a place and looked in. A heavy-set man, nude from the waist up with a pot belly and lots of freckles, was pointing to three small frogs swimming in a red plastic basin. His face was bloated and a hare-lip gave him a leering expression.

– All right ladies and gentlemen . . . Come closer and see my performance. A unique event. See frogs disappear into this Jonah's whale – and he patted his pot belly – but re-appear not in three days but in three seconds.

At his feet were three bottles of water. He picked up a bottle and drank half the water . . . He gargled with the water for a second, then threw his head back and opened his mouth so wide that a tonsil hung down trembling like a rooster crest. He grabbed one of the frogs – held it over his nose by one of its webbed feet – and in a split second swallowed the entire frog in a gulp. Exclamations rumbled through the crowd. He drank some more water and the two other frogs passed by the same underground tunnel. Turning he walked into the crowd.

– Here, ladies and gentlemen are the frogs – and he patted his swollen stomach. There were slight twitches under his skin like a baby at term. He bent over a small boy, took his hand and placed it over his stomach. The child pulled away and ran behind his mother's skirts.

– Now we will bring these three frogs up from the whale's belly into the light of day.

He took the red basin and held it under his twisted lip, drank more water and with terrific constrictions and the undulating movements of a feeding boa constrictor vomited up a frog, projecting it like a missile into the basin. The frog dived into the water and came up, furiously paddling its little legs. The man's face had darkened to the color of wine. Again his body contorted and jerking in spasms, vomited up a second frog which leaped out – regurgitated alive. Then a third time his stomach contracted in heavy labor pains, but nothing happened. Again and again the unborn child refused to come out. He opened a little satchel and pulled out a cow bell. He placed it near his stomach and rang it a few times, signalling no doubt to the frog that pasture time was now over . . . there was a small jerk under his skin. He convulsed again. Nothing. He took out a small rubber suction cup and placed it on his liver pulling on it a few times like he was cleaning out a plugged up drain. The frog might be sitting on his liver which it took for a lily pad. He drank some more water and with a last violent convulsion as if this was finally the ultimate birth pang, expulsed the green fetus which made a silent cry in opening its large pink throat, gulping in the water.

The man was trembling, sweat dripped over his forehead from his efforts. The three frogs were swimming nonchalantly in the basin, seemingly unconcerned by their dark night. The man, his hand shaking, handed an old hat toward the crowd.

– All I can say – said Arthur dryly – is this has given me a peculiar thirst . . . and I never liked frog's legs anyway.

They stopped for some drinks and then walked through the Luxembourg Gardens. Children in the distance were playing under the bald-headed statue of Verlaine. By Baudelaire's bust, a small boy was rolling a yellow ball. They passed a sculpture of a nude couple sitting on a rock with their arms around one another. Moss grew out of their asses as if they'd been sitting in this same position for centuries, mindless of time or weather and they would mold and crumble together – fingers, arms, legs, asses wearing down, their bodies falling in an indecipherable puzzle with moss covering them in a green billiard tomb.

They walked through the gravel paths under the proud and sad statues of Queens of France – pigeons resting on their crowned heads – and a monument of bronze masks with empty eyes where someone had jabbed a yellow marble into one of the sockets. By the gates, a man was selling ice cream in chiffony pastel shades. They stopped before McDonald's Hamburger Restaurant.

– Let's have a hamburger, Arthur.

They sat at a small table outside.

– Get me a cheeseburger – Arthur commanded.

– Why should I get it? Adrienne complained.

– Oh, go ahead you can move your big ass.

– All right – she mumbled, not knowing if she enjoyed being the slave or not.

She came back with the hamburgers wrapped up hermetically in little sacks. Next to them was an Indian couple drinking milk shakes through striped straws. The girl had on a turquoise sari with gold borders, her hair in a braid and a red spot on her forehead but no diamond in her nose. The man was fiddling with a camera. His fine carved profile was as classic as Krishna on a Hindu temple.

– I wonder if they have a McDonald's in India, I guess though, the cow's too sacred to make a hamburger out of – Adrienne reflected.

Just then an American Oldsmobile stopped before the curb. Out of it stepped the typical American family, so typical that they seemed ready to advertise soap, or breakfast foods. The woman was wearing a red cardigan and a plaid skirt. Her hair was tied back in a bun. The man wore a classic gray suit and a polka dot tie. His eyes were magnified under steel-rimmed glasses, his hair balding in the center. There were three children. A girl with a plaid skirt like her mother's; a boy in jeans and a white sweat shirt with LET'S GO on it, then a small boy with shorts and a faded Disney duck on a blue tee shirt. They were so impeccably clean that they could be advertising not only soap, but shampoo, deodorant, toothpaste and toilet paper on a television program.

Adrienne felt positively grimy, looking at them. Their washing in Europe was quite perfunctory. The French had it down to a system of washing the odorous areas, under-arms, feet etc and the bidet for the cunt. She saw Arthur and herself posing for a photo to be sent home – she in a striped St Tropez shirt, patched jeans, her long blonde hair in a tangle and Arthur in his spotted black corduroy pants and purple Indian shirt. He had once explained to her that when you were on the move a lot of underwear just got in the way. A friend of Arthur's who'd been back to the States after many years away, had said when he'd made it with some girl, she had had him take a shower before making it, and after that two or three showers a day.

– Quick – the woman said to the man – let's take our picture here.

They all lined up against the door of McDonald's. An African cleaning man was standing by the counter with a broom. The man focused the camera. They stood there with frozen smiles as if they were getting ready to deep-freeze their remembrances, so when they got back home they could dump all this into the memory freezer and pull it out and defrost it for future reference. Everyone was smiling except for the daughter who looked sullen. The mother saw her and called out in a nasal voice . . . "Lillian, please smile, otherwise when you see your photo back home, you'll regret it".

Here was a family picture in front of McDonald's in Paris not by Notre Dame, the Arc de Triomphe or the Eiffel Tower. No one would take pictures any more of these places, but now of a huge pop hamburger as big as the world with millions of smiling teeth snapping at it. Maybe even the sacred cow could be pressed between a roll – nice picture postcard to send home.

FOURTEEN : BLACK AND WHITE

Jackson dropped over to see Arthur and they spent the day and night swapping stories and drinking.

– Listen – Jackson said holding up his hand so he could have absolute silence – I heard from an African brother about this giant race of termites that once lived in Africa the same fucking size as a man. Well the whole race dropped dead 'cept for the queen, but this here queen termite was really a white chick under a spell, but to go on with the race she need a white dude who'd make it with her at midnight and she'd give him lots of loot. Well, you believe me it was darkest Africa and there ain't many whites hanging around. But there's this here black cat who think he take a chance so he paint himself white. The black cat's tribe get pissed off 'cause they think he should be satisfied with a nice black baby. Anyhow a brother go along to check it out with him; so one night he slip out before midnight and go to the tunnel. He crawl down there – that's where the white queen is holed up. His brother wait outside. Let me tell you though that this motherfucker is so scared the tribe could hear them teeth chattering two miles away.

Well, he go down in the hole, it's real dark, when he hear a kind of buzzing – Jackson puckered up his lips and blew inside an empty bottle by the bed – Man oh man, what does he see . . . but this here white bug with a horrible mouth and a lady's tits come straight at him . . . well he done passed out. When he comes to, he get his fucking ass off the ground and fly out of that there hole like he got wings. He scare the fucking shit out of his brother when he see this here white ghost shoot out. Well the cat go to the river and he scrub and scrub, but none of this white paint come off.

– Well I'll be a mother . . . how come none of this here paint don't come off? Lemme tell you if this paint don't come off it must be I is the wrong dude . . .

– That's why they say in this tribe a white man is really a black man not in his right skin and that's what he get chasing after them strange chicks . . .

– Yeah, well I'll tell you my side of it – Arthur said settling himself comfortably on the bed, taking a swallow of beer – There's this shoe polish salesman who the company sends down to Georgia to check on some accounts. It's late at night when he gets off the train and he tries to find a hotel – no go. All booked up. He goes to the slum areas and knocks on the door of a flea-bag joint. The guy opens the door looks at him and says . . . Sorry only for blacks here . . . This happens a few times. It's now real late. The guy gets an idea. He goes into an alley way, opens his suitcase, takes out a tube of shoe polish – black – and smears it over his face. He puts on black gloves and goes to the next hotel . . . Got a room? . . . Yeh, says the clerk and gives him no. 27 . . . Look here, says the salesman . . . be sure and wake me up at eight . . . I gotta get a train. The guy says okay and he goes to his crummy room, lays on the bed dressed and goes to sleep. Well, the clerk wakes him up late and he has to run like hell to get the train, but he just makes it. He relaxes, lights a cigar when the conductor comes by . . . Sorry, this car's only for white passengers . . . Suddenly the guy remembers the shoe polish on his face. He goes to the john and scrubs and scrubs . . . nothing happens . . . again . . . he's still black . . . Jesus Christ, he moans, I bet they knocked on the wrong door and woke up the wrong guy . . .

– Well, well brother, Jackson said happily, slapping Arthur on the shoulder – Howdya know a white man ain't really a black man covered over?

They went on and on. Adrienne listened to their stories while she made futile attempts to empty out ashtrays and arrange empty bottles. Where was the black man at? Across the courtyard she saw a Black Lion Shoe Polish billboard. The black lion now weather-beaten, but its dark nails exquisitely manicured – the dyed ebony skin waxed brilliant under a tin-lid sun. Every day under this sign, an imported Nigerian worker, in a red skull-cap, swept the gutter with his broom of twigs, unbandaging water from a black cavity, washing yellow phlegm metro tickets down the sewer throat. Today she'd watched him from the café – standing on a half-erased hopscotch where on the bottom square was still scrawled the word *ENFER*. She'd seen he had on a new gold watch – his dark face shadowing the dial. Suppose he'd been born on the day of a total eclipse – caught with a caul covering the sun – and maybe he could hear his mother's voice ticking in his ear . . . You are a cursed son of Ham . . . for darkness was born with you . . . You have hidden the sun . . . He stood there leaning on his broom like it was a branch . . . Did he see the sun-dial trees shadowing the scorching sand, or his naked brothers and sisters splashing their polished bodies in a muddy yellow river . . . ?

She moved out of her reverie, they had completely forgotten about her. She decided to polish her nails for once. As she brought out the red bottle, she saw Amsterdam and the port where the whores lived in large picture windows. In this one window in a stage set, sat this plump platinum blonde. She was wearing a rose satin gown, partly open, showing the putty swell of her breasts and the tops of her heavy thighs, her feet were crossed in white pom-pom slippers. She was polishing her nails a bright red. Her mouth was half-open, her tongue licking her upper lip in the sort of concentration girls have when they imitate a chore their mothers usually do. By her side was a night-table with a vase of plastic roses and in the back of a wash-basin was a mirror stuck with gold flowers. On the bed covered by a spread of white lace, sat a stuffed doll with platinum hair like hers. She was the perfect image of the woman as a doll object, framed behind the brown wood cross of the window frame.

Outside watching her was a tourist in a large dark cowboy hat, his hands in his pockets. She was a fata morgana – a mirage that reflected a reality projected out in a space seen transposed and doubled – the doll as object, image and herself – miles apart in space and time but viewed as the same moment.

That trip to Amsterdam had been full of consequences . . . It would be better if she didn't bring it up again. Jackson had gotten a gig with a bass and trumpet player – he was playing drums – at a small jazz club there for three days. Arthur and she had gone along for the ride. All the time, Arthur had been completely plastered on gin and beer. The last night he had just sat at the bar drumming along with Jackson and letting out a scream every so often. When the club finally closed at 4 am the bass player had stuck his bass next to the door ready to leave.

Outside was the canal, covered with powdery flakes from a compact moon. Arthur had watched the bass for a few minutes leaning femininely against the door, when he lurched toward the bass and plucked the cords – tearing at them as if they were corset strings to be quickly untied. They gave out a few desolate croaks and he stopped. Then suddenly without warning, he picked up the bass like the body of some ravished woman and began running with the torso over his shoulder outside to the canal. In a gesture of relief, as if he were getting rid of some great weight, he toppled the bass into the shining water. There was a splash . . . but no cry for help . . . as the bass slid on its back and floated down the water. It was a Magritte painting where the bass was both coffin and woman. It glided down the canal under the powdery moonlight. Everyone had rushed out to watch the bass, now the Lady of Shalott gently, crazily floating on the rippled current.

Before the bass came to a bridge, Jackson and the bass player ran down to a houseboat anchored on the quay and woke up an old lady with curlers in her hair. She didn't seem surprised and gave them a grappling-hook. They gathered on the bridge and, as the bass corpse passed under, they dropped the hook down and drew it up . . . water dripping out of the openings like small fountains. Because of all the oil and scum in the canal, little water had gotten into the bass. The next day when they were ready to leave Arthur had a colossal hangover and said he couldn't remember throwing the bass into the canal. In the car, the bass looked like a suicide victim with a white towel around its throat stump to keep it from dripping . . . She jumped. They were calling her.

– Hey, we're hungry . . . give us something to eat.

Jackson continued . . . Lemme tell you man. The black man had a supermarket in his backyard. He just had to raise his ass off his hammock and he stretch out his hand for a banana and he had it. It weren't till the white dude come along and start splitting up the land – building them goddamn walls and fences – labeling the bananas and coconuts on all them trees – that the trouble started. Man, we had it all together and on top of it they fucked up the religion, cause us blacks know that the whites gone torn out the first page of the bible where it say Jesus was black.

Then they started arguing about who the land belonged to.

She turned to go to the kitchen, Okay – she said grudgingly – I'll make spaghetti. The eternal spaghetti . . . one long snake spaghetti, anyhow it was cheap.

She went into the kitchen and she thought back to her summers in Long Island where her parents had a bungalow. Their black maid, Cleo, used to make them a lot of spaghetti. Cleo took care of her sister and her in the country; her parents only came out for weekends. Cleo couldn't have been more than twenty. Adrienne was about thirteen, her sister three years younger. It was at the time she was reading *Green Mansions* and *Wuthering Heights*. Cleo used to read all the movie magazines. The covers had Lana Turner with long blonde hair and vampire-red lips pursed in a kiss, or Rita Hayworth lying voluptuously by a swimming pool in a gold lamé dress. Cleo was teaching herself to read better by studying the magazines. She used to underline the words in red and then look them up in the dictionary. Words like . . . luminosity . . . vedette . . . femme fatale etc.

Sometimes she and her sister would sit on the front porch playing pick-up sticks and there'd be arguments . . . I saw you, you moved the end of the stick . . . You touched it with your fingers . . . or they'd play Monopoly . . . Collect $200 and go to jail . . . They were real little capitalists, each of them trying to get Boardwalk with its high rental. The moths flew in and burnt themselves on the light bulbs, falling down and struggling on top of the colored Monopoly money. A moon cake frosted the tops of cedar trees and the fragrance of honeysuckle and roses made them light-headed.

Or in August, they'd listen to the monotonous raindrops and dream of monsoons in India after having seen Lana Turner in the movies sacrificing herself for the poor Indians. Then she and her sister would play they were on rafts in their beds while around them was water and if they put their toes out of the covers, sharks would swim by and bite them.

Cleo had a large purple scar on her left cheek. Adrienne's mother had told her not to mention it. But one day Cleo was talking about her home in Alabama. Sometimes her parents went out and left her to take care of her five brothers and sisters. A fire had started in the kitchen and she had struggled to get all the children out. As she was picking up the last child, there'd been an explosion and her face had been badly burned. But everyone was saved. She became a sort of heroine to Adrienne.

One evening she and her sister were having a pillow-fight. Cleo who spoke rarely and very softly told them to stop, go to bed and be good because she was going out. She was wearing a white organdy dress which was so light that her satin slip made her body beige under it. Around Cleo floated a heavy perfume – Blue Waltz, Adrienne's first perfume bought at Woolworth's. Outside there was a big black Cadillac next to the gate. It was the black chauffeur from the big estate next to the bay. The chauffeur was looking up at the window. She could make out his strong white teeth and the white shirt under his dinner jacket. Cleo waved goodbye and like a nightmoth wafted down to the car where the chauffeur caught her, put his arm around her waist and helped her into the car.

Cleo was going to a party in the big estate next to the Sound. All the maids and butlers of the neighborhood must be going out and leaving the white children to take care of themselves . . . She could see all the servants in the spacious kitchen and pantry using the fine silverware and the crystal glasses. Maybe the white people were upstairs having their own party too; but the servants must be playing their own games . . . hide-and-seek on the marble staircases . . . and behind the satin drapes blind man's bluff . . . or maybe they even had a gigantic

Monopoly set where they bought the white man's land and his railroads . . . or they walked and hugged in the gardens.

She'd fallen asleep and dreamed that a whole lot of black men were standing on a Monopoly board the size of an acre. A white girl in a thin white dress was on the board holding an enormous pair of dice. The black men kept pushing the girl to throw the dice . . . She'd been wakened by a creak in the gate and the muffled sound of laughter, then the rustling of Cleo's dress like tissue paper followed by the tiptoe of feet. The car tires crunched on the gravel, the whining engine purred and drifted contentedly into the night. But not long after this. Cleo had gotten very sick. Adrienne's mother had taken her to the hospital. Cleo had asked for all the movie magazines and her white organdy dress. She'd never seen Cleo again. Much later her mother had told her Cleo was dying of skin cancer and she had asked to be buried in her white organdy dress . . .

She was interrupted by Arthur's cry.

– Hey, where's the spaghetti? Come on . . . we can't pick if off the trees.

There was a ring on the doorbell. Adrienne went to answer it. There was a black friend of Jackson's, Absalom Jones, called Absalom because he had a magnificent head of kinky hair that stood up like a bush on his head. He was a folk singer, with him was a French girl.

– Hope we ain't bothering you he said meekly jingling a bunch of gold chains hanging on his chest, his red shirt opened to his belly-button.

– No, no Adrienne said getting her strength together for new guests . . . You're just in time for spaghetti.

The French girl had a strange glassy look in her eyes and a smile that seemed stuck like the lower part of a comedy mask. She wore a plain black dress with a colored butterfly on the bottom and a tiger's claw on a chain. She was barefoot with violet polish on her toes and nails and her hennaed hair was long and stringy.

– Hello Ethel – she said staring ahead.

– No, this ain't your friend Ethel, this is Adrienne. This is Sylvette.

– Oh – was all she said. It didn't seem to matter to her if Ethel was Adrienne or not.

_ Could you show me the bathroom?

– Sure – Adrienne pointed down the hall.

Absalom sat on the bed next to Jackson. Arthur was sprawled out. Absalom repeated in a stage whisper – Sylvette's a real nice chick, but she just come out of St. Anne's loony bin. She's been tripping a bit too heavy. Believe you me, there's a bunch of nuts around. When I went to see her there was this here American guy, he walked into the Israel air office and tell the director he was Jesus Christ and he want to go back to Israel cause he got a lot of unfinished business to do . . . He look okay . . . a guy with beard and glasses . . . I even give him a cigaret . . . Guess there's all types in this world . . .

Adrienne raised her eyebrows.

– Well as I was saying – Jackson went on with his eternal stories. There's this here palace called Crystal Palace in Tombstone City way up on a mountain. There comes this black boy proclaiming he's the Messiah wearing an ermine coat, driving up in a purple Cadillac . . . and he comes to the place where there only be ruins now of an old dance hall, the Crystal Palace and he say . . . Up on this here mountain we gonna build a city of the Lord . . . only in glass so all can see God when he come down. Then he get all the dudes in the neighborhood to work for him and he has them take off their clothes and shoes and throw 'em down the mountain and he say . . . Being naked ain't no sin brothers, Amen, and let me tell you brothers and sisters, fornication ain't no sin either, Amen . . . and from below you could see them dudes crawling around like beetles carrying away dung balls of stone and weeds to clear that mountain top and build a glass palace . . . but let me tell you . . . there weren't no glass walls . . . only air . . . the Messiah waved a magic wand and they was building the Emperor's new palace. Nobody told them brothers and sisters there weren't any glass around them . . . they were naked as the fucking day they were born, so God could see right through them suckers . . .

Sylvette came out of the bathroom. Her long hair, now rust colored, was soaking wet.

– I love to put my head under the faucet . . . It so cools the brain.

– Don't you want a towel? – politely offered Adrienne.

– No. That's fine. I went into the kitchen and helped you with the spaghetti. I sprinkled the grated cheese on it – Sylvette said brightly – I'll bring it in.

Before Adrienne could move, she'd gone down the hall and came back with the spaghetti and the grated cheese like a mound of snow on top. As usual they picnicked on the bedspread. It had the universal stains of tomato sauce, oil and wine. Everyone started eating – then stopped suddenly.

Arthur gagged – Hey, this spaghetti tastes like it's been dry cleaned. In a second Adrienne realized there was soap powder on the spaghetti.

Absalom with a strong intuition turned to Sylvette, her hair still dripping.

– Sylvette, honey, did you touch anything in the kitchen? Now don't you jive me.

– No, only I saw some lovely grated cheese in a soap powder

box. It was so white, it looked much nicer than the other yellowish stuff on the table.

Sylvette had taken her Omo soap powder – appearances certainly weren't everything – Adrienne thought.

Absalom patted her arm – Now, Sylvette baby, how many times have I told you not to touch things?

– Why? – Sylvette said sulkily – Did I do something wrong?

FIFTEEN : NO BOUNDARIES

There were no boundaries to Arthur's world. His territory was only the extensions of himself. It was the watery element of low tide that changed with the moon. She on the contrary wanted definite answers . . . When will you be home? . . . Where are we going? . . . What are we going to do? . . . She wanted her ground charted, labeled. He gave no name to anything, while she belonged to the race that had named each animal, each insect, each amphibian and placed everything in its proper domain. He tore everything down. There were no frontiers he wouldn't cross, and for him the bar was the most democratic institution. Here there were no names, no races, because with names everything was made concise. His was the world of metamorphosis . . . the creeping fish, the flying lizard . . . It was before the Christian world, it was still Celtic, still drowning the new emerging identity . . . Before the dialogue with God.

Her parents belonged to the Old Testament, but not to the New of grace and forgiveness. "Honor thy parents" they agreed, but "forgive your children" they could not. Arthur belonged to a world of non-separation. He had not yet fashioned his limbs. He swam in an elemental, watery world. His baptism had been in liquid not yet named. He had not yet raised his head and looked around at the mounds of earth newly rising . . . the reeds shooting into the air, the birds trying on their delicate wings. He had the sense of democracy, but not yet of discrimination in its original sense before it became racial. All things were equal but not yet named. She belonged to the race of proper names where each thing had its aristocratic place. She born as a woman "was", he as a man had to "become" by forms, rites, initiations, metamorphosis. He had to prove himself even if it was often against imaginary windmills.

But now above all she wanted to save him, to assume her role of confessor. He was the prodigal son who if he would bow down, fall on her bosom, confess his sins – she would give him forgiveness; but until then she would admonish, punish him and deny him because he would not acknowledge her power. She was the Virgin Mary and Mary Magdelene rolled into one. But he acknowledged no one higher than himself. So she built a hedge of thorns around her and if she saw any buds about to bloom, she tore them off. She guarded herself in her sleeping palace.

She realized she'd gone down to the bitter hell of him – through his blood, shit, vomit, piss. Each day she took him down from his cross. A cross he built each dawn and destroyed each night but a cross built uniquely for his own private suffering in a "fucked-up world". He hammered his own nails into his hands and feet and against the authoritative voice of the father he revolted.

He was not the bridegroom who saved the good wine to the last, but as the evening wore on, his wine became less and less good till it turned to vinegar. He was always trying to turn water into wine but only by physical means. He gave of his resources prodigiously, to anything and anybody . . . He threw his pearls in every direction . . .

One evening she dreamed of a man in an immaculate white suit. Two side teeth were missing. He was blonder than Arthur, but it was him. He was an electrician and he had come to get her because he wanted her to watch while he put a light bulb on top of the Eiffel Tower. With him came an unknown dark woman. She had silver sparkles around her eyes. When they got to the Eiffel Tower, he left them and started to climb up the iron grid. He climbed nonchalantly. When he reached the top he waved to her. She couldn't look, he made her dizzy. He screwed the light bulb on the top of the tower and then started climbing down with large steps. Suddenly to her horror in the middle of the descent, he made a false move and started falling like a white bird. There was a hollow sound below on the ground of crunching gravel – and a thud. He had fallen on his back, his white arms outstretched cross-wise. For a moment she and the dark girl couldn't move . . . a police car appeared and a cop got out and called into a red emergency phone . . . Send an ambulance . . . Then they both rushed forward. He was lying on his back – his mouth open, she could see his pink gums – he had no teeth. There was no blood but he was in agony.

– Hold his hand – she cried out to the dark girl.

– But I've never touched him – the dark girl whimpered.

– Hold him . . . Hold him – she screamed.

She had stroked his head, sweat was pouring from his forehead. He writhed on his back like a wounded white bird which had broken its wings. Then suddenly he got up and started to walk.

– All right, leave me alone, I don't need anyone.

She had cried out – Lie down . . . lie down. You don't know what might be wrong with you inside. You must go to the hospital . . . a hospital . . . and she'd woken up shivering.

SIXTEEN :   DRUNKEN DAWNS

Often Adrienne had noticed scars on Arthur's back but she'd never asked him about them. One night when they were in bed, she'd traced over the scars with her fingertips.

Arthur turned toward her – So you'd like to know how I got my scars, uh? – Arthur said lifting one eyebrow and smiling ironically – Well they're from my old man. He used to beat me with a whip . . . those were the days when I was a kid and he used to drink . . . see, branded for life. And he turned away, not saying anything else, noncommital.

But inside him she could always sense a certain frustration. Most of his fighting he did in bars and then afterwards he became dependent on her to take care of him; to wash the blood off him, to mend his clothes full of cigaret holes and tears, to get his food together and buy him his bottles of beer. He'd leave her only to go out and get drunk and then come home at dawn, glassy-eyed, swaying – in a brute world where she couldn't go.

But those drunken dawns were something else. It was then all his barriers were down and his was the watery world of underwater sex, where for him she just became some deep dark hole . . . a wet slimy cavern that opened and closed with the tides. She became a sponge filled with spaces. She would have to go down on him sucking a red slug that throbbed and pulsed, or sit on top of him pumping and pumping as he watched her through his blue-green eyes – misty watery again under sea goggles. Then suddenly he'd become limp like a deflated jelly fish thrown up on an impotent shore, or he'd lick her in an odor of decay and rotting seaweed, a creature with a coral tongue. Sex at these times was completely undifferentiated . . . her arm pits, groin, asshole, ear, were all the same to him. When at normal periods he might be afraid to let go – now the dam broke, water overflowing carrying him along where he wanted to desecrate her, to curse her . . .

– Who do you think you are, the Virgin Mary? . . . some fucking princess? . . . you bitch . . . you whore . . . as he covered her with spit or sperm, his tongue rough sticky . . . his body sweaty and slimy like some great frog . . . Then suddenly as if the inner voice of his father should call out . . . and knock on the door . . .

– Is there someone in the bed with you?

And was it this – that knock – that inhibited the frog from metamorphosing into a prince?

But slowly the frustration and violence she was afraid of began to creep into their relationship. One day after a bad drunk, he lay in bed. It was about 5p.m. when the doorbell rang and Jackson showed up. He came in, his bottle of wine hanging from his shoulder. Arthur was still sleeping.

– Hey there, brother – Jackson called – Move over, – and he plopped himself on the bed next to Arthur. Suddenly seeing the two of them installed again for another drinking session began to infuriate her. She grabbed Arthur's foot.

– Get up, she ordered . . . Get up.

He turned his face bleary-eyed toward her as if coming back after a long swim underwater.

– What's this? – Little by little her words registered. He sat up in bed.

– What the hell are you trying to do, fuck over me? . . . Are you? – And he lunged toward her. She was shocked. It was the first time in her life anyone had really been violent with her. She ran into the kitchen. He followed her nude from the waist down, his sex red, flapping against his thighs. She was backed up on the kitchen wall. He grabbed a handful of her long hair and tugged at it, forcing her head back. Jackson jumped off the bed.

– Come on – he said soothingly – Let her alone, you and I need to go out and have a little drink.

He pulled Arthur back into the bedroom. She started to scream hysterically, – Get out . . . Get out . . . I never want to see you again . . .

– Fuck her, – screamed Arthur – I'm leaving – and he threw on his pants and shoes.

– Let's go – Jackson insisted and she heard the door slam. She stood stunned for a moment and then stumbled into the bedroom and fell on the bed.

And she remembered the reason she'd run away from home to go to Atlantic City when she was sixteen. She'd come home one night with a date, his name was Frank, a nondescript form now. She was necking with him in front of the door. She had smeared her acne with pancake base which had left a pink stain on his shirt collar – that had stayed in her mind for some reason – when her father had heard them and opened the door. He'd pulled her in by her hair and yelled . . . "You tramp" . . . at her. She'd been so hurt she'd locked herself in her room and the next day had run off to Atlantic City. Her father had felt real bad. He'd never touched her or made any reference to that scene again.

And what about Arthur's beatings? He'd told her it had all come to an end when one Sunday morning (Arthur had been about fifteen) his father had come into the room, pulled off his covers and ordered him to go to church. He'd grabbed his father and socked and socked him till Arthur had come to his senses, but his father had never touched him again. How much, though, of all this violence had reached inside him.

Then she felt she'd opened a forbidden door in Bluebeard's castle, seen something she shouldn't have and was left with a bloody key that wouldn't wash off . . . and she saw a young girl getting off a train and a man with a pasty white face, sunglasses and a large black hat staring at her. He went over to the girl, took her by the arm pressing her close to him, his leather gloved hand over her mouth, taking her to a dark barred bedroom . . . chaining her to the bed, opening her legs and shoving a Coca Cola bottle up her cunt as blood dripped over the sheets, other girls kidnapped, disappearing in dress shops where they were dumped down trap doors to the basement . . . drugged – their hair cut and dyed – sent far away to become objects like dolls. And she thought how easy it would be to become a doll . . . to be perfumed, bathed, dressed . . . no longer the pain of being human . . . the heart crushed out . . .

Looking back, she thought of a night when they had been sitting at a little bar in the neighborhood. The bartender, a black American guy, was working it with a French friend. On the back wall of the bar were two strange panels painted by some artist years ago and, though the bar had changed hands, everyone had left the paintings. One panel showed a middle-aged man sitting on a bench in a country square reading a letter. He had on a cap and a dark suit. The next panel showed a field with a young woman in a long pink dress kissing a young man; but behind a tree was the same man with a cap, watching them – and in his right hand he was holding a knife. They had endless discussions on the meaning of the panel . . . it was his wife, she was cheating on him . . . it was his mistress who was breaking off . . . he didn't know the couple but he'd been disappointed in love and wanted to get revenge on any happy couple . . . etc. She'd kid him and ask him what he'd do if a woman cheated on him. He always laughed and gave evasive answers.

That evening at the bar in walked two very elegant black men and a beautiful black girl in a pin-striped suit with a gray chiffon rose on her lapel. They seemed to be Africans speaking in a dialect. As she watched them she could see one of the men was getting very angry, he was shouting something at the girl. She looked frightened. Without warning he leaned over and slapped her on the face . . . then again. The other man tried to hold him back but he was infuriated. The girl held her face and started to cry then rushed over behind the bar. The man got up and tried to get to the girl behind the counter, but Harry, their friend, pushed him away.

– That's my wife – screamed the man – I have the right to do what I want.

– Oh yeh, well you don't in this bar – Harry said firmly.

The black man took a swing at Harry.

– Okay, you son of a bitch, if that's how you want it, come on outside. She looked at Arthur. He was turning his beer glass around in his hand.

– Did you ever hit a woman? – She had blurted out.

Arthur had watched her. A strange smile on his face.

– If I was a man – she muttered – I'd fix him –

– Look, Adrienne – he said sardonically – I'm no Prince Charming who has to come to the aid of all the lovely ladies in distress –

But when Harry had gone outside with the man, Arthur had slowly gotten up and followed them into the street. It ended quickly. Harry had an iron crank he used to pull down the iron shutter and the men backed out, running down the street. The girl, with tears dripping down her face, hailed a taxi – stepped in and was gone.

She began to see now a pattern in his violence. He took her more and more for granted. She was something that belonged to him, that was part of his territory. If he was drunk at a bar, a certain amount of outside space belonged to him. His space was not in the interior of walls, but around the bar where if someone pushed him or stood too close it was reason to strike out and defend it. Or it might work the other way, where he'd refuse to interfere in a fight because the principle they were fighting about was not his. But more than just hitting someone, it was as if he himself wanted to be hit and knocked out into unconsciousness.

For Arthur the world was just "fucked-up". It was insane where one had to be insane to understand it and all authority of any kind was something not to submit to on any terms.

That night he didn't come back, she dreamed he was wearing his green jacket but from the waist down he was nude and he came floating towards her imploringly, holding out to her tightly bandaged hands . . .

SEVENTEEN : "JE SUIS L'AUTRE!"

Of course they'd gotten back together again with new promises . . . etc. and it went on like the day of the black sun. No moon on the street of La Vielle Lanterne, the night Gerard de Nerval hanged himself on a lamp post with an apron string and a raven flying over his shoulder croaking . . . "I'm thirsty . . . I'm thirsty . . ." . . . "For dreams are a second life" . . . "*Je suis l'autre!*". The Hanged Man was in the Tarot cards and the I Ching predicted The Darkening of the Light, and in a total eclipse even one head can darken the sun.

In the café, the waiter had said – "Now I'm changing my role from waiter to lover. I'm going home and put on my pajamas. Ask the bright boys with silver trays to serve the left overs."

Later in the rue St. Denis, he hurried into a *tabac*, a coat dangling over his striped shirt. Inside a cloud of smoke, he'd made a call and when he came back there were shutters across his eyes.

Why in love is there always the taste of ashes?

Gerard de Nerval took an apron string out of his pocket . . . "Look, this is the belt Mme de Maintenon wore in her performance of Esther . . . I'll use it to promenade my pet lobster around the Luxembourg Gardens . . . It never barks, is never obstreperous and knows the secrets of the sea."

Walking through Châtelet, they looked for the Nerval monument and saw an effeminate muse trying to fling two wreaths over the sun and the moon. By the monument, a boy in a green jacket was sitting, staring at the poem engraved in stone:

"Je suis le Ténebreux – le Veuf – l'Inconsolé,
Le Prince d'Acquitaine à la Tour abolie:
Ma seul *Étoile* est morte, – et mon luth constellé
Porte le *Soleil noir* de la *Mélancolie*."

The morning of the total eclipse, he said he'd be right back . . . She stepped out into a falling rose petal sky. Flying pigeons circled around an old woman sprinkling confetti breadcrumbs. Across the street, a little boy played the harmonica spacing the pigeons into flying musical notes. A jet plane left a trailing rope of smoke fading like a fakir's trick. Saw no sun or moon. He had said he was going to buy cigarets. Waiting she saw him reflected in a cafe mirror . . . A man in a striped shirt leaning over dark hair and rose lips. But the mirror reflected impartially and the last black sun fell into the owl's pupil.

Why in love is there always the taste of ashes?

Before the cemetery, a short cut to the Luxembourg Gardens, they passed the window of an abandoned funeral parlor. Broken ceramic flowers trailed across the floor . . . wooden crosses piled up like sign posts pointing to a dead end road . . . a pottery head of Christ split in two against a broom . . . undone straw wreaths lay shipwrecked like life buoys left over from people long since drowned . . . two dusty plaques decorated with purple and red ceramic roses hung in the window . . . one said *REGRETS* the other *SOUVENIR* . . .

They stopped at Daudelaire's tomb slimy with snails of rain. Someone had left two purple wax roses. They passed by the black angel of death. He'd asked her the angel's name. It wasn't till much later she remembered it was Samuael. The dark angel held a wreath with gold letters . . . *SOUVENIR* . . . In a bin of faded flowers, he found her a red ceramic rose. She hid it in her paper bag. The guardian with sunglasses made threatening gestures.

How many roses had he given her as they went along those drunken nights, remembering . . . "They are not long the days of wine and roses"? . . . Once he had tripped in the gutter on a large plastic rose wet from sewer water and he had given it to her saying . . . "Here's another rose, you can bury someone with it," as he had laughed drunkenly. They'd walked through gravel paths of veiled statues and little cubicles with stained glass windows . . . "This is a planned city of death with streets and gutters . . ." he said.

They came to Alekine's tomb – *"Genie des Echecs de Russie et de France 1937 à sa morte."* A stone chessboard tabled his tomb in dinner napkins of dark and light . . . *"Ne m'attends pas ce soir, car la nuit sera noire et blanche"* . . . He had broken his bottle of wine. Later he was going to write a poem on Alekine playing chess with God, but he'd changed his mind.

Why in love is there always the taste of ashes?

The sun was very black in Paris that winter.

EIGHTEEN :   IN SEARCH OF A PAST

Adrienne was always going in search of a past she'd never had . . . Brought up in a city of supermarkets where all the products were behind plastic – where one washed dirt away with guilt, deodorized to get rid of the smell of flesh – wall-to-wall carpeting with no noise – heat always perfectly regulated. She often thought the janitor was a bit like God. When the plumbing fails, when the cockroaches come up through the bathroom pipes . . . call the janitor . . . when the lights fail call the janitor. It wasn't till she came to Europe she realized one could be cold, without light, if one didn't arrange it oneself. Here was a past she wanted to collect – the masks, old clothes, wigs, hats – everything to perpetuate herself in unending images. Her favorite spot was the flea market. Arthur used to go with her and sit in a café nearby, drinking – watching the "junk" as he called it. His camera on the table if he ever got inspired.

She walked along this collage world where nothing was linked together by any natural references. Plastic plates, lace tablecloths with coffee and wine stains, busts of Greeks and Romans in plaster, Christ in iron, silver and plastic. Buddhas in porcelain and wax. Clothes from every epoch – even a clown's outfit with his emblem of sun and moon showing his balance between two worlds.

Buttons that had given up trying to close things and lay exhausted in dusty boxes, knives and forks that belonged to nobody's hands or mouths – rusting . . . where in the pile a shiny silver fork linked up the image of some woman rubbing it with pink polish – and chairs that still had the marks of greasy heads – mattresses stained with urine, stamped with Pompeian forms of bodies. Soiled hats bowed with the weight of heads, gloves showing the agony of farewells in their crumpled fingers. And postcards . . . postcards from all the corners of the world . . . always saying, Remember me . . . Remember me . . . addressed to those who no longer had addresses or even bodies.

Among the relics had been a little sewing box in wood with tiny drawers. In the top drawer was a thimble, a spool of thread, bits of lace, and a pair of eyeglasses with a silver frame. In the second one, a lock of blonde hair tied with a faded red ribbon and a yellowed picture of a little girl in a sailor dress. She hadn't opened the other drawers.

What was there that couldn't be sold? – very little, perhaps the dead person's identity card and driving license, fishing license . . . his photos, his false teeth but not if they were in gold, his keys . . . there were always boxes of rusty keys that no one knew were for what doors, not even St. Peter's. It was a collage world, a decaying civilization where there was no archaeological ground to hold it in a knowledgeable order. In the earth one could dig down layer after layer in an orderly way and arrive at dates of existence. But here in this flea market culture, it was a hodge-podge of objects. It was a tourist culture that one was called upon to sort out for oneself . . . Dolls that had neither arms or legs, objects that cried out to be claimed, like in a Lost and Found, that someone had forgotten or dropped along the way. What was there that was not for sale? Yet at the same time couldn't one find a new identity under a theater mask, a wig or even a shawl?

There was a torn green shawl with an embroidered Chinese butterfly. She'd bargained with an old man and had gotten it very cheap. When she'd come back to Arthur, he was sitting in the sun with his eyes closed, holding onto his beer glass. He opened his eyes and Adrienne came into focus photoed on his pupil . . . a miniature butterfly swimming in a mirrored screen. His camera lay on the table. What was the camera but a witness. But was it really objective? There are no objective witnesses, if you are a witness, brother, you're involved.

Could the camera photograph – impartially – the battlefield of agony without coming to some assistance? The film was virgin but how about the guy who used it? The X who had taken a stand not to interfere and be entirely objective in the filmings of gas chambers, burning monks, hangings, murders, drownings etc . . . He really must watch out or one day the shadow trader would sneak up on him and take a photo on the sly. He remembered a film on "civilizing" South American Indians . . . to catch the poor bastards who were out of "touch" with civilization . . . the whites hung beads, knives, pots and pans and Mickey Mouse shirts on a line to be used as bait. But the most important thing they hung, to catch him, was a mirror. A pool of water, for him to look at himself, was still in his natural setting and attached to his jungle landscape extensions of himself, but the mirror removed, separated him from his camouflage and mimicry – made him face himself and become self-conscious, pointing out he was *naked* – in a hurry to put on a Mickey Mouse shirt. And with the left over crap of civilization – corn flake boxes, sardine cans, Coca Cola bottles – these the natives used as head-dresses instead of feathers and shells. Then he was fucked-up, over his balls into the white man's guilt. Luckily the white man gave him alcohol to try and forget about what he saw.

Sometimes, though, the camera was a witness even beyond death like some navigator who took off on a boat deciding to kill himself aboard by starving to death. Every day he stood in front of a camera . . . it ticking away as he got thinner and thinner till he couldn't move – the boat floating directionless on the waves with the camera still turning while he dropped dead and the film going on as a rat was seen nibbling at his ear in the last shot . . . or the guy found dead in front of a television set – it was still running and had been on for three months according to the autopsy of when the guy had dropped dead of a heart attack – and with all those images flickering before his dead open eyes . . .

– What is there that's not for sale? – sighed Adrienne sitting down and staring at a pair of old shoes next to a doll's head.

– My dear girl, everything is for sale, even us. I heard about a guy killed in Vietnam and he was shipped home, not in too good shape I'm afraid, as he'd stepped across a grenade, but anyway some G.I.s had stuffed his body with "horse". His corpse was worth its weight in diamonds. And don't think all those curses stamped on Egyptian graves kept the guys from helping themselves to the loot . . . Have some nice human bones just fresh from the grave (really chicken bones) hot enough to make the tourists come in their pants – He ordered another beer. He was getting lyrical.

– What you need Adrienne, baby, is a rock as a pet. There are instructions on how to take care of it. First you name it. How about Samson? But maybe it's a female. I wonder if you can tell if it's a male or female. It doesn't move and most of all it doesn't talk back. For another five dollars they'll send you a leather case if you want to travel with it. Can it "come" or can it only go? People in glass houses shouldn't throw rocks . . . get your rocks off . . . beat your head against a rock . . . rock your rock . . . or do you want to get stoned – he chuckled – I think we should send for two then we could make pebbles – he was now seriously playing his comedy.

– My God, you must have kissed the "Blarney Stone" – she

couldn't get away from his words – under alcohol they shot up like geysers, or volcanoes in eruption, an un-ending Finnigans Wake. She picked up the camera, focusing on him holding his beer glass.

They took the metro back. On a billboard in the station was pictured a man in a gray suit smoking a cigar sitting in an armchair, a drink next to him. Captioned under the sign was: BE PROUD, LET YOUR NEIGHBOR ENVY YOU WITH YOUR NEW SUPER FRIGIDAIRE. A KITCHEN WITH THE BEST CONVENIENCES GIVES YOUR WIFE MORE TIME TO BE BEAUTIFUL. DON'T MOVE. DON'T WASTE ENERGY. JUST PUSH A BUTTON FOR YOUR TELEVISION. DON'T LET ANYONE TELL YOU THAT YOU HAVEN'T THE RIGHT TO THE MOST LUXURIOUS EXISTENCE THIS WORLD CAN OFFER.

Arthur swaying a bit went up to the billboard.

– Adrienne, do you smell rotten eggs?

– No – she said wondering what was coming next.

– Do you notice a pitchfork next to this gray-suited chap? I see he has a tail and pointed ears.

– What the hell's the matter with you? Have you gone nuts?

– No, that man in gray is the devil. You know the devil always likes to be modern and follow the times. We really must become more worldly . . . Tell me aren't you afraid to lose your face or body and disappear in the too-shiny neon light . . .? What we need is to hold on to our beards, turtlenecks, sunglasses . . . We have to fish for a mask in the human aquarium . . . My dear, search for the myth of the happy hero . . . find him in the metro . . . a giant plastered figure against the picture of the deodorized sweet-smelling self.

How about the three *clochards* drinking wine under a billboard advertising water 100% pure . . . Do you know about that Irish lady who arrives in London and the customs officer opens her bag and what does he find hidden but three bottles of wine . . . What is this, sternly says the officer, you know wine is not allowed in . . . And the Irish lady throws her hands above her head and cries out . . . Oh, Glory be to God, it's indeed a miracle . . .

She couldn't help but laugh as the train roared into the station and they walked in through the door.

– Look Adrienne – he continued as the door shut – everyone has on a rubber mask. They carry it with them when they sit on buses or metros or walk in the street. It makes their face a blank. Everyone's got the same blank expression . . . the drunk's got a special mask, it's bright red.

She looked around. It was true, every face was a blank as if they'd erased every emotion from it, even if children, sweethearts, parents were dying of cancer at home. But once she'd seen a woman in a station against a pillar. The time for the metro door to open and close. The woman stood crouched in upon herself like an accordion, her shoulders puffing up and down, her face a crumpled mask of tragedy. Then the metro closed leaving the woman salted to her pillar . . .

She had to be fair though, there were times when he was everything she wanted. Even a short walk in the neighborhood meant something . . . a sudden opening into a courtyard with a cat sunning itself, or he'd stop and buy her a rose. Days when he could forget about drink, short as those times were. But there was no real solution, outside was still the fire exit which one used only in case of emergency, but even that in times of riot could get blocked up . . . because if he didn't drink for a certain time, he was more sensitive to alcohol and became drunk immediately on a few beers. In those dry periods, usually after terrible drunks, he had to keep away from cafés, old buddies, wandering the streets at night. He stayed home close to her, never leaving her, reading, fooling around with his photos. She lit candles and incense and they made fires in their old fireplace watching the red shadowed flames kaleidoscope on the ceiling. They had meals on the bed and she supplied liquids in pitchers and bottles in all corners of the room so he could consume his habitual watery intake. Then they'd lay in bed making love. He was quite shy when he wasn't drunk . . . tender . . . while they listened to a record of Jackson Browne with the record cover of a cloudy Magritte sky, a lamplight, the last lit window and the stolen Chevrolet . . . where he could take off with her, crossing all the borders . . . on and on.

But all this was short-lived. A buddy would show up, or they'd be invited out and it would start all over again, hanging around the cafés as usual. They'd go to the Select where there were always people leaning on the bar watching the door like they were still waiting for Hemingway to show up, or at the Closerie des Lilas with engraved copper plaques nailed to the tables as they rubbed their sweaty fingers over Gide, Mallarmé etc., even Lenin had sat, and maybe plotted, there.

They stood at the bar, but even if he had decided to drink only a few beers that night, someone would lecture . . . What's the matter . . . a little drink never hurt anyone . . . best thing for a hangover . . . Come on I'm buying . . . Don't let me down . . . and how could he refuse? Then they'd argue who could hold the most . . . or how many day and night drunks they'd gone on . . . Superman exploits of drinking that raised them above the universe . . . I got so drunk in Kansas City, I thought it was Chicago . . . I took a train to California and I woke up in New York . . . I fell asleep under a bridge, nearly fell into the Seine . . . Don't know how the hell I got there . . . You know I woke up with this strange girl in my bed . . . I'll be damned if I know how she got there. She even said I fucked her three times . . . sometimes you miss all the fun . . . I told her, baby, wait till I'm sober . . . and so on . . . and so on . . .

NINETEEN :   NOTIONS

One day after coming back from Galeries Layfayette, Adrienne thought of her job in the Notion department of a big New York store – a hundred different items . . . notions, whims, knick-knacks gimmicks of – mothballs, hangers, needles, thimbles, sanitary napkins, hair curlers, rubber bands, candles . . . whatever *notion* ran through your head . . . rubber fruit, corn plasters, falsies etc. In whatever order you happened to dream these things up. Remember NO DESIRE MUST GO UNSATISFIED IN A CONSUMER SOCIETY . .
We allow no frustration to exist on a material plane . . . Think of the horror if every fifty years or so we burned all our possessions like in certain primitive tribes . . . this fantastic holocaust of objects burning higher than the Empire State Building with nothing left except unleavened bread and burnt bones. Who could stand this? And all over the city naked hermits sitting on top of apartment buildings under television crosses, staring at the sun with white eyeballs like Stylites and being fed a handful of bird grain time and again . . .
All day long in the department store she had stood there giving out *notions* . . . "Yes, madame, you name it, we have it as long as it has a NAME . . . *notions*. . ." A mental apprehension of whatever may be known or imagined . . . No dildoes, madame, for that you must go to a sex shop. We have however, kerchiefs with pinned false curls on them in red, blonde or black hair so you can safely go down at 4a.m. to the supermarket with a respectable appearance so as not to offend

your neighbor, with your curlers covered over. Supermarkets were opened all night long so every whim and desire could be satisfied at every moment . . . dreaming of chocolate, chewing gum, deodorant . . . YOU DESERVE THE BEST THE WORLD HAS TO OFFER YOU . . .

Later she had been transferred to the Complaints Department. Here on the switchboard she received thousands of complaints but only about clothes. It was as if the whole world had become one big dressing room . . . Hello, this dress they sent me is too big . . . too small . . . there's no button on top . . . the zipper's stuck . . . I asked for blue... I got green . . . My husband says I look like a maid in the dress . . . Yes, Madame (never lose your temper or you lose your job). The customer is always right . . . If I could just cut off my head, the dress would look okay (laugh politely at the jokers). The dress fits so tight you'd think it was a salami skin. If I went swimming in the dress, in that size, I'd float . . . There's a button missing near the you know what . . . (take down everything carefully). Remember one button missing near the cunt could be fatal . . . for want of a button virginity might be lost, then pregnancy and who knows if this slip might not be another Hitler etc.

She was also connected to the fur storage department. Clean your fur coat so moths do not destroy those earthly treasures . . . Remember her mother . . . "A fur coat in our society is a status symbol".

How about the animals, were they satisfied with their fate? What if the turtle should call her up . . . My shell is too small . . . I can't get a fridge in it, or the frog . . . I'm soaking wet, I'd like a nice green umbrella, or the snake . . . I can't stand my new skin, I want one in gold . . .

Even God or whatever *notion* it was that ran the universe had gotten sick of some of his creations. The dinosaurs had been cut out of such large pieces of skin that there wasn't much left over for a decent head. The *notion* department had switched to smaller sizes. Lizards fitted with Batman wings and that dodo a "dead notion" that laid eggs and suckled its young, and the fantasy trip, where things resembled one another and hid in each other's ethnic group. Caterpillars that metamorphosed into frightening carnival masks of crocodiles that even horrified monkeys . . . Mimicry . . . Travesty staged a permanent performance. Every animal ran around clothed or metamorphosed into a costume where it played its appropriate part.

Only man was born naked.

And Adam and Eve saw they were naked and Eve now felt she was equal to Adam . . . Decidedly God wasn't having better luck with Eve than with Lilith, Adam's first beloved, who had asked for equal rights (the first liberated woman) and had been immediately kicked out of paradise . . . And here was Eve beginning it all over asking to put on dungarees . . . just like men . . . these dungarees the proud symbol of the working class, because hadn't God said you shall work and suffer by the sweat of your brow . . . And remembering this, the Dungaree Co. made a large billboard of Christ and the twelve apostles, after all weren't they workers?

. . . Christ stood in the middle with white dungarees and the eleven apostles were in lovely chiffony ice cream colors, but Judas he stood aside wearing black ones, and since all men were equal, the rich as well as the poor, everyone wore dungarees.

What a heavy burden had been put on clothes to hide the human form, to try and make it into something else. The round shouldered, hunchbacked, flat-chested, flat-assed, flat-footed, knock-kneed . . . the ideal Hollywood form was dressed in an ideal size and the skeleton arising on its day of resurrection with trumpets blasting would be out there searching for its ideal flesh. Be careful to take the right arms and legs and try them out for size. But somehow it was as if there was nobody under the clothes, only more clothes piled on top of clothes like the *clochard* with three overcoats. And beneath all this the perfect ideal – a shroud – stitched in gold thread.

A friend had told her that when she'd gone to India if she wanted to photograph the family they always brought out proudly the member with the most infirmities . . . the leper with a nose eaten away or no eyes etc. All these infirmities seemed to be a mark of beauty to them. But here it was the Hollywood ideal of the stretched and labelled model spread out on the billboard of the world.

A blind man worked on the ground floor in the department store, his chair and a table placed next to a marble column. He demonstrated a small gadget – a *notion* that threaded a needle. He showed that one could be blind and with this gadget succeed in getting the thread through the hole. He sat up very straight in his chair. On the table were spools of thread, packages of needles and these little silver *notions*. He wore dark glasses and his face had deep pock marks. All day long he threaded needles with his silver *notion*, slipping the thread into a wire and feeling the needle's eye with his fingertips, then pulling the thread so quickly through the hole that it was as if one had seen a flicker of a mousetail in the back of one's eye. How many angels did he displace on the top of his needle that were quietly sitting there thinking they weren't going to be disturbed?

But hard as it was for a rich man to get into heaven – like putting a camel through the eye of a needle – there was always a loop hole . . . a gimmick – and if one couldn't enter heaven by the front door, there was always the back one. Because the rich man wrote CAMEL on a tiny piece of paper and with a *notion* slipped it through the eye of the needle, and maybe even St. Peter standing at the gate with his golden key would have to smile admiringly at this ruse and mightn't he then be persuaded to sneak the rich man to heaven through the servants' entrance?

But in this idea of *notions* little by little nothing seemed to hold together anymore. Thread was lighter and lighter, seams opening up in the most embarrassing places. How many times had the blind man's thread snapped as he was threading it . . . leather, rubber, nylon, aluminum, paper were not made to last. Everything was only "temporary" there was really not much sense in the word "eternity". Neither did love, as she saw it, last . . . "eternal marriages" or "eternal couples". The glue for this combination seemed to be made of brittle stuff.

Once in the Louvre in the Egyptian Hall, she'd seen the life-size statue of some Ramses with crossed arms holding his symbols of eternity. His black kohled eyes reminded her of a racoon she'd seen once under a nightclub table. Ramses was staring across the room at an old black guardian in sunglasses sitting on an iron chair. They had probably been facing each other for over twenty years and, as the old black man and the statue looked into each other's eyes, she thought that maybe that old black man might understand a bit about "eternity".

Downstairs in the basement of the store was the Fur Storage Department and she'd met Simon who worked there when he'd brought her up a box to put a coat in. His mother had been a well-known modern dancer and he had inherited a sinuous tension as if he was always ready to spring . . . maybe in her last days of pregnancy she had kept looking at the Discus Thrower . . . He wheeled the carts of furs over the cement floors like a Roman charioteer coming back with spoils . . . Simon said he put the furs in storage to keep them from the earthly moths.

He used to call her up from the basement. She was on the top floor,

– Hey Angie – he called her that – short for angel living on the top floor – I want to complain, will you get God on the phone for me and tell him a Luciferic angel would like a pair of wings to fly up to you?

They dated.

They went to Child's on the morning break to have Martinis . . . ready to join hands and fly over the buildings together. People who called to complain after she got back were soothed and calmed as she flew on a cloud in a white mink coat and he on another cloud in a golden chariot.

But she was puzzled, even after going out and bringing her home, he never made a pass at her. She never tired of watching him, his supple movements. His mother in her dance poses must have studied all the forms of Greek statues and concentrated everything in him, so that when he was born he had leaped out complete like Athena from the forehead of Zeus. Even when he just put on his coat, as he turned to catch the sleeve, he seemed ready to string a bow. He had auburn hair that fell into carved waves.

Once when they had gotten the same day off, he invited her to his apartment. He lived on Twenty-Third Street in an old building. He said he roomed with a black dancer. As they were going into the building, his friend came out. She suddenly realized he was a homosexual. He had a red band around his kinky hair, a heavy gold bracelet around his wrist and purple tights. Maybe this was the problem with Simon though he gave no outward signs of effeminacy, except perhaps this over aesthetic refinement in his movements, but nothing really showed anything to her since she had had no experience in these fields.

The apartment was furnished with old Victorian furniture – dark plush velvet, lamps in opaque glass with painted grapes and birds, a picture she supposed of his mother, in a Greek toga standing on a pillar shooting an arrow, maybe Diana. The window looked out into a courtyard where along a fence someone had painted yellow sunflowers which were now fading. He mixed some drinks and put on a record, she remembered it was *Red River Valley*, and they sat on the brown plush sofa. Since her experience with Chris, she'd been very closed with men, more on guard than ever.

He leaned over and kissed her but without passion, tenderly then he looked at her and played with her blonde hair.

– Hi, Angie – he said quietly as he gently put his arms around her and kissed her cheeks, her neck. He opened her blouse, kissing the top of her breasts, loosening her bra. She could feel, little by little, warmth running through her body, his hands were firm, massaging her and she responded. He had taken off his shirt and pants. It was an entirely aesthetic experience, as if a statue should come down from a pedestal and make love to her, a Pygmalion in reverse. He was gentle and affectionate but not very passionate. When he came, she thought she saw something like astonishment cross his face.

He took her hand.

– Angie, I have to tell you, you're the first girl I've ever slept with. I don't know what it is, but ever since I was a child, I used to fall in love with all the Greek statues of men I saw, the women's bodies never interested me. I didn't think it was possible or it could be like this – he put his head on her breasts.

After that they saw each other every night. She never asked him about his black friend and he never mentioned him. One morning they were sitting at Childs having their Martinis. She was twisting an olive with a toothpick. He was pale. He put his hand over hers.

– Angie, I didn't want to tell you before, but I'm taking a plane for Hollywood tomorrow. My mother has made a connection for a screen test for me. Maybe when I get settled you could come out . . . Anyhow, I'll write to you . . . I won't forget you . . . My Angie who's flown me out of the basement . . .

She didn't say anything. She picked up the olive and ate it mechanically. The next day he was gone and there were no more calls from the basement. No one to fly away with. Just complaints.

A week later she got a letter from him at Beverly Hills . . . Trying to get all my connections together . . . If I can get it as I want it would be great if you could come out here . . . Maybe I'll make you a star in my life . . .

Then she never heard from him again. When she went to the movies she looked for him on the screen but never saw him. She put his letter away in her little gold box of souvenirs . . .

Souvenirs wrapped up in a lavender handkerchief to pull out on a rainy day . . . but souvenirs rot and spoil faster than food. When she opened the box much later, the letter had faded, photos were bleached. Nothing in the box had been preserved hermetically.

TWENTY :   MASQUERADE

That summer, for her week's vacation from the Complaints Department, she decided to go to Provincetown on Cape Cod. A friend had recommended Mrs Janis's rooming house, a wooden frame house of two stories, the back part overlooking the Sound. She had a room on the ground floor in the back, with two large windows. The water lapped in and out on the sand making her feel that a thousand tongues were licking and licking at the shore. At night, lit up ships skittered on the water like Jack O' Lanterns and a fog horn croaked in endless repetitions. By the entrance stood an iridescent violet lamp that Mrs Janis lit precisely at 9p.m. each evening. It seemed to be a mysterious space ship that blinked on and off. Mrs Janis belonged to a sect called the Purple Light of the People. There was purple all over the house, the toilet paper, the dishtowels, the curtains. She even wore a purple dressing gown that went admirably with her white hair covered with a violet hairnet.

Fog like a veil covered the Sound and she could only see the line of the beach where seaweed, fruit rinds and sometimes a shipwrecked case of bottles floated by as a consumptive pale foam coughed up over the shore.

The first day she took a walk down the narrow streets. A traffic cop was directing the few cars lazily winding by. He was dark, well built with a full sensuous mouth and a red scar over his left lid. His eyes were yellow with brown specs. As she crossed, he whistled after her and winked – very uncoplike. When the light was changing he came toward her.

– You're new here – He had an insolent Rhett Butler manner – Where're you staying?

Surprised at herself she answered meekly

– At Mrs Janis's boarding house

– Oh, the purple light place. Hey, baby, tomorrow night there's an artists' ball. I'm the summer cop here but I do carpentry and work in the fish factory in the winter. How'd you like to come with me? Dress up in some kind of costume and I'll pick you up at eight.

Intellectually she considered herself a liberated woman but a primitive approach always took her off guard and, even though she hated to admit it, really turned her on.

His amber eyes were faun-like, mocking

– My name's Georgio, my father was a Portuguese fisherman, gave me a Portuguese name. What's yours?

She told him and timidly answered okay. She waved goodbye. Walking back she was annoyed with herself for giving in so easily. Oh well, what the hell, but what should she go as? For some reason a ghost or a phantom appealed to her. She passed a store and bought some white shoe polish.

About seven the next day she decided to dress. There was a heavy fog outside. That would go very well with the costume, a background of mist she could fade into. She took the white shoe polish and rubbed it over her face – a white mask stared at her from the mirror. Tying her long blonde hair on top of her head, she put on a white bathing cap with rubber ridges of rose petals. Then took a sheet from the bed, hoping Mrs Janis wouldn't mind, and wrapped it around her Greek style. As luck would have it she'd gotten her period. Over the top of the sheet she slipped on a white sweat shirt, spread a smudge of violet eye shadow on her lids and contemplated her disguise. With the gray fog in the background of the mirror, in her white sheet she seemed to be thrust forward, born on the foam of a wave, an imploring ghost leaping out of the water before the surf crashed it down into tiny drops again.

She heard the doorbell ring . . . that must be Georgio. Mrs Janis knocked at her door.

– Have a nice time at the ball dear – she coo-ed – I've been to so many nice balls in my day.

She saw Mrs Janis in her Isadora Duncan robe wafting through the ballroom in a purple flame.

As she floated down the hall, the purple light was making her sheet fluorescent. Georgio was standing like a Bacon painting with a butcher's apron of red spots for blood and a chicken leg strung around his neck. The purple light made him surreal. She suddenly saw the old alcoholic lady who lived in the neighborhood at the butcher's, but when she left, the butcher had pinned, as a joke, a chicken leg to her coat.

Georgio stood there all lust and blood as if he'd taken a transfusion and drained her . . . as if the poet and the butcher should meet in the market, he a bloody butcher, veins bulging on his neck as half a rump masturbated on his shoulder . . . His apron spotted and dripping like a Jackson Pollock painting. She, the poet, was chalky white, the color of bismuth, afraid to be reminded of unredeemed red. Her lambchops, fitted with little ruffled pants, well done, the poet-ghost is sensitive. She sees the mocking butcher appraising her anaemic skin and hooked outside the shop hung an audience of embryonic pigs' heads sticking out their obscene tongues at her slender green shoots.

They went down the street, the ghost and the butcher. Strange forms walked by them – an assemblage of characters from an insolite Hollywood film. The ball took place in the mayor's colonial office. Inside was a cross-section of civilization for the last two thousand years, Roman warriors, cowboys and

Indians, two Cleopatras, one with part of a matted floor mop on her head and a selection of colored dish towels arranged coquettishly around her, the other in black wool braids and a gold mini dress. There were two Supermen and something between Batman and a vampire, a clown in a checked suit and a false red nose had shoes too big for him which he kept falling over, a bird catcher with an explorer's hat and a net with a stuffed parrot inside. He kept going up to people and cackling . . . Polly want a cracker . . . A woman with curlers and a bathrobe had a box of cornflakes and cat food in a basket. An exhibitionist opened a raincoat, flashing his naked body under the startled eyes of girls who snickered at his prick. A fisherman with a line dragged off hats and wigs in a free-for-all. Someone even came as The Mask of Red Death . . . black and red spots painted on his skin, and gays, there were plenty of them – in bathing suits, gold lamé, black silk dresses, boas, beads, holding onto each other with rouged lips and colored wigs. One gay was crooning *My Man* while clutching on to a hairy Mae West . . . but "he" was strange, not really a woman, something disturbing like those mustaches boys put on pin-up girls on billboards making them freaky. There was a gay in a white suit, a roll of wallpaper under his arm and a Nazi cross on his chest. It took time to catch on that it was a young Hitler as a paperhanger.

– Come on let's dance – ordered Georgio as he led her expertly around the room. He pressed her tightly against him, the chicken leg scratching her breast. He swung her around and around among all these unassorted costumes resurrected from some flea market of time. The red paint wasn't quite dry on his apron and silk screened onto her sheet. She hoped her period wasn't showing but no one would be able to tell. As she danced, she began to feel flushed and her face started to itch. Under her eyes she felt a swelling, realizing suddenly it must be the shoe polish. Feeling faint she told Georgio to stop and they went over to a table by the window to sit down. Under the fog outside, a faint fingernail moon showed and the boats flashed in the distance like ruby rings.

– I'll be right back – she murmured as he ordered some beer.

She went to the ladies' room and poured cold water over her face. Then she scrubbed and scrubbed the white polish. It came off unevenly. There were patches of white and red welts over her face. She pulled off the bathing cap, some white had dyed the front of her hair. She had aged overnight. She pushed as much hair as possible over her face to hide it, then made up heavily. In the mirror was a ghost who didn't want to disappear but hung on to its mask before its ectoplasm sadly disintegrated. She walked out into the world of freaks and everyone's private nightmare. Georgio looked at her unbelievingly.

– It's that damn shoe polish, I'm allergic to it – she moaned.

– My God, you look just like a lady clown – he said as if he expected her to jump up and down or something – Let's go out and get some air.

– Yeah, that's a good idea, at least it would be dark enough to cover her face she thought.

They went down to the beach. It was a warm muggy night. The mist hung down like thin layers of tissue paper. There was a small cove. He leaned over and pushed her down on the wet sand. Her face didn't seem to bother him.

– Hey, I've got my period.

He laughed, – What's a little more blood?

He took her hand and put it on his penis. It was as hard as a rock. He pulled up the sheet and rubbed against her. She felt feverish . . . trying to push him away but he continued moving on top of her.

– Wait, wait – she cried as she pulled at her Kotex tail, tearing it out like some bloody white mouse. He went on, his hard flesh pressing in her, when suddenly he came.

– Jesus, I'm sorry – he apologized – I was too hot.

She felt wet in the back, was it the foam moving in – was it blood or sperm?

– Look I really don't feel too good, I have to get home – she said in a weak voice.

She wrapped the sheet around her as if it were a bandage and the butcher and the ghost dragged back. He kissed her good night at the door.

– Take it easy, I'll see you tomorrow – as he went whistling down the street.

The purple light winked on and off like a silent alarm.

The next day she stayed in bed with a high fever. He went to see her a few times and they made it, but he always came immediately. The last day he didn't show up and she took the train back.

TWENTY ONE : FALSE MESSIAHS

On the train back from Provincetown, she had sat next to a Merchant Marine Officer. He had some gold on his shoulder but she didn't know what rank he was till they started to talk and he told her he was first mate on an oil tanker. He looked a bit like Cary Grant she thought, except his eyes were more slanted and his skin a sunburned color like he could have had some Indian blood. His name was William and he was rather shy. She felt good with him. He was very protective asking her if she was in a draft, or if she wanted a drink or a cigaret. He took her to eat in the dining car and they had wine with their meal. It felt nice to be fathered for a change. When they got to New York, he had to leave for his ship but he said he'd call her.

In a month's time she heard from him. He took her out to some swanky nightclub and bought her an orchid and dinner. In the cab he kissed her respectfully. They went out a few more times but he only fondled and kissed her. As he was much older maybe he thought she was too young. Once they were sitting in a nightclub when he turned pale and his hands began to tremble. He called the waiter . . .

– Quick bring me an orange juice . . . He held her hand hard, squeezing it, his fingers were bluish. When the waiter brought the juice he gulped it down and smiled at her.

– I'm diabetic, but I'm okay now . . . You know what . . . How'd you like to see my ship? She was already feeling lightheaded from too many cocktails, he always liked her to drink a lot.

– Oh, great – she cried. He took her in a cab to a port which might have been Staten Island. The tanker was in the harbor like some rusted whale that had floated too near land. A three-quarter moon hung hazily above, its orb eye fishy. Water gushed out of the back of the ship in satin ribbon foam. He helped her up the gangplank. They went into the officers' mess-room. In it was a large oval table and on the wall a picture of a clipper ship. The copper portholes shone like gold rings. There was a sense of order and masculinity about the room with its dark wood panels and stark chairs chained to the table. Then he took her to his cabin, small with a neatly made white bunk and a tiny bathroom with a large mirror.

– Honey – he said softly – Why don't you take your dress off.

That evening she had been wearing a champagne-colored dress with little silver stars sewn on it. A dress sample from her father's company. She dug William. He was gentle, ready to please her. He opened the bathroom door. His white shirt was open at the neck. He had laid his tie and jacket neatly on a chair. She slipped her dress over her head. He took it from her and placed it next to his things – standing in back of her, watching the mirror. He picked up her half slip and put his hand underneath, a fingernail catching on the top of her stocking. He loosened her bra strap and lifted her up as if she was a child, onto the bed. With his foot he kicked the door open wider, the mirror reflecting them.

– I won't hurt you darling – he said soothingly. He lay on top of her still dressed and rubbed up and down over her pink pants, meanwhile watching their mirrored image.

– Just let me hold you, it's all I want – he moaned.

He stroked her breasts, her stomach, her hair but didn't touch her below. All that time he kept turning to look in the mirror. After a little while he got up and kissed her. Nothing had happened. She felt as if she was an actress in a movie set and at the same time watching her film but she didn't feel bad. It was like a child who had been soothed before it went to bed, before however, it would have its recurrent nightmare.

He pulled out a bottle of scotch from a drawer and made drinks with the tap water. He sat by her, stroking her hair, smoking a cigaret, the smoke curling upward immaterial as if once Aladdin's lamp might have been underneath. Her eyes turned to the small dresser. There were two photos, one was of a young man slightly resembling William, the other was a blonde woman about forty. He saw her watching the photos. There was a certain sadness in his face as he looked at the man.

– That "was" I say with quotation marks, my younger brother, Dan. He disappeared ten years ago on a 425 foot freighter near the Tortugas. That's the area in the Bermuda Triangle, which is roughly from Florida to Bermuda . . . Yes, the whole ship literally disappeared into thin air – cigaret smoke trailed out of his lips and vanished as if it were being taken as a witness to this undeniable possibility. – They say it's a magnetic field that cuts through time and space – there was a dreamy look on his face – Well anyhow, that afternoon, the weather was clear, no waves . . . but the ship vanished like a magician's act . . . no wreckage . . . no bodies . . . nothing. They sent planes, ships to search the area but absolutely no trace of even a bottle. The sea was as calm as if it had been oiled. It vanished like a toy ship. Who knows – he mused – I always get the feeling he'll show up one day and though it was more than ten years ago, he'll be the same age as when he disappeared . . .

William opened a drawer and took out a paper

– You see this? – he said shaking the paper at her – This is a U.F.O. form given to all the captains of ships and planes to note on in case anything strange is seen in the sky . . . Look here's some of the questions . . . "Did the phenomenon – move in a straight line? – stand still at any time? – suddenly speed up and run away? – break up in parts and explode? – change color? – give off smoke? – change brightness? – change shape? – flash or flicker? . . ." He put down the paper – sometimes when I'm on watch, I've seen a few bright objects that roll along the sky . . . glow and disappear . . . and crazy as it seems, I wonder if Dan could be on one of them . . .

She didn't say anything. He took another drink. He seemed far away. She stared at the photo of the blonde woman and thought that in some years she'd resemble that woman.

They went up on deck. A gray mist covered the ship. A foghorn belched in distress. The moon, a whitish mass of gelatine, was disappearing. He held her waist as they went down the gangplank.

When she got home two silver stars were missing from her dress.

That night she dreamed she was sitting on a beach when suddenly a fiery object raced through the sky and a ball of yellow light, smaller than the sun, wheeled through the sky. In the distance was a full ghostly daytime moon and above a plane – when to her horror, she saw it had lost control and was hurtling straight down to where she was. It was an army plane, khaki color with red letters and numbers she couldn't decipher. It was getting larger and larger as it fell, smoke coming out of the back. She ran to a cave nearby and hid inside. Looking out she saw the plane crash, then explode sending up great white waves of spray that filled the mouth of the cave and drenched her . . . She woke up, her heart beating furiously.

William took her out one more time . . . On the way home, he put his hand up her leg, uncovering her in the taxi, looking in the driver's mirror. She remembered being very embarrassed. Then for Valentine's day he sent her an enormous red satin box, heart shaped, filled with chocolates and after that she never heard from him again . . . She had kept the box for years to put her make-up in. The bottom was stained with powder and rouge, till one day she spilt a bottle of nail polish over the box and she threw it away . . . like all her lovers maybe he had crossed the space and time barrier.

So she hung on, waiting for all the men who had never found her. The false Messiahs – for the one who would pass through her hedge of thorns, she who was not awake but constantly dreaming. But none ever found her. Each of them had made some fatal error and the hedge closed around them – putting them through a hundred humiliating trials to test their fidelity. Was it possible one had come to her with a revelation she hadn't understood? Maybe she needed distance to understand his cryptic message – time to decode the last symbol scratched like a claw-mark on the yellowed paper – or would it be a message inside a milk or whiskey bottle floating unexpectedly outside her door . . .?

TWENTY TWO :   COUPLES

In the apartment house in New York City where she had lived as a child – on floor twelve and a half – there was no thirteen or no one would have lived there – in the dining room was a large lacquered Chinese cabinet. There were two doors. On one of the doors stood a Chinese mandarin in a purple robe and on the other door, a Chinese maiden in a red robe decorated with pink shell flowers. Below on a pond on a painted leaf sat a frog. Its belly was inlaid with mother of pearl so iridescent it seemed to be still dripping with water. The frog's back was lacquered green and the eyes bits of yellow shell. A white swan, also with mother of pearl feathers, glided in the background and a tree of cherry blossoms hung over the edge, its white pearl flowers floating over the pond. The mandarin and the lady stood eternally staring at one another. Their separation in space was fixed – static – there was no bridge across their pond. Nothing could help them cross the water to each other. Through all her childhood breakfasts, lunches, suppers, she'd watched them staring at one another. Once she had made a bridge of colored matchsticks and taped it across the pond hoping somehow if she closed her eyes and then opened them she would see them together. But on opening her eyes, they stood in their same fixed positions. Their moist shell eyes far away from one another.

Then she'd sit on the window-sill looking over the roof tops. Across was a roof with a man who kept homing pigeons. He had a wire pigeon coop. He'd unlatch the door and let some pigeons out as he waved a long stick back and forth in his hand and the pigeons flew above, then landed on his weathervane stick. These were domesticated pigeons which always came home.

On the dining-room floor was a valuable Chinese rug with oriental designs and, in the middle, blue and yellow woven flowers. One Easter her mother had bought a white rabbit for her sister and her. She could see the rabbit – its pink trembling nose, the watery red eyes and its ears raised and lowered like train signals at any sign of danger – the white angora fur so soft they used to rub their faces in it. It lived in a box in the kitchen but one morning it escaped into the dining room and when they had come in for breakfast, the rabbit had already nibbled off the leaves and the yellow flowers in the middle of the rug leaving little bald patches. Her mother had been so mad she'd given it to a friend in the country and the poor rabbit had died eating real grass sprayed with D.D.T. Where was that rabbit's sense of reality? It would have been better off having a watch and a pair of gloves.

In the morning, her mother would force her to eat oatmeal with pimply lumps in it. When her mother went back into the kitchen or to bed, she'd throw it out the window watching as it dribbled down the building like obscene vomit; or she'd dump it into the dirt of the snake plant. This monstrous snake plant, that thrived on oatmeal lumps and her father's crushed cigar butts laid around the calloused leaves like turds . . .

One night she dreamed she had gone to look for her father though he had been dead already seven years. She had gone to the cemetery and there were *clochards* eating baguettes and drinking wine on a tombstone horizontal like a table. She walked through overgrown weeds but couldn't find her father's grave. She passed by a tomb with a profile of a man carved on the stone with an inscription ANCIENT OF DAYS. Then she came across an old man in a pin-striped suit who told her her father had been murdered by a child, but who the child was she never found out.

Now it was as if she was searching for the ideal couple that Plato said had once been both man and woman, joined together. She was only half. She thought of her friend Muriel who had been in a car accident. She'd been picked up in a coma and taken to the hospital. After a month she was still in a coma but her beautiful green eyes always stayed open. The nurses treated her like a doll. They washed and brushed her light-brown hair, put a ribbon around it and dressed her in lovely nightgowns. They even manicured her nails and cut them. She grew even more beautiful except her eyes were glassy like a doll's. She even had her normal period every month. She never moved or spoke and no one could tell if she felt anything. Her face was a blank, a mask that seemed to be covering another face underneath. Her husband Marvin was heartbroken, he adored her. Every day after work he came with flowers, perfume and chocolates. He held her limp hand and stroked her hair as she lay there propped up on her pillow like a sleeping beauty. Her green eyes staring like a doll when the mechanics get stuck and the lashes can't close. Except for a slight breathing under the sheet by her breast, there was no movement. Little by little Marvin stopped going to see her and after a year he sued for divorce.

Three years later Muriel was still alive. She had seen her then, but couldn't stand to go back again. Her skin was as white as if it had been dusted with rice powder. She was heavier, a little bloated and her hair was down to her waist. The nurse still manicured her nails. But her eyes were always staring in the direction of the door – as if some day someone would pass, make a sign and maybe wake her up.

Adrienne now felt she herself was in an iron lung – a mirror hung over her face reflecting the image bathed in the humid silver moisture of her labored breath clouding the glass – the oxygen pumped in and out. She was rigid, unable to move . . . a narcissus placed in a vase grew in the mirror, its white petals staring at her pale sweaty face. All the sterile equipment was arranged against blank walls, steel basins, oxygen tanks, silver hypodermic needles, clamps. A white curtain blew in from the window in a bandage as clouds drifted through the sky breaking up into globs of phlegm.

She lay as a silver mummy in her sarcophagus . . . entombed alive . . . fixed at one point. Her universe reflected in on herself . . . a moon satellite of dead light. Her breath oozed in and out dripping on the mirror in shiny bubbles from underwater fish. She was walled alive in her Noah's ark . . . carrying her species with her but only one by one . . . Each thing was alone like one goldfish reflected in a mirror. She lay waiting for the sterilized dove to appear above her with the hope of a potent green twig . . .

Then there were certain other days filled with "time" as she put it.

There was that afternoon at the Planetarium watching the stars reflect on the dome sky, thrown out by the special time machine projector. Along the edge of the dome was silhouetted – the Empire State, Woolworth's, even her neighborhood in the eighties scaled to the dimensions of the dome. It was a moment of expanding consciousness, a frosted picture of a magic landscape seen inside a candied Easter egg for peeking inside there was this "moment" always held onto, always there, floating in an egg of time. Once looking in Arthur's eyes that "moment" had opened up . . . and she saw them swimming under water, going down and down into shadowy water, bubbles rising from their mouths till one of the bubbles broke and she saw Arthur crawling through a coral hedge, but she couldn't distinguish his features – as if there was an overexposed spot across his face . . .

TWENTY THREE : IS THERE ANYBODY OUT THERE?

Arthur arranged his photos. He was waiting for Jackson to come by and pick him up to go to St. Michel. Hopefully they were going to make some money, he with his photos and Jackson playing bongo drums. The bell rang.

– Okay, brother, let's get going – Jackson called out tapping staccato thumps on his drum. Arthur gathered the photos under his arm. Adrienne was out teaching English. It was a sunny June day. Boys had rapt looks on their faces as they lounged on corners watching girls in light butterfly dresses waft down the street. Jackson's hair stood up, braided in little pigtails, a beaded band around his forehead.

They found a sunny spot on the boulevard under a linden tree dripping its white snowflake flowers over the street. Arthur spread out his photos on an old cloth . . . a tongue spitting gargoyle from Notre Dame, a statue of a naked woman, Psyche, lounging under a waterfall from the fish pond in Luxembourg Gardens, a 1920 slinky carved cat from a doorway in rue Guenegaud, the "Quinine lady" lying naked on a pedestal, her arm flung over her forehead, as if suffering from a bad hangover, the three stone muses holding on to one another, from their neighborhood, and other assorted monuments. Across the way, an African in sunglasses stood over a series of masks laid out in repeat copies – effigies pressed out like chocolate cookies. Next to him was a stand of

Indian scarves, jewelry and bells tinkling with every breeze.

Jackson began drumming hard when a small boy came up to him. His parents had turned to look at the masks. The boy was about five or six in a sailor suit with a head of tight blonde curls. He stood watching Jackson, his mouth half open, chewing on rainbow colored candies. Suddenly he took a few candies out of his sticky hand and laid them next to Jackson. Jackson smiled. The parents turned, yanked the child's arm and went on. Jackson stopped playing.

– Man, I got a joint – he murmured – There ain't no cops around. He took the joint, lit it, inhaled deeply and handed it to Arthur. Arthur sucked in the smoke, closing his eyes. The smell of grass mingled with incense from the Indian stand. They sat idolically in the sun. Just then two French students came up to them and whispered in broken English

– You got . . . LSD?

Jackson looked at them. They were out for kicks, a bit naive. Certainly Arthur and he seemed like the right connection. Jackson thought quickly.

– Yeah, man – he said excitedly, rolling his eyes – I got great stuff – and he put his hand over the child's colored candies and held them up – New shit, just come from the States, all colors – and he held out his hand seemingly stamped in chocolate with bright frosting of violet, green, yellow and red beads.

The two students stood there hesitantly

Last night buy LSD . . . bad . . . no well . . .

– Look, brother, I just took some myself, it blows your mind – he tapped enthusiastically on the drums, rocking his head from side to side – Tell you what, I give you this red one – and he held it out temptingly between two fingers, something like the witch holding up the apple to Snow White – for twenty francs

. . . then you come back and I give you the other three for fifty francs . . . a real hot bargain . . . you'll be spinning, believe me man.

Shuffling their feet back and forth they whispered to each other, finally one of them pulled out twenty francs, gingerly took the sticky red candy and they walked off – looking behind them as if Jackson might be a mirage and disappear at any moment.

Arthur laughed

– Hey, pretty smooth. How'd you like to be my manager? Hope they don't come back pissed off.

– Listen – Jackson said emphatically – Suggestion is a mighty powerful gimmick, when you hustle baby, you gotta be right in there.

Jackson went on playing the drums and with the twenty francs Arthur got beer and wine. About half an hour later the two students stood before them. They were holding each other's arm and seemed exhuberant.

– Very well . . . we chop red LSD in two . . . we flippé . . . and they handed Jackson fifty francs. He gave them the rest of the colored candies.

– Head big . . . big . . . see colors . . . up . . . down . . . They echoed like a stereotype of what one was supposed to feel.

– Have a good time boys – Jackson called as they went tripping down the street – Come on there, move your ass, we's gonna eat and drink baby.

They packed up the stuff. There was one green candy on the cover. Arthur put it in his pocket. They went to the cafe across the street and ordered spaghetti and drinks.

With his mouth full, Arthur mumbled.

– Show's you how man can be fed on illusion.

Later on when they got home, they were both high. Arthur took out the green candy to show Adrienne and then put it back in his pocket like a talisman. They sat down and started on more drinks which they'd brought back with them.

– You know man – Jackson expounded – we all gotta get wise. Remember that Little Black Sambo story, well I'm gonna re-edit it . . . "Give me your pants Little Black Sambo or I'll eat you up", threatened the tiger. But there was a day in Alabama when that there sun rose like a lump of butter and a one-eyed nigger's school house in conjunction with that melted Sun – cause an instant eclipse . . . And the whole world go dark and them repentants knelt down to pray. Then that there sun froze into a great white lump and Little Black Sambo showed his teeth, "Like hell I'll give you my pants" he snarl, "Just you come over here and I'll poke your fucking eyes out and I'll knot your tails together till you knock each other out into one striped Aunt Jemima pancake, and I'll eat you warm under a frying sun with the whole family by the open school house . . . yes sir, that's what I do."

– You know what – Arthur interrupted – speaking of blacks, I was just thinking of Aldos Solomen. He was a real brother of yours before I'd ever met him.

Jackson assented thickly

– He sure were, and I'd go out on the town every time someone buy a painting from him.

– Remember when I first met him? It was at the Select. It seems he'd been over here from the States for more than twenty years, even something of a celebrity with his painting.

– That so – Jackson nodded, his eyes closing.

– Yeh – Arthur continued – at that time he was into coffee, before he'd done a bit of drinking till his nerves cracked and he began hearing voices and seeing strange guys around him.

Once he said he heard voices outside his door whispering all sorts of bad things about him, and one time the devil had come into his house and asked him to sign a paper. He'd seen one of the names on it – Beelzebub – but he'd lit a match to the paper and the devil had gone up in smoke. And you know what Aldos said . . . He said all the guys who were bugging him were white. Sometimes he'd get that strange look on his face, turning to the side like he was talking to someone, mumbling. Only I couldn't see anybody. He was still good for a binge once in a while and he'd have to be taken home and that's how I ended up in his pad one night . . . though I'll be damned how I got there . . . The only thing I know is when I woke up in the morning there were all those paintings staring at me. Boy what a trip.

Jackson was out of it, nodding gently, his wine bottle in his lap. Arthur went on loquaciously – Adrienne had heard the story but there were always new variations to it.

– Right on the wall smack in front of me was this painting of a middle-aged black dame in a rocking chair with a yellow flowered hat and a little bitchy pekinese dog on her lap, its pink tongue sticking out. She was on a porch and the old gal seemed to be staring across into her neighbor's backyard with her mean little eyes to catch all the gossip . . . In the painting next to her sat an old black woman on a bench with torn shabby boots, one on top of the other like her corns ached, and a large paper bag at her feet. Maybe she was a maid coming home from work waiting for a bus. Snow was falling. Her battered hat was white on top. The only other thing in the picture was a red fire hydrant and a bare tree. The woman sat with her hands crossed on her lap waiting, but at the same time expecting nothing . . . not even the bus – maybe just to get her goddamn shoes off and dunk some bread in her coffee, the other painting I remember well was some old bar in a

Southern town . . . a big pot-bellied stove, a bright green pool table, a couple of guys standing at the bar and an old black man with white hair staring into his glass . . .

– Let me tell you though, Aldos always took his paintings seriously. One night we'd been invited to dinner by a friend cause now I was living with him, I didn't have any other place to go, it was before you honey – he said tapping Adrienne on the knee – On the wall was this life-size portrait of a well known black saxophone player in a green sweater and purple pants holding his sax over his knee like a gold fishing rod. Well this here guy had been on the jazz scene a hell of a long time . . . a heavy guy with kinky hair, not too dark and a damn sexy mouth, you could see his mocking eyes were taking in the whole scene – as if a good looking chick might be walking to a seat in front of him at a concert, but there was a kind of cool in his drooping lids and around his lips – a guy who was no longer in the running – an old time fisherman holding his horn rod over his knee who now only entered big-time competitions . . . small fry no longer interested him. You could hear him on his sax wailing . . . Baby I dig you . . . do I dig you . . . but staring ahead into a mirror of himself playing. Once in a while his eyes caught on fire and his thick lips blew out sparks that sent the audience; but he was a pro who'd been through the scene so many times that everyone knew it was a game . . . a fucking sophisticated game, but even so the music turned them on. It was damn good . . . maybe a bit mechanical but still better than someone inexperienced.

He stared out of the canvas, somewhere in a space above cause some great chick might be floating out there, even though he knew better . . .

– So Aldos turns to this here painting and waves his hand at him . . . Come on down from there, we's invited for dinner, now get ready . . . of course the painting didn't move . . . it ain't polite to keep them folks waiting . . . Still the painting didn't move . . . All right then we's going without ya . . . and Aldos turned his back angrily at the figure . . . You know I felt a little sad . . . This painting was sure the man, but a man who didn't want to go to dinner. I can see Aldos now – Arthur stretched out his arm – Looking like some old black monk with his white cropped hair in a torn gray turtleneck sweater and I swear to you when he raised his fingers in the air, it looked like the fucking pope's sign of blessing . . . it sure wouldn't have surprised me to see a bud hop out of his brown branch finger. And you know what he did when we left, he put a plate of cookies under the picture . . .

– On top of it, believe it or not, he was the only damn person who could get me out of bed in the morning.

Adrienne raised her eyebrows in disbelief. His voice seemed to be on tape, going on and on and if he got stuck at some particular place, he'd adjust the mechanics and go on, – his eyes were far away.

– Aldos had insomnia and when I'd be out after a good night's drunk sleeping away, he'd sit in this here red plush chair of his with all the straw stuffing sticking out like an old bird's nest, a striped blanket covering his shoulders and one of those wool hats with pom-poms on it children ice skate in. His shoes were full of holes, wads of newspapers around the room where he'd torn out pieces and stuffed them on the bottom. In back of him was this huge avocado tree he'd planted from seed a few years ago, and that fucking thing kept growing and growing till it hit the ceiling ready for Jack and the beanstalk. It leaned against the studio window – those windows were always dripping – I said he needed a windshield wiper. I swear it was a scene from that painter that does jungle scenes. I was always expecting a lion to leap out from behind the chair or a snake or two but the only thing was this damn mouse that came to nibble a piece of candy that had fallen on the floor. Aldos had a big sweet tooth like lots of guys that give up booze – Maybe I'll like candy one day . . . when he heard the mouse under the bed he'd look at me with a straight face and say . . . What's that under the bed, a pig? And out would come this tiny mouse. Everything was a mix-up there, drunk or sober it was another world – a real fly on the wall seemed false and the yellow flowered hat on the dame and the red fire hydrant real.

– God how Aldos stored everything. He never threw anything away . . . old pieces of bread turned into cement . . . letters with money from America were forgotten in books . . . doors in the wall that were stuck and couldn't be opened, or doors that looked real but were painted . . . old bunches of keys that no one knew what they opened any more . . . jars of outdated metro tickets, and I remember there was a dried bunch of flowers on a table I picked up one day that just fell into dust.

Jackson, his head slumped on the side of the chair, was snoring. Adrienne sighed. Whether Arthur needed an audience or not, any inattention on her part always made him mad. She wondered if she shouldn't make a dummy of herself and sit it up so she could go to bed, and then save it for other occasions, but she went on listening patiently.

On he droned.

– Aldos sat in his chair doing some drawing or took a tiny snooze, and then around seven in the morning he'd pull my toe and dance around the end of the bed like some crazy striped bug and get me to walk down to Montparnasse . . . It'd still be dark, the dawn just coming up, I might have a hangover, but I'd feel good and we'd go to a café where there'd be two or three other hungover guys sitting like statues in a corner and the grumpy waiter brought us our coffee and me a calvados, sloshing the coffee all over the saucer . . .

– Once after it had been raining, I remember seeing a rainbow with the moon going down on one side of the street and the sun coming up on the other . . . Then on the way back I'd buy some beer, whatever money he had he'd give me, and I'd make it back to bed and Aldos would take out his palette juiced with those hunks of colored toothpaste and start some drawings with orange suns and yellow flowers . . . he had drawings all over of arms and legs, African masks . . . tiny heads . . . umbrella bones . . . evolutionary abortions that ended in a new species . . . black guys against yellow suns, a new sunburned race . . .

– But in the end his house was condemned to make place for another fucking tower . . . we'd have to get out. Little by little they walled up all the windows except for his, and Aldos didn't want to go home any more. He'd sit in a café staring ahead, then he took to dragging around the streets talking to guys when there weren't any next to him.

– Hey Jackson – and he poked Jackson who opened his bloodshot eyes – you remember when we carted his stuff away to the new room Jerry had found for him? . . . but he never made it to the new place, cause he was found wandering around the streets after three days, and they stuck him in the nut house . . . he didn't remember much after that. Boy it was some job getting his stuff out.

– It sure was – Jackson nodded, taking another sip of wine – It took us and two other dudes to drag that fucking alligator plant down the stairs with them guys behind it like it was some kind of jungle camouflage covering their asses.

– And how about those paintings in the closet . . . painted in a sparkling gold dust . . . cities of Eldorado . . . chicks in gold turbans and robes . . . paintings of suns and stars. Everything was in yellow and gold by a black guy who wanted to make it to the sun but had been too burned by it . . . well they stuck his stuff into the new room under white sheets and there it is to this day. Then they began walling up his window with gray brick and plaster . . . that was it . . . those motherfuckers – Arthur cried.

– And then at the nut house of St. Anne's . . . that was another story . . . who knows maybe Sylvette was there at the same time. Jackson had gone to sleep again.

– Boy that was the end there. It looked like a self-service cafeteria where they'd put Aldos, except with bars. There was a television set that blasted away with people lined up in rows only they weren't looking at those images. Aldos was in a chair in a corner with striped pajamas and a pair of old slippers, his hands folded on his lap and godamn it, if it didn't hit me he was the maid in his painting, waiting . . . but waiting for nothing. I went over to him. I'm not sure he recognized me. I'd brought him chocolate and some flowers, at that time I thought he might still be painting, they were yellow daisies. I gave him the flowers. He broke off two of them and before I could make a move, he'd eaten them . . . petals and all. I was kinda flabbergasted . . . I had once read Van Gogh had eaten his paints . . . the color must have made him crazy. The flowers were like little gold suns.

– An old guy in a terry cloth robe came up to him and said, "Have you seen my red sock? Don't forget we have to get out of here before night, the truck is coming . . . "

– Just then a nurse came and took him away. A young thin girl was looking in a mirror and putting on make-up – that was cool – but she kept putting on rouge and lipstick them rubbing it off and putting it on, over and over like a clown in a quick change act. Next to her an old lady with long gray hair, looking like something watching the guillotine in the French revolution, was knitting but she'd knit one line and then take it out and begin again . . . An Indian guy kept walking around the room shaking hands and saying "thank you" with an English accent . . . another guy with a black patch over one eye, in a silk bathrobe would walk to the middle of the room, his hands in his sleeves like Fu Manchu, spin around like a robot, self-wind himself up and begin again.

– It was a freak circus where no one could finish his act . . . But the most spaced-out trip was this old dude with twisted skinny legs in a white smock, everything seemed out of joint – made of rubber – like a tight rope walker who'd fallen into the rope – knotted in it . . . crying out "Help . . . Help . . . Help . . ." in a doll's mechanical voice . . . "Is there anybody out there?"

– I sat next to Aldos. He didn't say a thing. He kept staring ahead of him. Slowly his head bent over to the side . . . listening . . . God knows, maybe he heard a magic voice whispering to him . . . enchanting him . . . cause little by little it was as if he was being hypnotized by something I couldn't see . . . his eyelids were weighed down like a line with a sinker pulling at them and his head fell on his chest, his hands still crossed on his lap . . . I left him . . . dozing with that son of a bitch television blasting away in front of him . . . and boy did I get fucking drunk afterwards. Then they shipped him back to the States to some institution . . . that was . . .

The doorbell rang. Adrienne got up wearily. It was Vivian, a good friend of hers; an American who had a sweater shop around the corner from her. Arthur called out .

– Hey, Vivian, where's my hat? Vivian was making him a green wool hat.

– You'll get it one of these days as soon as I can find where I put the rest of the wool. Adrienne made a sign to Vivian with her hands as if waving her back. Vivian understood. Adrienne went up to her.

– Look – she said in a low voice – I want to get out of here, let's go to your shop.

– Okay – consented Vivian. Adrienne turned around. Arthur was stretched out on the bed, his head to the side already asleep. Jackson, on the chair, was snoring heavily.

– Well, I guess they really won't need me – Adrienne said sarcastically.

TWENTY FOUR :   WRONG NUMBER

Vivian's balls of wool were all entangled. Vivian felt that clothes could not be cut from a pattern any more than life. There was always a problem with her of having too much material, too litttle, or the wrong kind. As if life could be folded over and basted with seams. She had boxes of half-finished sweaters . . . imploring sleeves hanging over the edges of baskets in drowning gestures, colored backs and sides metamorphosed into creatures that seemed to be developing from tails to webbed feet, or knitted wings that were no longer good for flying. Dislocated mannequins lay about the shop – outstretched arms with colored bracelets and gloves, plaster heads with green and purple hair . . . amputated legs sticking out of corners, white masks with knitted scarves around their half-heads.

Nothing was definite or finished. People who ordered sweaters came back a month later to find odd pieces attached or four arms. It was as if Vivian was no longer interested in the complete human form. She only saw parts of it. She could not seem to "knit up the ravelled sleeve of care". She couldn't detach herself from an empathy with her clients and friends. She suffered from their infirmities and had to cover them up. It was almost as if she wanted to make a magic cloak for each person, to hide them from their disabilities, their nakedness and she quickly had to spin the material for this cloak to cover up the sudden pink birth of confused innocence from those strong projectors that filmed their faults on a life-sized screen.

So she suffered with them in her own guilts by developing heavy asthma attacks.

Once they had gone to the rue Bassano where Vivian had to get her work card, it was a respectable office, modern windows, desks etc. But leading up to the second floor was an old staircase with a worn red rug. On top was an iron eagle. Suddenly Vivian had started to suffocate.

– Get me out of here – Vivian gasped.

Adrienne had dragged her outside. Vivian was gasping – leaning against the building – when Adrienne noticed a bronze plaque . . . "In this place the Germans tortured the Resistants during the forties war". It was more than an attack, Vivian had said she'd seen the carpet covered with blood and the suppliants being dragged up the stairs – their cries and all their breath had been enclosed in a vacuum . . . this breath of theirs that had not entirely left the place but sighed and moaned through the cracks and the crevices asking for respiration from the living . . .

It was a bit like all the heavy trips Vivian was always stumbling on. Hanging in her shop window was a rainbow crocheted cape It was so bright, like a Joseph's coat – it seemed to give off light. Vivian was very superstitious about this cape. It had been ordered about six months ago by a model, Cynthia. Cynthia was a bleached blonde with very fine white skin, impeccably made up. She was always looking at herself in windows, mirrors, metallic sides of cars, puddles of water – all the polished surfaces that reflected her image. One had the impression when one talked to her that she bent over to look in the other person's eyes to be again reminded of herself. She watched desperately for any wrinkles to appear. She took massages, saunas, spent all her free time in the beauty parlor and her money on creams and masks. She had been modeling for magazines for about ten years. Each day she made up as carefully as an African getting ready for a magic dance. She changed her eye-shadow with the time of day, from rose to green to violet or she made a rainbow lid of seven colors and then little silver sparkles around her eyes like drops of rain before the sun. Her lips were designed sometimes in dark purple, downcast like a mask of tragedy, or she'd paint smiling orange comedy lips. Her fingernails could be green, black or gold and were as long and useless as those of a Chinese Empress.

She was married to an Englishman (she was French) who adored her. He was an older man with gray hair and a mustache, distinguished-looking, who had been lamed in the war. He used a mahogany cane with a carved jade parrot on the handle and was always elegantly dressed. Rumor had it that he had become impotent from a wound in the war. He ran all Cynthia's errands for her. He'd even go to the drugstore late at night if Cynthia had a whim to have bubble bath or powder – a familiar figure at night with his perfumed packages.

Nigel cut out all her pictures that appeared in the magazines and kept them in a red leather scrap book. The house was filled with Cynthia's image. There was even a blown-up photo of Cynthia nude behind the bathtub. Nigel seemed like a gray shadow beside her – reflecting her light of gold and pearl. It was hard to say just how old Cynthia was. She claimed to be thirty. Her face was a mask. She rarely showed any emotion as if it would wrinkle her skin and give it lines. An occasional smile would flicker across her face like a Mona Lisa image, then the mask fell back into place like a carved cameo.

Six months ago she had ordered the cape before taking a trip to Germany to model for some show. What exactly had passed was never really known, but she wouldn't show her passport at the border. She had gotten hysterical and the news leaked out she was forty-three. That night she had taken a hotel on the French border and when they found her the next day, she was in a red negligée her hair fixed and her face carefully made up for her last rendezvous . . . a bottle of sleeping pills empty beside her.

At her funeral there were all her elegant model friends in veils and large hats bringing roses and lilies. Nigel was inconsolable and it haunted him, this idea of letting Cynthia rot in a grave. She would have hated the idea, so he got a permit to have her incinerated at Père Lachaise. It took time to have her exhumed. However, over a month later it was arranged – But what was the horror of it – When they opened the coffin, there was no question – she had been buried alive – Her hands with the long nails painted dark purple were lifted under the cramped space above her – she'd torn slits in the rose satin of the padded coffin – threads hanging from her nails. Her blonde hair had grown . . . it was black at the roots . . . What was her sudden moment of revelation telegraphed inside the coffin on awakening alive in a cellar of darkness – the lid sealed . . . one moment to scream, to be aware as her fingernails tore at the rose quilted satin . . . could anyone hear her? . . . Was there anyone outside? . . . Then nothingness . . .

It seemed the sleeping pills had just put her in a profound coma. She was cremated as planned, but Nigel was now in a mental hospital. He was always trying to telephone Cynthia . . .

– Are you down there? Just wait. I'll come down and get you
– Then he'd hang up his imaginary telephone and begin again.

– I'll come down and get you . . . Why don't you answer me? . . . Wrong number . . . Wrong number . . .

TWENTY FIVE : PIGEON MORALS

Vivian had all sorts of strange orders. Once she had to crochet fifteen straw garden hats, each with a colored rose, for some rich ladies outside Kuwait whose Arab husbands had struck oil. But in the town they lived in, there was only one road, the rest was sand, so the ladies drove around and around on the same road in a circle in their husbands' chauffeured Cadillacs, or they sat in each other's courtyards drinking forbidden scotch on the rocks. Then they took picnics on an oasis with dates and figs served on gold plates, wearing Vivian's floppy hats shading their faces against the sun, as they sat on an oriental rug by a palm tree – a tag hanging down from their hats saying – Made in France . . .

Often on sunny days, Adrienne and Vivian sat in front of the shop. One day an old lady walked by holding a basket. Her hair, dyed henna, stuck up in little hedgehog points over her head and she was wearing gold ballerinas with sparkles on them. Vivian's cat, Sphinx, a red Persian was living up to his name, one paw crossed over the other staring into space with an enigmatic smile on his face. The vet said the cat suffered from psychological asthma and at night the two of them would gasp for air together; but Vivian had to be careful because often he sat on her chest when she slept. Even though he was castrated, she called him her Prince Charming in disguise – he never left her for one moment. Suddenly Sphinx came to attention, his marble green eyes fixed on the basket.

– Oh, no, *mon mignon*, this is not for you – coo-ed the woman as she opened her basket covered with a cloth. Inside was a pigeon quietly standing without fear, its bright beady eyes staring over the rim.

– I found this pigeon by the church down the street. It had a bad wing and I've taken care of it for a year but the wing hasn't really healed and it still can't fly, though it's tame as a cat, eats out of my hand and sits on the back of my chair when I look at television; but now I'm bringing it to the veterinary to have him give it a shot . . . If I leave it in the park the cats will eat it – She pushed away Sphinx whose whiskers were too close, and at the same time shoved back the pigeon which was trying to raise itself out of the basket.

Adrienne looked at the pigeon. There was grain at the bottom of the basket, it pecked at the seeds half-heartedly. After all what could she do with a pigeon that couldn't fly, keep it cooped up in the apartment and give it beer to drink?

– I guess you don't know anyone who would like to take it? – the woman said sadly.

Adrienne and Vivian glanced at each other – a sudden guilty look as if one of them should take it, but they answered no.

– You're sure it wouldn't be better to leave it in the park? Maybe it would be okay – Adrienne asked.

– No, I couldn't do that, it would be too cruel, maybe the doctor will know someone – She put the cloth back over the pigeon, stroked the cat and shuffled down the street, her gold ballerinas sparkling in the sun. They watched the woman disappear down the street. Adrienne turned to Vivian.

– It's a funny thing but a few days ago, I thought I heard shots outside the window and sure enough someone in the upper stories had gotten a pigeon . . . It was lying on its side, the eyes covered with a pink film and its claws kind of tightened up under its chest . . . Can you imagine the bastard who did that? . . . I was afraid to move it so I told the concierge. You know how old she is, well she hobbled out, put her glasses on and looked at it. And you know what she said to me . . .

– You mustn't eat it, these Parisian pigeons are no good, they eat too much garbage . . .

I really had to laugh, so I told her it wasn't for that I'd called her, I had no intention of eating it, but I didn't know what to do with it . . .

– Well – she said – put it in the garbage can . . . But I cried, it's not dead yet . . . She answered, then shoved it in a corner, and before I could move, the old lady limped over to the pigeon and with her cane pushed it against the wall. This time I saw the pink film had covered its eyes completely like a tight sausage skin and its claws stuck out. She picked it up by a claw and threw it in the garbage can . . . Eat it, funny how the French see everything on the table . . .

Vivian was arranging a tapestry on the wall.

– Have you seen Hyacinth lately?

– No, for a real long time, haven't seen Daisy, I mean Hyacinth still can't get used to calling her that, since Arthur dumped the plate of spaghetti on his pants. She left me this tapestry. You know she's the only woman who can travel two roads at the same time, when she came and left me her tapestry – you wouldn't believe it – she showed me her stockings, one was red and embroidered on it was "absence makes the heart grow fonder", and the other was purple with "out of sight out of mind".

– Paradox is her stuff of life I guess – sighed Vivian.

– I wonder if it's because she once told me when she brought a date home to neck, her mother had hidden an alarm clock under the sofa and after ten minutes it would go off and frighten them like a time bomb. She said if she ever hears a phone or a clock ring when she's in bed with a guy, she can't come.

As Vivian sat knitting, Adrienne saw heads, falling – guillotined in the French Revolution . . . knit one pearl two . . . as the skeins of red wool unwound from her lap like blood. She remembered that under the store was an opening into one of those innumerable sewer catacombs. During the German Occupation, a Jewish family had hidden there until the Germans caught them. There was a graffiti of a Jewish star scratched on the wall in a corner, and there had been a tin cup, a child's doll without legs and an old coat Vivian had found on the floor, but she had closed off the cellar and never went down there.

– Do you believe in dreams? – Vivian asked clicking her knitting needles.

– Why? – Adrienne demanded – actually she did.

– Because I was thinking back . . . Remember when someone smashed my window last month? – she looked up at the window reassured to see the new pane of glass still in place, – Well, at the moment the guy broke the window, I'd been dreaming a thief had stuck his hand through the window. Of course there had been a crack in the glass I should've fixed, I'd only taped it, and probably I unconsciously knew that . . . well in the dream the thief's got his arm through the broken window and I take a knife and cut his hand off.

– My you can be blood thirsty, Vivian, back to an eye for an eye, a hand for a hand.

– Yeh, well just let me read you a little case from the newspaper I saw yesterday.

Vivian put down her red knitting, laying it on the ground like a tail of blood.

– Listen to this, I'll stick it into English . . . This woman kills her husband because he has a mistress, all right a classic scene . . . plus she has five kids, he rarely comes home and doesn't give her any money. One day he comes back to get a change of clothes, the kids are away and while he's bending over to change his shirt, she comes up from behind – knifes him and he drops dead . . . Okay, but now comes the problem of how to get rid of him, so she decides to cut him up into pieces so it'll be easier. First she cuts off his head, and listen to this, she puts it on the mantelpiece next to her clock with the two angels on it. She admitted she had to close the eyelids as his open eyes were a bit too much for her. Then she cuts his arms and legs off of his torso. After, she goes down to her sister who lives below with her niece of sixteen. They both thought it had been the right thing to do as he was a real bastard . . . so what do they do? . . . they put the pieces in a blanket, but not the head, and wheel it all in an old baby carriage to the Seine and dump them in. But the head is a problem . . . It's a real Poe story . . .

The next day is a sunny autumn day. They wrap the head up in waterproof paper, covering it over with newspaper, and then the wife and the sister (the niece stays home) get on a bus and go to some cemetery where their parents are buried in the suburbs. Can you see those French housewives? . . . One in a gabardine coat with a string of pearls and a flowered dress, and the other in a nice starched blouse and a pleated skirt – the wife sitting with wrapped up husband's head on her lap like she had just come back from the butchers. After they got to the cemetery, they threw the head down a hole where a grave had crumbled in, and when no one was looking kicked dried flowers and earth over it.

Almost the perfect crime, except the niece gets married and tells her husband the story on their wedding night. He keeps his mouth shut till he wants to get rid of her and later on the whole thing comes out. They found the rotting head, but still identifiable in the old grave . . . and do you know what the wife said at her trial? . . . I don't regret anything, by his running around like that he was a bad influence . . . he was corrupting the morals of the children. There's a real lesson for you.

She was interrupted by an old lady in a blue worn bathrobe with curlers in her hair. She called from across the street.

– What time is it, please?

– My God – Adrienne exclaimed – she looks like the March Hare, her white curlers look like ears. Vivian turned to her.

– Please say you don't know the time, every night she comes downstairs to ask what time it is. If you tell her we're in for an hour's conversation, if you don't she'll cool down.

Adrienne waved and pointed to a non-existent watch on her wrist. The old lady mumbled and like the March Hare disappeared into the hole in her doorway.

TWENTY SIX : S.O.S. SEX

A few nights later, she, Vivian and Arthur went to have drinks in a neighborhood Arab café. It was one of Arthur's favorite spots. Tonight he had a heavy hangover so he just slowly sipped at his beer. At the bar a few Arabs were drinking, having forgotten about Mohammed in Paris.

In the back room was a couscous restaurant, the walls decorated with camels and palm trees. The odor of spiced lamb floated deliciously into the café.

– If we had any money, it'd be great to eat here – Adrienne commented. Arthur groaned.

– I couldn't eat a thing.

Vivian, even her eyebrows were knitted together, was counting stitches. She was making another one of her creations. Arthur leaned over; there were tangled skeins of every color wool.

– What are you making, an octopus? Arthur inquired. Vivian looked up

– It's a sweater for a baby but the woman wants legs on it.

– Mmm – he sniffed – When am I getting my green hat?

– Next week, I found the wool.

Arthur was wearing his purple Indian shirt and Adrienne's scarf tied around his neck. His hair was standing out on his head in two celtic wings, his beard had studied shades of red gold. Adrienne was rubbing her feet in the sawdust on the floor making little castles. Just then, out of the restaurant, came two girls and two guys dressed in hip outfits, one of the girls had an Afro hairstyle though she was white, and the other had short cropped hair and big gold ear-rings. The men had the classic leather jackets and jeans. They passed by the table and as they did, the short-haired girl whispered something to one of the guys. He nodded. Outside they piled into a small car stationed just in front of the café. But they didn't leave right away. They seemed to be watching the table. Then one of the guys got out of the car. He had dark curly hair and a space in the middle of his teeth. He came over to Arthur who had his back to him and was facing a mirror.

– You speak French? He said in English, tapping Arthur on the shoulder.

Arthur lifted his head up, looked at him in the mirror and grunted.

– No.

It wasn't true, he understood a lot more French than he let on.

– Well, the girl in the car – and he pointed to the short-haired girl – she like you, wanna fuck you, okay?

The girl in the car was demurely smoking a cigaret and staring at him.

There was a stunned silence at the table. Vivian dropped a stitch and Adrienne kicked her feet so hard on the table leg, sawdust flew out of her shoe. She narrowed her eyes and stared at the girl. Arthur didn't say anything for a moment. He just slowly turned his beer glass around in his hand.

– Excuse me – he said – but I happen to be with a girl.

Adrienne swallowed her breath. The guy leaned over Arthur's shoulder looking at him in the mirror and slightly sneered.

– You mean you no fuck nobody else? It was a real male challenge.

Arthur stiffened a bit.

– That depends – he muttered.

The guy a little mollified looked at his reflection.

– Well I give you her phone number.

Before anyone could say anything, Adrienne opened her bag and pulled out a pen and a piece of torn paper.

– Here – she said her face a blank.

The guy scribbled down the phone number, tapped Arthur familiarly on the shoulder and got into the car. The girl with the gold ear-rings watched them, the cigaret at the corner of her mouth, the smoke veiling her eyes. As they drove off, a slight formed around the edge of her lips.

Arthur took the piece of paper, folded it without looking at it and put it in the pocket of his purple shirt.

– Well, well – Adrienne said a bit jocularly – Why didn't you go off with her?

_ Would you have liked me to do that? Arthur replied, a strange mocking light in his eyes.

She answered coyly.

–It's not my affair.

He got up.

– I gotta take a piss – and went to the back.

Vivian gave Adrienne a knowing look and went on knitting.

– Just think – Adrienne said gritting her teeth – He couldn't say to the guy . . . Look I'm living with a girl or he would have been blacklisted. It's like those guys that say to you . . . Why don't you want to make it? . . . You're not frigid are you? . . . What's the matter, you're a liberated woman, no? . . . So the first thing you're supposed to do is spread your legs apart to prove you're a hot-blooded female.

Vivian looked at her.

– What would you have done if he'd gone off with the bitch?

– Well you goddamn well know I couldn't say anything. I'd have to play it cool . . . but when he came back I'd probably go wild and make a scene . . . It's so fucking modern to play it cool. Smile and say why don't you do it again. But I guess I'll never learn.

Arthur came back. Everyone felt the evening was over. They walked Vivian to her shop. Arthur didn't say anything and Adrienne ignored him. Just before the house, Arthur broke the silence.

– You didn't like the girl wanting to fuck me?

– Oh, don't be silly – she said noncommittal – you're a free human being – her voice cracked.

– Come on, tell the truth and stop playing games. I wouldn't the hell have dug it if some guy did the same thing to you, so I'm gonna tear this fucking number up. He took the paper out of his pocket and stripped it into tiny confetti pieces that blew in a quick flurry of snow around them.

Adrienne felt a strong rush of emotion go over her. She took his arm and squeezed it against her. He was silent as they walked into the house.

The next day she told Vivian what he'd done. Vivian smiled.

– Did you ever think, dear girl, that he'd already memorized the phone number. Adrienne looked at her astonished for a moment, and then they both began to laugh.

TWENTY SEVEN : THE SNOWFLAKE

When all the other bars and cafés closed at night, everyone went to the Snowflake. Its windows were covered with a facsimile of frost and inside, the walls were lined with white satin. Red lantern lights hung from the ceiling giving the place a hellish effect. When the bar was filled, everyone crowding together, the walls seemed to be covered with hot ice that burned and froze with an incandescent glow.

It was a white limbo for people who couldn't be alone at night, who suffered from an insomnia that no pills could cure, people on the prowl who were looking for their nightly ration of sex, or those who needed to drink till the last moment of oblivion, and the people who needed an ear to talk into, a telephone that connected them into some under-hell . . . with numbers pasted on the walls . . . S.O.S SUICIDE . . . S.O.S SEX . . . S.O.S FRIENDSHIP . . . S.O.S HELP . . . All the numbers one could call to know there really was a voice out there – before one called HELP and crashed into the void . . . and those that sat at the bar, their hands held across their eyes to blind themselves before the coming dawn.

Against the back wall of the Snowflake was a large picture of the *Titanic,* just before the iceberg was about to hit the ship. The iceberg, as large as the ship, was only partly above the water, most of the wall of white ice treacherously floated below. In some way, it was as if everyone in the Snowflake was aboard ship . . . drinking, music playing, ice clinking in glasses . . . all unconscious of what was going on below them, thinking they were still on solid ground while everything was swaying – a red light might go off, a rat would be seen leaving by the back door – a sudden cry for help in the corridor . . . and outside . . . was there anyone out there? While they were in their Noah's ark going down into those layers of flesh, down into the stokeholds of selves burning in the gigantic furnaces . . .

One day a man had dived into a pool, taking for granted it was filled with water, but the pool hadn't been filled with water that day, nor would it be in the future.

And ships didn't just sink, even when the chairs and tables slid across the floor and glasses broke and the water rose to your ankles, it must be from a busted pipe. But they were getting ready for their shipwreck, they were preparing for it – going down into the Scandinavian underground with the crashing and crackling of icebergs, high mountains of ice booming thunderously as they hit against one another, for underneath them were the catacombs – the Snowflake rested on bones.

The barman, Raoul, jiggled the drinks, crushed the ice, squeezed the lemons, juggled cubes, filled glasses with red wine staining the walls in spots of blood – shaking the Martinis in a frosted silver shaker and pouring the pale yellow liquid into curved glasses. At one of the tables was an American buying a round of drinks for his friends. Adrienne thought he had a dog on a leash at his feet, but when she looked closely at it, she realized it was a baby raccoon. Its black ringed eyes stared at her as if suffering marked hangovers from too many parties.

Suddenly she wanted to scream out to Arthur – we're sinking, can't you see the water rising, the icebergs cracking around us, as he sat there guzzling down drink after drink. Then the waiter, like a steward in a white jacket, brought her a cocktail ordered by the already drunk American with the raccoon. There was a large white ring of ice on the bottom and a small blue ring on top. She drank the cocktail and as she looked into the ice she saw Arthur's face – it seemed to be enormous and they weren't sitting in the bar, but somewhere in the Himalayas on an icy cliff looking down into a frozen world. It was dawn, the sky was flesh-colored with swirls of purple-veined clouds forming into an embryo. Arthur was looking off into the distance, staring at something very intently. His hair was flowing behind him in the wind like on the prow of a ship. His lips were set in a tremulous smile and his face was soft and open, expressing love and compassion, but the love was not of a human sort but blissful, rather it didn't seem to be directed toward a human being but expressed cosmic emotion and would have been directed to her only if she could have turned into a goddess.

Where she was she could only see his profile, his breath curling out of his mouth in streams of smoke. She could not see what he was looking at. She felt a great love for him, almost a form of worship. Then she saw he was staring at a nude woman standing on a pinnacle, but the woman was made out of ice. She was so realistic as to be almost human. Her long icy hair was sculptured strand by strand and her arms seemed to be stretched out in a gesture of longing – so fine and transparent one could almost see blue veins pulsing in the ice. In some way, the woman could have resembled her. Then the sun, an orange fire, rose over the mountain directly in back, and as its rays hit the statue, she began to melt, tears flowing out of her whole body and as the sun rose higher and higher, she melted faster and faster . . . she was a white burning candle with the sun flame above her, until only a reddish pool of water was left. Arthur became sadder and sadder, the illumination disappearing from his face and with a shudder he bent over and put his hand over his eyes. She tried to pull at his sleeve to say she was there, but she couldn't move. She felt a chill run through her heart, a sliver of glass from the Snow Queen's magic mirror. She sat frozen at the table . . .

Arthur looked down to his feet at a pool of ice and alcohol running out of a broken glass, fallen from his hand. The liquid made little paths in the sawdust. He heard the waves outside his father's bar in Atlantic City – inside there was always sawdust mixed with sand dragged in from the beach. Ever since he had been a child how many old men's and women's stories had he listened to over and over again like a broken record that had stopped at one point and then begun repeating the same thing all over again . . .? It wasn't my fault . . . It wasn't my fault . . . He was no good . . . She was no good . . . He left me . . . She left me . . . In my day . . . In my day . . . One old woman who came to drink always gave him money. He'd arrange to put the big bills on top when she asked him to get change for her, and as she couldn't see too well, she'd give him a large bill. Since the customers always bought his Cokes and candy, he had been fat as a child.

Here it was like listening to a row of parrots perched at the bar. Each one using his keyword . . . I'll knock him down . . . I'm thirsty, give baby the bottle . . . Hello sweetheart, when did you blow in? . . . In the early days when his father was building the bar, one of the workers who had been a literature prof but kicked out of his school for too much drinking and had gone into construction when he was sober enough, and he and the old man, before he'd quit the booze, used to get drunk together and Ed, the prof, had said that drinking was in the Third Circle of Dante's beginning hell, and the old man named the bar just that. He saw the sign lit up on the boardwalk, its red lights flashing on and off   *The Third Circle Bar.*

One particular day stood out in his mind. It was the day of his twelfth birthday. There'd been a big storm . . . the sea a raging cauldron of beer foam. At the bar door, in his imagination, he saw a Disneyland of umbrella handles of ducks, lizards, dogs, dripping wet. The bar was filled with people shaking water off them, pools of water growing at their feet as if they'd been resurrected from the sea. A woman sat at the bar in a low wet blouse, her nipples sticking out in points. An old man in a sailor cap and a wooden leg was leaning next to her.

The rain had stopped and the sun came out, the drafts of beer foamed over the tap into cool amber pools, he almost expected to see little starfish wriggling in them. For him the wood of the bar was a prow of a ship that had settled there from some old wreck . . . shadows and smoke made cloudy underwater reflections. People sitting at the bar were cut-off figureheads, bubbles rising from their mouths. One sailor had blue eyes and a flat nose, as if his face had been pressed under a diving helmet. A fat blonde in a rose satin dress was watching a guy in a striped suit twirl a rose; he stuck it under her chin, then dumped it into her whiskey glass. She laughed, pulled the rose out and bit off the red petals one by one with her large white teeth. They fell all over her lap. The man put his hand on her thigh to brush them off and to this day he could hear the satin rasping as his nails snagged on it . . .

It was summer and the life guard, off-duty, was there, all sunburned in a tee shirt, curly blonde hair looking like an ad from *The New Yorker*. He thought of how later on that image of the life guard had focused – himself as this image – of how when he passed beautiful women lying on the beach they would open their legs wider, or he, a Superman, flying some ravishing blonde in his muscled arms, triumphantly over the waves – a hero. He had later decided to pass his lifeguard test. He'd learned to row raised on the swell of the treacherous waves and then shoot out with the oars to catch the crest of the next wave, feeling the rhythms, but he'd gotten drunk the day of the test – the boat turned over and a life guard had come out in a boat. However, he'd been dragged by the waves onto the beach before they got to him. That was the end of the sunburned masculine dream of himself as a hero . . .

His mother had arranged the birthday party for him in the room behind the bar where they lived, their bedrooms were upstairs. There was his older sister, Edith, and her girl friend, Sylvia, who always used lots of make-up and his buddy, Hank, who had later married Liza. His mother and father were out, but his mother had left a strawberry shortcake with twelve candles, snappers, candy and Coke. There was a donkey tacked on the wall next to a kindergarten painting of his that they still hadn't taken off the wall. He remembered the painting – it was of a little house that looked like a shrunken suitcase for some reason ready to get up and move, a small bull-frog flat as a child's deflated rubber toy and those lollipop flowers that children always paint, melting like all day suckers under a rayed sun.

They were supposed to put the tail on the donkey. With a handkerchief over his eyes, he'd held the donkey tail with a pin in it, his outstretched hands before him as they turned him around and around. He'd tried to orient himself where the donkey's ass might be. He felt the wall and pinned the tail, he heard laughter, he'd put the tail on the mouth. Then they played blind man's bluff and tried to catch each other. On the sideboard were crystal decanters of rye and scotch.

– Why don't we have a drink for my birthday? – he'd said casually, as Edith lit the candles and brought the cake over. He'd remembered he'd blown them all out except one.

– You won't have your wish – Edith had said spitefully.

– Yeh, but I'll have a drink – He'd never drunk before. As he picked up the bottle of scotch, it seemed to give off rainbow-colored lights like danger signals,

– I don't want any – Hank had said.

– Okay, you sissy.

– Yeh, is that so – Hank had said angrily grabbing the bottle. But Edith had butted in

– You'd better quit that, or I'll tell Mom and Dad.

– Is that so, well I'll tell them you took ten dollars from the cash register.

– And how about you and Mary playing with each other in the laundry room, I saw you. He remembered Mary, the girl next door. It was the first girl's cunt he had ever seen. Edith was very prudish.

Suddenly he felt woozy and ran into the bathroom. The door slammed outside. He could hear his father, he was drunk, he hadn't stopped drinking yet. His mother was pleading with him.

– Please, Jim, don't make a scene in front of the children. It's Arthur's birthday.

– Goddamn it, aren't I boss in my own house? – and he heard them go noisily up the stairs, their bedroom door slam. His mother crying. He knew how brutal his father could get but he was afraid of him, he'd been a coward till he was fifteen when he hit back.

When he came out of the bathroom, he'd let out a scream. His sister in a black mask was leering at him . . . He saw himself about four years old. His sister was six. Their parents had left them alone for a little while one afternoon. He was in a play pen, when coming toward him he saw this horrible witch with a black mask and red curls. She leaned over the play pen and muttered in a crackling voice . . . I'm going to kill you . . . He'd screamed with terror and the witch slowly glided out. A few minutes later his sister appeared, picked him up and soothed him saying . . . Wasn't that a nasty witch, are you sure you're a good boy? . . . It wasn't till later when he saw the red wig in his mother's room that he realized it was his sister who had played both the parts, who had tried to scare and soothe him in a double character. Adrienne had given him a real shock when she'd put a red wig on once. That experience with his sister made him very mistrustful of people. It had certainly marked him in some funny way, as if there were two sides to everyone and in some unguarded moment they might show another horrible side.

In his mind, birthday and Halloween parties were linked together. The mask was always there. That night when his sister had played that trick, he had had a dream within a dream. He'd woken up and found himself in bed with his double, a dummy of himself but as he touched the dummy's arm, it was his arm he felt . . . little by little he came back to the present, his eyes focused on the pool of water at his feet.

Adrienne sat unmoving at the table, she realized she was somewhere where she couldn't communicate – as if she was shut off, frozen in her own iceberg, what was language – she used to tell her English classes – but communication. She had recently compiled an article for her students about the *Titanic* from various sources.

". . . The night the *Titanic* hit the giant iceberg, the lights went out on the ship and in the black water the other icebergs floated like veiled phantoms. There was screaming, crying, shouting, bells rang. Lifeboats thrown overboard – women and children piled in first. There were all kinds of stories of cowardice and heroism. As they lowered a lifeboat, a woman screamed.

– Let me get into the lifeboat . . . my two children are in it . . . I'm their mother . . .

The officer who was rowing the boat filled with women and

children bowed his head.

– I'm sorry madam, but one more person in this boat and it would sink. I must take the responsibility for everyone in here. I deeply regret it, but I cannot let you on – and he bowed his head lower.

The woman began to cry hysterically. Suddenly a low voice came from the lifeboat and a young woman said – I will change places with her. I am alone with no husband or children.

Everyone looked at her in a misty night. The officer raised his head.

– If that is what you want and the other woman is willing, we will hoist you up on the rope ladder and exchange you with the children's mother.

The other woman looked at her with an imploring look and cried

– Oh, my God . . .

They hoisted up the young woman. The children's mother threw her arms around the young woman's neck – I will never forget you. What is your name?

The other woman put out her hand and said simply "Miss Evans".

The children's mother was hoisted into the boat – everyone was laughing and crying hysterically.

– God bless you – called the woman squeezing her children next to her. The lifeboat moved backward through the inky waters.

Miss Evans stood at the rail of the *Titanic*. It was lowering into the water. Her pale arms waved to them till they disappeared like fine mist.

Later that night more lifeboats came to pick up what survivors there were struggling in the icy water. Where the *Titanic* had been, there was nothing, only dark heavy waves and a few empty buoys. Miss Evans was never found. Nothing at all was known about her except her name and that she came from Boston. If you go to Boston you will see a statue erected to this unknown heroine..."

What is language? Language is communication... The shipwrecked people swimming in the icy water cried out each in his own language... HELP... *SECOURS*... IS THERE REALLY ANYBODY OUT THERE?

She had written for her class words from the story on the blackboard:

> HELP SHOCK ICEBERG LIFEBOAT BUOY
> SHIPWRECK LADDER SURVIVORS PHANTOMS
>
> Make a sentence with each of those words. The blackboard represented the inky water as she drew the white chalk marks of letters – icebergs scratching the surface. How much was still hidden, lay underneath in the meaning of language... Language is COMMUNICATION... IS THERE REALLY ANYBODY OUT THERE?

"On August 10, 1977 the space ship *Voyager* was launched from Cape Canaveral, Florida. In it will be a record of Beethoven's *Pastoral Symphony*, a poem in French by Baudelaire, a passage in Arabic from *The Koran*, Rock and Roll music, American and African folklore etc... It will be a bottle floating in space, in an attempt to communicate with extra-terrestial beings. This space bottle will be sent on a message of "PEACE" blessed in the name of the Earth. *Voyager* will travel across the whole universe, through the entire solar system and beyond. The space bottle with its message has been constructed to last for more than a million years."

IS THERE REALLY ANYBODY OUT THERE?

TWENTY EIGHT : A PILGRIM AND A TOURIST

The difference between a pilgrim and a tourist is in Webster' . . . "a tourist travels from place to place for pleasure or culture . . ." The pilgrim is . . . "one who travels to some holy place or shrine". The pilgrim is looking for an energy that has been generated and left behind. Hermits who have sat in caves meditating for long years, their bodies so still that green moss covered them without their knowing it – and the isolated temples . . . bells ringing at dawn, monks bathing in clear pools and bowing down in veneration at the thought of a new day. Ancient monuments and tombs containing sacred energy as powerful as atomic rays but unused, gathered up after long years of meditation . . . energy so powerful that it would blast mountains and make them move. Steep cliff passes with man-made steps where thousands of footsteps had worn deep paths in stone. Stylites who had sat for years on columns, their bodies as highly-charged as lightning bolts.

And there is the voyage of the lover who goes back to his trysting places where the image has become doubled, for to keep a goldfish from dying of solitude in its lonely bowl, a mirror put behind it, makes it see itself again and again, but it is not itself it sees but the other and slowly chases this vision – turning around and around in the clear silver water on a new solar trip.

Afterwards . . . She had sat by the long pool in the Luxembourg Gardens. The pond lay covered with scum, old newspapers and goldfish drifting by like bits of orange peel rising to the surface. A faded rose eddied in the ripples and a child's green plastic toy, crushed out of shape, floated on the water. Moss covered the wall. The water was olive green, oily.

In the back, a cascade of water dripped down over a marble pair of lovers, Cupid and Psyche. Next to Cupid stood the two stone vases taken from the two fountains of sweet and bitter water. Over Pysche's lips he rubbed the bitter water and the sweet water over her hair. Was it feminine curiosity that had ruined her? Daring to look at her naked lover when he had warned her he must never be seen and only came to her at night. She was lying nude on her lover's knee, butterfly wings rising from her shoulder, her head thrown back, her eyes closed. He was tenderly embracing her. Was this the scene before she had leaned over him with her candle and had seen his incredible beauty only to lose him as the hot wax fell on his shoulder awakening him to her loss of faith and then disappearing for good – and was not the prophecy made that she was to be the bride of no mortal lover but that her future husband awaited her on the top of a mountain – a monster whom neither gods nor men could resist? But she could not believe her lover existed without her "seeing" him. What was love then but an act of faith? Psyche, the butterfly soul, the beginning of psychoanalysis – for who was this dark monster that lived with one, but exactly where should one shine the candle so as not to awaken the dark side?

They had sat on the iron chairs watching the olive water, saying nothing but she could feel his presence beside her. They had not touched or looked at one another. His eyes were fixed on the marble statues, a cigaret at the corner of his lips gave out a slow streamer of smoke.

But it was difficult to go back – the cafés, houses, rooms were constantly being torn down. On the demolition lots, only imprints of wall paper and shadow pictures of strange forms were X-rayed on the walls. A pigeon with a pink iridescent throat came and sat on Psyche's hand. Perhaps one of the homing pigeons of her childhood flying over the roofs and seas to return again to her. Could she tie a message to its foot and send it back to her childhood?

Look, I'm grown-up now. I tried so hard, oh lady of the Chinese cabinet, to let you cross the pond and meet your mandarin. Here I am now watching these marble lovers sculptured out of one block of marble and they are together always, but they are not flesh and blood. They could only be a monument on a tomb of lovers who have now crumbled away – yes marble is solid but flesh separates.

She stopped the message she had been writing in her mind. He had been next to her in the chair, so close but not touching. A linden blossom fell on the pool scum, a yellow metro ticket sailed along the water. She seemed to remember he had taken a photo of the lovers, then a black guy with sunglasses had come along and taken pictures also. After it had begun to rain.

TWENTY NINE :   LA DAME DE MIDI

That summer they were going to go for a couple of days to Provence with an American friend of Adrienne's, Linda, whom she'd met about five years ago teaching English. Since then Linda had married a rich Frenchman, Jean, who worked with his father in an agricultural enterprise. Linda wasn't too happy with Jean and was glad to take her friends with her. She had been a fervent communist from a very poor family in Southern California and couldn't adjust to the intricate manners of her rich French in-laws.

They left late, at the end of the day, and decided to spend the night in a motel as Jean had a business appointment in Chartres early in the morning. Jean was generously sponsoring the trip or of course they couldn't have made it.

They drove along the autoroute. The oily sun burned endlessly along the horizon. They stopped at a picnic lot with a few trailers at the side and a motel surrounded by a wire fence and stumpy trees. A public toilet door was open and a broken mirror reflected the setting sun which was slowly going out like a smoldering cigaret butt dropping ashes of darkness – newly ignited by a flickering moon striking on the tinder sky.

In a trailer a couple were eating out of red plastic plates while a radio wail hooked up to a howling dog lost in the woods, and a rat leaped on a toilet seat and drank out of the bowl. Along the highway a Cadillac – shiny black panther – glided on a macadam road far from the jungle, speeded on deluxe feet of rubber and dropped spoors of gasoline. Behind the car's green shades sat two black men camouflaged – closing out the crescent moon.

The next morning they arrived in the square in front of the Cathedral of Chartres. Jean and Linda left them. They'd meet later. The rays of the sun flowed out like yellow liquid splashing on the mandalas of stained glass windows into a kaleidoscope view with bits of glass fanning out into different shapes, then cracking up into other jigsaw puzzles of color. Here were hints of a biblical vision of the world juxtaposed into images of shiny left-overs, but one could have imagined as having been seen completed by Adam and Eve – now squinting their eyes against the tiny forbidden hole in the gates of paradise after having been kicked out – taking one last desperate look.

On the top step of the cathedral lay a dead pigeon, its wings stretched out, its head turned to the side as if it had been impiously dashed from the head of a saint – having failed to leave the city and bring back the far green leaf. At the side of the church sat an old bearded *clochard*, his head bent over his chest, a bottle of wine sticking out of his pocket. To Adrienne, the pigeon and the *clochard* were really domesticated to cities. They both hung around the monuments, churches and old buildings. She could not imagine wild pigeons, they always came with cities, like the *clochards*. Once in a while, the authorities dumped the pigeons and the *clochards* into the country to get rid of them, but they both always came back and nested again by the monuments and churches.

Inside the cathedral, they raised their heads to the stained glass windows – the world was turning faster and faster in a carousel of colored lights. Shadows of birds silhouetted behind the glass dome gave quick glimpses of a holy ghost spoked around the heads of stone saints. A plane thundered overhead vibrating through the stone walls. Microphones were placed on raised podiums announcing God's words to those who might still be deaf. Motorcyclists in striped sweaters and high black boots held on to their colored plastic helmets as if they'd landed from another planet. A blind man with a white cane was bumping into stone statues until an old lady finally guided him around. A Portuguese family had brought their new born baby sleeping peacefully in a straw basket, its humid mouth slightly open.

Everyone had clustered around the statue of the Black Virgin. In front of her hundreds of devotional candles were burning, the tiny flames shimmering like birthday symbols. The dripping candle wax fell into a tray hardening into wax ex voto objects of deformed ears, fetus, fingers . . . the Black Virgin, in a niche, reddened by trembling flames. For most of the tourists perhaps they only saw the Virgin blackened and sunburned by a long celebration of candles – the black not really intrinsic to her skin. There was a legend that the three Marys had crossed the sea from the hot countries, maybe Africa, with Joseph of Arimathea who had brought the holy grail holding drops of Christ's blood from the crucifixion. When they had passed by the Cathedral of Chartres, they left the veil Mary had worn at Christ's birth. In the early days, the Black Virgin had been put on display every spring but when autumn came they put her underground in the crypts – swallowed by winter like Persephone. Arthur and Adrienne watched the candle flames. In back of the Virgin, soldiers had left their iron crosses and war decorations. They passed by stone statues in reverie sprinkled by freckles of colored light.

Stepping out into the bright sunlight, they walked to the back part of town till they came to a canal where there was a sign: CANOTS A LOUER.

– Hey, that's a great idea, I'll show you my rowing – he said pulling on her arm – and we'll take some beer with us.

By the canal there was a little café in a pebbly garden. They sat down at a rusted table to wait for a boat to come in. Arthur ordered a beer. Two dogs were attached to a wire that ran from one end of the garden to the other. Their leashes moving up and down on the wire like trolly cars racing back and forth or mechanical dogs in a shooting gallery. Arthur put aside some beer to take on the boat. She could see him becoming expansive. He had brought his camera but had not taken any pictures of the statues in the cathedral. His eyes had a mossy film, a bit like the oily water. There were a few fading water lilies and a waxy candy wrapper floating flower-like on the scummy canal. A boat arrived. It was partly filled with water. They took off their shoes and socks, Arthur adjusting the oars.

– Now don't get carried away and turn the boat over like you did for your life guard test in Atlantic City – she jibed.

He dipped his hand in the water and splashed her. Then he built up a rhythm and the oars passed smoothly over the oily water. They passed great round sewer pipes blocked with mud leading down into the water, modern buildings with terraces overlooked them, but little by little disappeared as they drifted on, and small houses arose with glades of trees, their overhanging branches sweeping into the water. In the far distance, a swan glided as tiny as inside a plastic globe that children take into the bath with them.

They passed boats with boys and girls lying sprawled out, the girls' hands pink fish trailing in the water, their faces and hair wet after a water fight. White petals were falling like snow flurries over the water.

– Dandruff from snow queens – Arthur said, shaking his hair, the petals flying out in clusters of moths from his beard.

He picked up his bottle and took a swallow of beer. Butterflies landed on the canal like water skiers and quickly took off again. Suddenly Adrienne felt something at her toe. It was a little green frog gazing at her, its round yellow eyes fixed. Then it turned abruptly and leaped under Arthur's seat. He leaned over to catch it when he made a false move, before he could get his balance the boat rocked and he fell in, head first. He splashed around, coming up with an astonished look and began moving the boat up and down. Adrienne shrieked afraid she might join him. Finally he heaved himself into the boat and shook himself like a wet dog spraying the water over Adrienne.

– Well I'll be goddammed – and he began to laugh. Adrienne joined him, laughing so hard she began to cough.

– You'd better watch it or you'll be next – he admonished.

The frog seemed highly amused and on the trip back kept jumping from one end of the boat to the other.

When they arrived back at the café, the man looked at them in wonder. They informed him there was a frog in the boat. He leaned over the murky boat water and deftly caught the creature. Then letting it go – the little legs kicked out in a practiced scissors' stroke – disappearing into the water. There was a splash, a few ripples and it was gone under the candy paper flower.

They met Linda and Jean and continued their drive. When they had almost reached their destination, they stopped for a picnic at an abandoned chateau Jean knew about not far from his house. They climbed over a broken stone wall following a labyrinth of shrubs at one time certainly arranged in strict grammatical precision with exclamation points of thin shrubs and commas of ivy now lying in a stream of consciousness landscape.

Adrienne bent down among the weeds whispering – Maybe I'll see the Red Queen followed by the March Hare – as she wriggled her fingers above her ears.

An enormous rusty flower pot had wisps of dead palm brooms brushing against the sky. In front of the château, stone columns braced the ornate roof. The windows were shuttered. On the veranda lay rotting wicker chairs on their backs and in a corner a crushed colonial helmet. The great bronze door had inlaid sculptured angels in mossy green, blowing horns. At the end of the labyrinth stood an orangery with broken glass panes. The wild orange trees in wooden crates still had little gold balls on their branches. On the mosaic floor lay a dead pigeon, a long line of ants crawling out of its beak.

Back in the garden was an empty stone pond with weeds growing out of the cracks in the cement. Two bronze frogs that used to spit out water were dry, their mouths open, gasping for air. Cedar, mulberry, umbrella pines and exotic shrubs grew about now in jungle style. Jean said the house had belonged to a Frenchman who had built railroads in Ethiopia. Haile Selassie had even come to dinner here one day (lazily eating dates on gold plates, thought Adrienne). Jean's grandfather had visited the house and he had said there were stuffed lion heads, dried lizards, eland horns and an enormous stone falcon the man had found in the sand in Ethiopia. There was red velvet furniture, carved chess sets of bone and leopard rugs on the floor. There had been a photo of the owner in a colonial helmet, maybe the one outside, standing against railroad tracks in Ethiopia, holding a whip, snapping it at the sand bidding it like the red sea to open up a path and let his tracks stretch out across the country.

But even this house had not been enough for him. He had started to build another château against the stone wall but death had interrupted him and, as Jean's grandfather said later, an architect more omnipotent had taken him to his domain. Yes, Adrienne reflected, there was something about high buildings God didn't seem to like. Now the new ruins were old. Large fig trees grew out of the cellar foundations and stones had already tumbled down from unfinished pillars.

They sat down at the edge of the stone pond, took their shoes off wriggling their toes in the dry dirt and then opened up the picnic basket. Arthur took out the wine Jean had stocked up on and began drinking. They sat statue-like each in his own reverie, when a bottle of wine rolled off the edge, splashed and broke, the red liquid trailing on the cement floor. Arthur moved dramatically into the middle of the pond to try and catch it, waving his arms and bowing.

– Who am I Kubla Khan, Haile Selassi or am I Superman? – He leaped in the air – that is to be not to be, or am I the Great Gatsby waiting for this pool to fill up with the waters of memory? . . . This blood that flows out of me – and he lay down on the cement next to the spilt wine . . . Oh, Daisy, the illusion that vanishes . . . See who I am.

Suddenly he ran over to the porch, grabbed the crushed pith helmet, stuck it on his head and jumped back into the pool – No, I'm the Consul, beneath the volcano waiting for my desires to erupt – he put on a pair of sunglasses and held up his wine bottle – and this, dear friends – and he pointed downward – is the place of hell . . . God I'm drowning in all this air . . . Give me to drink, said the Ancient Mariner . . . Who am I floundering in these depths? . . . Ha . . . Ha . . . I weigh a ton I'm bright green . . . Who am I? Why you win the twenty dollar question . . . I'm Moby Pickle the last preserved American that sank in the twentieth century . . . And where was I captured? In the supermarket and cut up in a package deal for the frozen food department and who is the manager but Ahab stumping through the store on his ivory crutch, swearing a final frozen vengence . . .

Adrienne felt her hand touching something soft. It was a squashed tennis ball. She played with it idly, then threw it into the pond at Arthur. It fell with a thud. Arthur kicked the ball with his bare foot onto the grass, threw off the helmet and flung himself on the stone ledge. Linda applauded . . .

. . . Sand lay rising beside them and smoke from the new railroad smelled sooty and acrid leaving a black cloud behind in the wind. Vultures swooned in the sky, lions roared from behind Rousseau dunes, damask tents rustled, clanging the entrance bells, oriental rugs lay across the sand. A pair of lions crouched sphinx-like, held by gold chains. The ruins of the palace began to fill with sand. Hourglasses of sand kept spilling and spilling. There would be no more towers just a confusion of tongues. Peacocks brushed their elegant feather duster tails along the dry brush and trumpeted a forlorn cry. The desert sand clogged the modern plumbing . . .

A portrait of the emperor had once hung in the salon. He was wearing a leopard skin. His piercing eyes and hooked nose made him look like a bird of prey. He could have been a combination of an Egyptian god and a falcon. Crouched at his feet brooded a lion with a gold chain.

They lay there listening to the sudden blanks in the late afternoon. The cicadas fell asleep or forgot to sing. The clouds unraveled on the empty stone walls heavy with sunlight, dropping splashes of unexpected shadows. Whites of eyes fell behind slits of lids and the light chinking through the shutters on the veranda played on the tiled terrace in slots of yellow and black – a mimicry of the beast stalking its prey in a dim twilight.

It was early evening when they arrived at the house. Jean's parents owned acres of fruit orchards, but Jean didn't get on too well with them. The parents didn't appreciate his choice of a wife – a poor American with communist tendencies.

The mistral had begun to blow. The wind had a metallic sound moving in waves of static. It blew so heavily along the border of pine trees that it rippled them in seeming swells of water. From the lavender patch on the side of the house, there was a heavy odor of lavender sachets placed somewhere in hidden drawers or in closets as if ladies with white hair, or young girls in organdy dresses, might steal out of corners to greet them. The orange light was just going out softly like a candle burning down to its final flicker. A lost bee zig-zagged across the lawn, hysterical at the loss of its honeyed light. The frogs began their evening trio. Adrienne imagined them in white starched shirts with guttural horns, squeaky violins and a few rumbling basses. A butterfly tossed by the wind gave up and let itself be blown around like a white petal.

The house had been closed all winter. An odor of cellar mushrooms filled the rooms. The bookcase was filled with bits of yellow paper chewed up by the mice for nests. Adrienne picked up a book idly. It was Goethe's *Faust*, as she opened a page a black beetle fell out dropping on to the floor like a blot of ink. Linda came in and dumped down a load of American pocket books she'd picked up second hand in Paris. Outside stripes of violet and red lined the sky.

Arthur and Adrienne had a room upstairs. Arthur crawled into bed and fell right asleep, his mouth partly open breathing heavily. She opened the window wide. The moon was coming up, part of a crescent ring. The wind raised the clouds in billows of foam racing across the sky and the smell of lavender overpowered her . . . She felt drugged as she drifted off to sleep. Suddenly she outside the window. She put up her hand to her head and felt something sticky and soft. She held it up in her hand – a pink fetus object. She let out a scream, it was a newborn mouse.

Arthur sat up.

– What the hell's the matter?

– A mouse – she said trembling.

Then she saw the silhouette of a cat on the balcony. Its green eyes shining like peeled grapes. Certainly it was the cat which had crawled over her without even waking her. She looked at the window behind her, there was a nest of cotton and disappearing down the ivied wall was a tiny gray mouse clutching a pink baby in its mouth.

The next day the sky was very clear. The mistral was still blowing but was losing its breath. After coffee they walked around the grounds, inspected the big swimming pool but because of the wind settled in beach chairs by the lavender patch. Arthur lay on the grass and fell asleep. The lavender rippled in violet waves and bees buzzed over the flowers drunk with the odor. As Arthur lay there he saw a woman with a long black dress and a dark veil bend over him, she whispered question after question . . . what has four feet in the morning . . . two feet in the afternoon . . . and three feet in the evening? Her voice was far away, mumbled like a bad phone connection from a foreign land. Suddenly the wind blew up her black skirt and he saw she had furry sphinx paws with red manicured toe nails . . .

Arthur sat up and rubbed his eyes. The woman was so real he couldn't believe it was a dream. He told the dream to Jean beside him. Jean laughed and looked at his watch.

– You see – he said – It's twelve clock. His English was good but not perfect.

– Ah, *mon pauvre*, you see *La Dame de Midi*. She come to people who sleep in noon sun. Often the peasants get her visit. She also the *Demon de Midi* when old men go crazy for young girl . . . Watch – Jean said laughing and shaking his finger at him.

As Adrienne listened she thought of the Demon. However, Arthur's infidelity to her was *always* there. Where ever she went she had to count on a third presence. The lady . . . the bitch . . . the other woman . . . the whore . . . the mistress . . . the temptress. She was "Lady Alcohol". Not a flesh and blood woman which might have been simple, because when he really got drunk it could happen he might have a one night stand somewhere, but he'd always come back to her feeling very guilty. It was this "she" though who gave him everything that no ordinary woman could fulfil. It was the ancient proud Lilith who embraced him and took him down into infernal regions where she could never get to. There were no outings, bars, cafés, parties, conversations that he didn't stop to refresh himself on her. She stood there as a mirage beside their bed when his eyes were filmy and he was fucking her, he was not looking at her but above and beyond her. She was a twelve year old girl, a princess, a whore, a Mohammedan houri fucked not here, but only in paradise – not of this world. Yet she was caught in some strange reflecting labyrinth. He needed her to conspire, to mirror, to catch and also in some perverse way to make "Lady Alcohol" jealous to keep the oasis of her liquid coming.

She turned to Jean, he was pointing over the hills to his father's peach trees.

– This year peaches too low in price so my father cover the orchards in gasoline and fire them. Only most perfect fruit look like ruby and topaz he keep on trees. After the smell of peaches burnt over the country for days smell like jam brulé . . . those new made peaches so perfect they look like plastic. You know every year they spray the bugs and every year they spray more. They spray and spray and less birds and one year no bugs, no birds around and no fertilization of the fruit. A *vrai catastrophe*. One morning in the village the people not believe their eyes. In one garden big red apples, golden pears, lovely vegetables and the farmer who grow all this he say . . . "Look I save so much worry . . . Everything that grow here is in plastic . . ." and Jean stopped and looked at them with a straight face. They all stared at him and began to laugh.

– I tell my father to grow plastic fruit – Jean sighed, but I afraid he is not amused.

Since the wind had dropped, they got into bathing suits and went down to the enormous swimming pool at the end of the garden. Its wall had been painted a turquoise blue giving the water a dyed look. They sat around in beach chairs with drinks on the orange tiled floor. Adrienne and Linda took their tops off.

– You boys got it lucky – she said handing around the ice cubes – just think you are in a topless bar back in the States – she grinned.

Linda had straw colored hair, freckles on a stub nose and slightly protruding teeth which gave her a babyish look. They sat back listening to the cicadas and the wind. She snapped on the radio. A rock and roll scream of drums and guitars shot out. Linda jiggled her ice cubes up and down restlessly. Adrienne knew in spite of all the money, Linda wasn't happy with Jean and her in-laws; they made her feel inferior. Not that they were in any way impolite, it was the general tone. Linda said they had a fit if she ate her salad at the same time as her meat.

The girls rubbed sun tan oil on their skins. A butterfly attracted by the odor sat on Adrienne's knee. Its little green head and antennae staring at her like a visitor from Mars. They all lazed around, swam, ate, drank, then went back into the pool and watched the sickle moon come up reflected in the water.

– You know how much water's in that pool? That amount of water would cost a worker four months of his salary to have it – just plain water filled up new every month – Linda remarked. She still liked to gripe about affluence.

– It's a moon shining solid gold in the swimming pool, a gold moon slipping into its watery platinum setting – smooth as Cartier's jeweled window – said Adrienne, waxing poetic.

Just then some leaves fell into the pool breaking the precious gold moon into unprotected pieces. Bats whirled overhead and a few dogs howled in the distance.

As Adrienne looked at the pool she thought of what Arthur had said about Gatsby, the vision of the American self-made man looking for his dream again, his blood dyeing the pool red . . . and she saw more and more around her the disintegration of the couple. Each couple that broke up was a threat, for the moment Arthur was beside her reflected in all her mirrors, but she could see leaves tumbling down from the trees and soon they'd shatter their watery image into all those broken pieces.

She remembered Vivian had told her when she'd broken up with her boyfriend, Steven, four years ago, it had been so terrible she used to set the table for two, put another pillow by her side in the bed, and have long conversations with him. She said she wasn't crazy; she knew he was gone but it was a bit like a compensatory dream. She had heard about a woman whose husband had been killed at Auschwitz, who had made her room into a miniature cell with a life-size dummy of her husband which she put at the table and into her bed. She lived only in her past, never went out, the neighbors brought her food. It was as if she, now an old woman, had taken a photo of herself today and had erased all her wrinkles, smoothed out her skin, dyed her white hair black – but her face had become a mask. Present time was locked out of her room.

And when the two by two reached the promised land, what then? Did they go off and start all over again looking for someone else?

The next day Adrienne and Arthur took a walk down to the nearby river. It was polluted. On the other side was a chemical factory that dumped a steaming urinal acid through large pipes into the water. A sign was posted:

PAS DE NATATION – DANGER D'INFECTION

They watched white bellies of floating fish bounce down the river like swollen prophylactics. In back of them was a crossroad with a rusty statue of St. Peter holding two keys and guarding a fenced field of dry dirt and stones. Behind St. Peter, nailed to a tree, was another sign:

PAS D'ORDURE – STATIONNEMENT INTERDIT AUX GITANS

To the right stood an abandoned mill with its large stone-grinding wheel cracked in two, scales of yellow water flowing over it. By the side some stranded roots uncovered from a fallen tree, writhed by a dead water rat, its claws stuck upwards like twigs and the pink tail trailing obscenely in the mud. A torn billboard showed a smiling blonde girl drinking beer in a car over a cemetery of wrecked cars. A little farther on lay the village cemetery, its Brillo cypress trees scratching against a metallic sky. Arthur was lying down, chewing on a blade of grass, his head on her lap.

– Just think, in that neat little garden of tombs underground, God is busy scrubbing all those bones so white and clean . . . That girl drinking beer is making me thirsty – and he took a small bottle of beer out of his pocket.

– Hmm – Adrienne pointed across the river – see those metal constructions – Jean told me that's an atomic plant.

– Jesus Christ, take a look at that yellow piss-water – Arthur muttered . . . "clean old prime Nantucket water which when three years afloat the Nantucketer prefers to drink" . . . Shades of *Moby Dick* . . . It's a world of polluted oceans and universe . . . the white whale's been caught, the world's just one big fucking garbage can – even the air's polluted with second hand ideas and all the damn chlorine and disinfectant in the world won't whiten those lost words again . . . maybe only tons of poet's words dumped into dirty landscapes and water can purify all this crap. I once read a thing on the poet Rossetti. You know what the hell he did? When his wife died, he sat in the room with her corpse and stuck his poems under her head . . . and he sat there three fucking days watching her rot – those poems laying under her decaying head with the juices starting to flow over the pages. Well on the third day he couldn't take it and he screamed . . . Christ no, give me back my poems . . . And he dragged the sopping mess out from under her slimy hair . . . because without his words she was nothing but a fucking corpse. He pulled on Adrienne's long blonde hair and stuck a strand in his mouth.

The next day was their last day. They lay around the pool. Adrienne's breasts were sore and very sunburned. She hoped they'd turn brown and glossy looking like those pictures in *Playboy*. There was a reddish glow around the distant mountains as if surrounded by infra-red tubes. Arthur was sitting at the edge of the pool dangling his toes in the dyed-blue water. He'd been drinking all afternoon – making boiler makers, scotch and beer, then beer and scotch. Adrienne was picking up slices of saucisson on the point of a large bread knife. She gave a slice to Linda who took it and shading her eyes from the sun picked a pocket book from the bunch at her feet, laying her head on Jean's leg as he dozed.

– Hey, look at this frog hopping around like a pig in shit.

Arthur had just caught a frog and stuck it in a large pitcher after dumping out the ice cubes. The frog jumped up and down, its webbed fingers slipping as it tried to hold onto the glass. Arthur was staring at the frog and seemed to be trying to remember something. Adrienne could see his eyes – out of focus – a malicious gleam in them, his lips red, over sensuous. She knew at this time he was not to be crossed, one false step and it would be like going into enemy territory. Now she could see he was getting prepared to go on stage. His role was half tramp, a bit Chaplinesque, funny then breaking down into a pathetic imitation of how mother never really loved him, to a quick change of cops and robbers – he of course was the good robber and tried to get the nasty cop – or there was the heavy torturous scene of how no one really understood him. He was on stage and he played his act out, gradually drawing the spectator onto the platform and before the spectator knew it, he was given a subordinate role of acting butler who kept handing him the whiskey glass, or changed the ice or swept away the rubbish behind him; or the spectator could become stage manager where a single rose in his hand symbolized the whole garden, and soap powder sprinkled on the set, a raging snowstorm.

Each of Arthur's gestures was enlarged into his own symbolic act – a raising of his hand and he could draw liquid from a stone.

But while he was on stage he could stand no boos – he was the star. The play was by, about and for him.

– You know what the kids used to do back home to frogs? They'd put straws up their ass and blow through them till the fucking frogs bloated like douche bags . . . then they'd dump 'em against a wall and they'd explode . . . Bang . . . Bang. What d'ya think of that?

Adrienne didn't answer. Linda continued to read and Jean to doze.

Arthur leaned over Linda's pile of books attracted by a cover with an orange creature on it titled *The Monster*. An orange horned beast held two naked squirming women in his claws and hanging from his jaws, two others. Some green demons were hopping around in the background. Written on the cover was . . . "The biggest sinner the world has known – a black magician who put a spell on the entire universe".

He thumbed through the pages. Suddenly he stopped, his mouth opened, he tensed. His body seemed to gather in upon itself as in the first sniff of some hunted animal.

– Well if this isn't a bitch . . . Hey, listen . . . 'I, the Monster, killing this man Jesus, will be the servant inside the shape of this being of a frog, while making the sign of the cross in the name of the Holy Trinity' – he leaned over swaying a bit and made the sign of the cross over the frog in the pitcher – 'And giving the power of the Trinity to this frog, I swallow its power inside myself and it will be my servant . . . Then I pierce the heart of the frog with the blade of the satanic word of Samuel and into my body passes the Holy Ghost with the blood of the frog flowing over me . . .' Arthur stuttered – Jesus . . . 'And at that moment with three gold nails I crucify the bloody body of the frog . . .'

He dropped the book. It seemed as if something had clicked in his mind . . . photoed from the eye to the lens . . . I dreamed I got a letter from my mother and inside it a cut-up frog . . .

Almost as if his arm had become a magnet to attract steel, the bread knife slipped into his palm – with the other hand he grabbed the frog out of the pitcher and like a doctor doing delicate surgery, placed the point of the knife on the frog's belly . . . with a quick flip upward the pale skin ripped open like a ripe fruit, without removing the knife point, he jabbed it into its heart . . . the frog convulsed . . . pink slime and guts dribbling out.

Adrienne screamed. Linda pushed Jean who sat up abruptly. Arthur, glassy-eyed, stood up numb as if he had put a finger into an unknown electric socket – the orange sun blazing over him. Before anyone could move, he staggered over to a large pine tree. Hanging from a nail on the tree was the black top of

Adrienne's bathing suit. He tore it off and jammed the back of the frog onto the nail. It hung there obscenely, its split white skin enveloped open. Making the sign of the cross, he took the frog's arms and stretched them out as on a crucifix.

– Look at this all you bastards . . . Look at this, – he leaned over the frog – It's a goddamn fucking world . . .

He was still holding the knife. Raising his hand on the knife handle as if he was going to play a game of darts, he flicked it into the pool. Suddenly his body convulsed and vomit poured out of his mouth, – heaving and heaving as if his own guts would shoot out, he fell down under the tree into a stack of pine needles and passed out.

The others seemed stuck to their places. Jean finally got up, grabbed the frog, its legs still twitching, and threw it into the bushes. Dusk was falling. The red sky had become violet. The knife glistened in the dyed-blue water but no one made a move to pull it out.

They brought the books, glasses and food into the house. Adrienne picked up *The Monster*. The creature stared at her with its red eyes. Now she was the stage manager, butler removing the props from the end of the play, but she was going further – she was going to get rid of them for good so there could be no repeat performance.

She went into the living room and put some newspapers and twigs into the large fireplace. She lit a match to the paper. Flames shot up. She tore *The Monster* apart, throwing the cover in first, watching the orange beast blaze red. The pages crackled. Finally only black flakes and convoluted forms were left . . . clusterings of harmless black mushrooms but because they still looked sinister were tagged Trumpets of Death.

Still beneath it all, was this great "dread" of him . . . was he her "Angst", that philosophical bugaboo? It was as if she would be swallowed up by him – eaten like the monster with the woman in its mouth. She had to be on guard. He would drop her down to some muddy sickening bottom and there would be no more backbone that in its evolutionary climb had been so painfully won to hold them up – all this slime and gook of disintegration.

She went out to see him. A curved silver moon was coming up over the burnt out mountains. He was lying on his back, his arms stretched out, some pine needles in his hair, bits of dried vomit stuck in his beard. Oh, how she hated him when she saw him like that . . . back into the beast . . . his eyes were not completely closed – slit like a voyeur behind a half-raised shade. She felt a sense of shame, and also a sense of superiority and righteousness at the same time. She wanted to kick him . . . Circe turning her man into a pig . . . how did she feel? Triumphant? . . . Scornful? As she flung her acorns at him. She could remember nothing of his soft sensuous lips, his clear blue-green eyes . . . mocking, affectionate . . . his warm hands careful on her sun-burned breasts. It was like watching the beginning of a decaying corpse. He lay far away from her in a land she couldn't enter. A soft wind was coming up. She walked back to the house, got a blanket and threw it over him. He wouldn't be moving tonight. He was breathing hoarsely. Crickets in the distance sounded like the creakings of a hundred rusty doors.

She went to the pool. The thin moon looked sharp and cruel, lighting the knife that shivered flabbily under tiny ripples. Yes, he'd sleep the night through, but how much would he remember, or want to remember, tomorrow?

The next morning they were all having breakfast in the glassed kitchen when Arthur came in, shivering, hung over, the blanket around his shoulders. His hair was full of pine needles.

– You look like a porcupine – Adrienne quipped.

He gave her a murderous glance, and groaned. His hands were shaking.

– God, I need a beer. – He went to the fridge, took out a beer and sat at the table. No one said anything. They were busy sipping coffee.

– I can't remember a goddamn fucking thing except I was sitting by the pool . . . then woops . . . blackout.

Still nobody said anything.

– Christ, what a dream I had . . . I'm lying in this coffin on display in a funeral parlor . . . the coffin lid is made of glass. There's a bottle of whiskey on top of it but I can't move . . . I'm dying of thirst and there's this fucking bottle of whiskey on it placed right over my lips. A bunch of people are laughing and pointing at me . . . the next thing I know is I wake up on these damn pine needles . . .

– I guess I'd better get our stuff ready if we want to get going – Adrienne got up.

The mistral had started up again. The cypresses and pines crouched over with cramps. Epileptic clouds frothed through the sky. The wind whined and whistled like high tension wires. They piled into the car. Arthur leaned heavily on Adrienne, a pine needle still in his hair. He had a sour alcoholic smell. It was a silent trip back to Paris.

THIRTY : THE TOWER

More and more towers were being built in the world. They were rising higher and higher – stretched up in enormous erections against the sky, phallic symbols of power and the mighty father. In these hotel towers all nations came as tourists. Japanese next to German or French next to English or American next to Russian etc. Each one speaking in his own language, locked in his own room with his special combination lock – watching television.

On every tower stood a portrait of King Kong beating his chest and proclaiming his primitive might. The higher the tower the more the sunlight was cut-off from the lower dwellers below and those in these shadows of the long phallic towers banded together in committees demanding reimbursement proportionate to their lack of sunlight.

In the Montparnasse Sheldon Tower, the Tibetans had come to Paris to give the sacred Black Hat ceremony. They had picked a glassy and slippery mountain tower, a man made Himalaya where at night the rose-lit windows set the tower on fire.

The lobby of the hotel was spread out like a grand crematorium of cement and gray marble with potted palms in the corners. The clerk in the black suit sat at his desk, the king of the judgement hall, taking down names and numbers, giving out gold keys. Upstairs was the large salon where the Black Hat ceremony was taking place and downstairs was a ready-to-wear show for New York buyers.

The buyers were drinking in the Tropicana Bar decorated with pictures of pyramids, tropical birds, palm trees and a few lions. The ready-to-wear contingent were decked out in safari outfits; hunters in khaki outfits, colonial helmets, models in exotic turbans and tight jeans. The theme was adventure – the safari – but everyone had a glass in his hand instead of a gun. The buyers blended into the murals, strapped into white tight suits like resurrected mummies. Models with caked make-up, gold chains, baubles and trinkets jingled in gestures of harem slaves performing for an auction and eunuch salesmen preened like exotic birds that had been forced to land for water in an oasis but discovered all this was maybe a mirage, but cocktail after cocktail made the promised land seem very near, however not touchable. Models in curly, kinky, fuzzy, straight wigs rustled their nylon, dralon, orlon and stood crane-like – one skinny leg on the bar ramp, beads and chains strangling their necks as if they'd been made queenly captives. Screechy voices called, "Darling . . . and could you . . . and would you . . . and how much?"

Salesmen were feeling material and pinching asses with shrieks and guffaws of laughter.

– I'm getting ready, with my new line of tee shirts this season – said one bald buyer to a fat man. After Gilmore's LET GO . . . and YOU GOTTA KISS A LOT OF FROGS . . . and an Arab and a Jew on the same sweat shirt, – I got my new model stamped out with the spaceship *Voyager* meeting an extra-terrestial being holding a flag saying PEACE . . . he rubbed his hands together.

Suddenly from upstairs there was a blast of Tibetan trumpets and the judgement of clothes assembled in checks, prints, flowers, plaids, Paisley, stripes, zigzags, in a camouflage of the human form with bands of linen holding the mummy together – the flesh embalmed on the spot.

A salesman nodded philosophically,

—Take the clothes off and we're all the same, believe me Sam — He shook his whiskey glass.

Sam, a man with sunglasses, pondered looking into his ice cube

— Take the flesh off and what have ya got? . . . nothing but a skeleton.

Upstairs in the grand salon the Tibetan ceremony was being prepared. Wind blew in through the arched windows floating the crimson drapes into banners and crystal chandeliers tinkled their lobules. A blood-red carpet covered the room up to a raised podium with a microphone and a mass of yellow and red scarves rose fluttering like gigantic butterflies. Tankas of gods and goddesses floated on dazzling silver clouds, deer grazing at their feet. In the corners devils in flames — snakes burning their hair. Above, blissful hermits meditated, golden auras shining around their heads as sticks of incense blew streams of perfumed smoke through the room.

Arthur and Adrienne had decided to go to the ceremony. Adrianne still had a soft spot for the occult and Arthur thought he might take some photos. Unfortunately no photos were allowed. The place was already packed when they got there. Distinguished men and women looked as if they had studied Tibetan history in air-conditioned libraries, or bi-focaled scholars in gray suits who might have sat cross-legged in monastery gardens shaded by black umbrellas held by bowing Buddhas. There were the androgynous couples — unisexed . . . long hair, beads and jeans.

A few barefoot children ran up and down the aisles, one did a somersault, fell on his face and began to cry. Adrienne and Arthur found seats in the back next to a black American in a business suit and a Japanese in a purple kimono. In front of them were two heavy American girls with long flowing dresses, the earth mother type. A small almost naked baby was sitting on the lap of one of the girls. The other was complaining.

– I wanted to take the kids to Tibet, or as near to it as I could get, but after my divorce my ex went to California and when it was his turn to have the kids he used to take them all the time to Disneyland, and since then the kids don't want to go to Tibet with me, but stay with him and go to Disneyland.

Two Tibetans in saffron robes advanced into the room holding trumpets and letting out blasts. The trumpets were so long that they reached like divining rods ready to bring forth water from unknown sources.

Everyone got up as a large, fleshy Tibetan came in escorted by a retinue of more saffron-colored monks. He was wearing a red pointed hat with earflaps. His face was as smooth as a china doll and he was smiling. He looked like one of those fat happy buddhas one sees in curio shops. His yellow robe was decolleté on one shoulder. He composedly sat down on a throne-like chair. Incense snakes curled over his head. Adrienne whispered to Arthur

– I read this is the sixteenth re-incarnation that he can remember.

Arthur suddenly saw the broken mirror in the bar with all its thousands of reflecting faces all the same and in the midst, the grinning ape.

Then the incantations began, voices and music came from far away as if the back walls of the Sheldon Tower had opened up into an immense cavern where piped music wailed across the loud speaker from another time. The door opened and some Zen monks filed in and sat down in Buddha postures along the side of the podium, their hands crossed, their black robes still as shadows – austere, unmoving while the Tibetans exploded in rainbow rockets of fire – the dark and the light.

All the time the fat Buddha-like figure on the podium kept on smiling . . . a smile like a crack in a garden door that opened into some wonderland . . . a sparkling jewel of light. It was the jewel inside oneself . . . the "OM MANI PADME HUM".

As the incense smoke filled the room, things became hazy and she saw herself as a child in Central Park. She was thirteen and she had gone with her younger sister to visit the Indian Cave which was on 72nd Street. Many times later she had gone back but she could never find it again. Maybe it had been covered over. It was a small empty cave with wide iron bars across it.

That afternoon she and her sister had climbed over the bars and into the tiny cave. A young blonde boy stood watching them through the bars. If it had been once an Indian cave, there was nothing left to prove it. It stank of piss. There was a rotting comic book of Superman, a rusting bean can, a gold bottle top and some ashes where maybe a bum had camped on a rainy day. The other entrance to the cave led over a mound of dirt to a small creek and back into the park. She had said in a low voice to her sister there certainly must be Indian treasure or jewels in a cave like this and she had begun scratching under a stone. Her back was to the boy. The boy stared at them, then climbed over the bars and came up to her . . . I heard you . . . You've found some jewels . . . You've put it under your dress and he picked up her dress and tried to pull down her pants . . . She had been very frightened and had mumbled . . . I . . . I was only playing. Her sister stood there, her mouth open. Just then a couple came by and peered through the bars. The boy took off through the back entrance. After that she kept imaginary treasures to herself – only the smile –   could that be an indication of the jewel inside oneself? OM MANI PADME HUM – the jewel that must be washed constantly to keep it from clouding – purify the eyes, the nose, the mouth.

What of the smile of the Mona Lisa? That smile of mystery, a smile that does not communicate the secret. It is the smile of the Western world but not of the Eastern one, that was the smile of compassion that gathered and went forward to harvest. Think of all the smiles . . . the smile of the idiot communicating nothing "full of sound and fury", smiles of detachment, smiles of involvement . . . and how about the drunken smile – that leap into the absurd – no waiting for anything, time goes by on roller coasters and carousels – it voyages on credit in spaceships, it is not the smile of bliss which is self-contained future time, the immersion of self into some divinity – it is bliss without grace. . . the drunkard's smile is a step into the absurd where all contradictions are cancelled . . . where space and time are right now . . . no waiting, it's happy birthday every day in a universe of presents . . . except on waking up and finding only empty boxes and torn tissue paper . . . being fixed on one point – blindfolded, to put the tail on the donkey – only one can't find the donkey . . . it is the release from contradictions without the divinity as its focal point. And how about the beatific smile . . . the smile between saints and God . . . and the smiles of superiority . . . the leer, the smirk, the mocking, the supercilious, contemptuous, sardonic . . . The smile, my dear student, is communication. A man alone does not smile i.e. exceptions: the saint, the lunatic, the drunk and the idiot, even the baby only learns to smile at someone. What was this smile of Buddha and the smile of Christ?

Shadow lights of cars whizzed through the room and reflected into a mirror where broken colors of yellow and red flared out. She thought of the aligned double mirror in their neighborhood café which reflected the back street. People who seemed to be coming forward were going backward and as the cars rushed ahead in the mirror another car was going down the street and it seemed they would crash, but the mirror image passed out into space and the cars never met head-on except in her mind. She had once seen Arthur in this mirror and she thought he was coming toward her but actually he was retreating.

She was always looking backward as if in an auto watching the scenery from a rear window. There was no beginning or end and finally was it only death that limited the image of this familiar horizon? . . . There was her father stretched out in his coffin with his smile of death, his swollen hands folded over his breast on his maroon tie, so carefully shaved and powdered as if he would rise up and go to a business appointment, and her mother in complete hysteria wanting to give the undertaker his tortoise-shell glasses to put on in his coffin and still continue to see out of his now closed eyes . . .

The slow Tibetan chant, the mournful blasts on the trumpets and the ringing of bells brought her to temples of Buddha statues . . . She saw Arthur and her embracing, their legs plastered on two columns, a snake circling them and the sound of OM like the long drawn out moan of after coming.

Once someone had pointed out Henry Miller standing in front of La Coupole. He was bald with silver rimmed glasses in a dark turtleneck sweater. He was holding a blue and yellow box with red stripes under his left arm and she could see the words OM . . . till she saw his hand move and another O appeared. It was OMO, a soap powder.

In '68 boxes of Omo had been dumped into the St Michel fountain – below a bronze statue of St Michel victorious, taming the devil with scaly wings and a snake's tail. The students had emptied boxes of Omo soap powder into the fountain and billows of suds flooded it, washing out the dragon's mouth . . . Omo for grated cheese . . . or thrown over the stage for a snow storm . . . OM MANI PADME HUM

... And when the first Karmapa arrived at illumination, the Dakinis, those celestial beings, offered him a miraculous crown made from their divine hair ... Each Karmapa was coiffed with this invisible crown which only the illuminated could see. But one day an Emperor saw the invisible crown on the Karmapa and he asked to have a copy made to show other people so they could also become enlightened. A hat was made from the mane of a black horse and this Black Hat was the visible crown ...

On the podium, the red hat was being removed from the Karmapa whose smile had not diminished in intensity but seemed to be shining across the room. From a silk box a monk took out tenderly the Black Hat. Adrienne couldn't see the hat too well but, dark as it was, flashing lights rayed out like hidden jewels set in its band. The hat was placed on his head with the blasting of trumpets. Just then one of the large salon doors opened and two gays with sun helmets looked in, "Oh my ... we have the wrong door," they giggled, closing the door quickly.

The monks then passed around a silver dish with rice in it, a symbol of the universe. In the Karmapa's left hand he held the feminine bell and in his right hand the masculine thunderbolt. A monk came forward with a white scarf to put around his neck and with another blast of trumpets and a ringing of bells, the ceremony was over. There was a rush forward, almost a stampede to be blessed by the Karmapa and have a holy red string tied around their necks. Discreetly ushers came around with little wicker baskets. In one basket, Adrienne already saw a hundred franc note.

– Okay, let's go down to the bar, I'm thirsty – Arthur motioned to the door.

They walked down to the Tropicana Bar. It looked like an oasis of drink where everyone had indiscriminately gotten together at the water hole after a day of thirst in the desert and all sorts of strange creatures brushed heads, tails and wings in that first euphoric democracy – hippies with Indian jackets and long hair, the safari group in linen suits and helmets, some Zen students in black robes, Tibetans in saffron robes, professors in tweed coats and glasses, some elegant old ladies in fur jackets and as Adrienne watched these women she saw. . .

Preserved American women greased with cosmetic opulence voyaging in that foreign sunset of life menopaused inside splendid hotel lobbies and served anaemic tea under crystal chandeliers that lit the stamped array of cattle showing princely marks of ownership. Hotels where crowned heads of Europe once madly skated on marble floors. Bourgeois princesses, gliding on the fluttery red carpets of waiter and hotel clerk who bowed to their hidden sovereignty, changed at twelve into pumpkin coaches, their swollen tourist feet cramped into gold sandals.

Wicked ladies clothed in the perfume of "My Sin" spraying themselves with a past cultivated with memories from someone else's garden as they sat feasting on tiny larks cooked in winey sauces, while feeling the discreet dark eyes of tired counts glancing at their beaded bosoms. Heady with burgundy they belched out bubbles of an undigested vintage country. Finally after a decoration of princely gout, they took the baptismal baths at Vichy and filled their thermos bottles with holy water from Lourdes, a souvenir of undeclared *aqua vitae*.

She came out of her reverie as she noticed two Tibetans at a table pouring salt into their tea. Arthur squeezed in at the bar next to the gays who had looked in the salon door. Beside him were the earth mothers, one had her baby in a sling over her back. Her friend was saying

– Sunday is chocolate day for my daughter. I told her she can't have any chocolate during the week, then on Sunday she can stuff herself even if she vomits . . .

Arthur was crushed in but had managed to get his beer. One of the gays moved too quickly and threw Arthur's beer over him.

– Hey, what the hell do you think you're doing . . . fucking fag.

– Now, now mister – he said turning red like he had heat stroke under his helmet – I'll buy you another beer.

– You'd better . . .

Adrienne began to feel goose pimples rising on her back, it was probably better to get out of there.

– Oh, by the way – she said sweetly – let's go home, I got some beer in the house

– Yeh, then let's get the hell out of here.

They tripped over the fauna of the Tropicana.

– Who the hell do those fags think they are? I remember when some gay in a bar picked me up and I went home with him to try it out but nothing doing, couldn't get anywhere near a hard on, guess I'll have to stick to girls.

As they walked away from the Sheldon Tower, she looked up at the rose-lit windows.

– Look, honey – he said expansively, putting his arm around her waist, – we'll get a room in the Tower and order champagne and caviar and we'll just stay in bed, keep the curtains closed and make it on the nice white sheets and take bubble baths together. She sighed . . . it's a nice dream . . . she thought of a girl friend who'd freaked out on an acid trip and had the nightmare that no matter what part of Paris she'd run to, the Tower would fall on top of her and crush her with its great stone penis.

But wasn't she always living in a tower where if she let down her long yellow hair she might just have the witch climb up and not the prince?

THIRTY ONE : FISHER KING

One night they went to the movies to see something called *The Fisher King* about a man who could breathe under water. Arthur had brought a bottle of beer with him in a plastic bag. The sack made irritating noises as he dragged the bottle in and out. She could dimly see his profile in the low light. His strong throat moved up and down as he gulped the beer. She felt goose pimples on her arms and legs and she thought of Cliff her childhood sweetheart just before Chris, she'd never gone all the way with him. Cliff lived on Long Island where she had gone for the summer. He fixed cars, and on his day off he'd come to the beach. Her first image of Cliff had been of him sitting on the small wharf, his blue shirt open at the neck, fine light hairs shimmering at his throat, his sunburned face thrown back gulping down a bottle of milk à la James Dean . . . white drops trickling down the corners of his lips and as she watched him she had thought what would it be like for him to suck at her breasts . . . but she was never to know with him . . .

Much later there had been Sebastian who only came at midnight and left at dawn. He had been in some anarchist organization. She remembered he'd gotten up one night naked from bed to take a drink under the faucet . . . his mouth and face dripping like under a diving helmet. He had come to her through all the seasons . . . with wind and leaves blowing through the door, his cheeks like a sunburned apple . . . or he came in a trench coat, his sleek hair dripping with rain, fog in his eyes, – and in bed all was mist . . . or in the snow with flakes melting on his duffle coat and in the morning the only trace of him were wet footprints on the floor, or in the spring, opening the door to him with a new moon in back of him and red kerchief flaming around his neck. But then he didn't show up again. In the blazing heat of summer he had melted away and she never knew what had happened to him . . . and he faded slowly as she left another scarecrow in her field – an effigy to scare away something that no one was afraid of . . . till the figure was only rags and tatters . . .

The movie began . . . The scene opened on a deserted beach, there was the scientist who had implanted fish gills in the hero so he could live under water and only breathe on land for short periods. Along comes the heroine, a romantic girl with long hair, collecting shells. By chance the hero is swimming around, he sees her, of course falls madly in love and she feels the same. Alas, how are they going to make it as he can't live on land. Solution – she goes to the scientist and he implants fish gills in her also. Then she dives down to the hero and they embrace.

He makes her a house under the sea, no problem, no walls only fish net to keep the sharks out, sand-to-sand carpeting, coral sculpture in the finest tradition of modern art, a free aquarium with all kinds of fish floating by, a large shell bathtub where they bubble-bathe together and he washes her back with a live sponge. They even have television as he's found a mirror and arranged it at the end of their seaweed bed where they can see all sorts of sea creatures reflected in it.

But unluckily her fish gills get clogged and she dies. The last scene shows the hero swimming to shore with her body putting shells around her and disappearing back into the water. On quiet nights people say they can hear wailing coming up from the sea.

The lights went on. There was a lot of noise and screaming in the front row. A young girl with bushy hair was laughing and crying. She got up and ran down the aisle then back to her seat again. She was very drunk. She fell on the floor. Two boys carried her out mumbling and gasping – "I want a drink . . . I want a drink"

She remembered a story about a monk in a Zen monastery who had taken to drinking, but found the drinking interfered with his duties, so he went to his teacher and asked him . . . "What do you think is the best solution to stop drinking?"

The teacher looked at him intently for a moment, stroked his chin and answered . . . "Don't be thirsty . . ."

Arthur turned to her

– Come on, let's get out of here, I'm thirsty.

THIRTY TWO : INSTANT GOLD

With alcohol, like alchemy, he wanted to make instant gold out of himself. It was no accident that it was the alchemist who had discovered the distillation of alcohol, ardent water . . . *aqua vitae*, for distilled spirits was a form of acceleration of matter. The alchemist hurried up the process of time in his transmutation of matter. Arthur hurried his process of time with alcohol by trying to burn himself up in a sort of ecstasy, but he changed matter by physical not spiritual means. Everything had to be now, no waiting, not even for love . . . love was based on a chance throw, hit the lucky number and you win the doll in white on the wheel – but she wanted a love where there was transmutation, a metamorphosis where her love could change him and her into new beings.

There was nothing he would use of the ordinary world of rites and habits. He slept in his clothes or threw them off as he felt, – he awoke, slept, ate as he pleased. There were no formulas or conventions to break day into night. It was before biblical time, breakfast by moonlight and dinner at dawn. Those superficial guardians that were vague barriers against chaos were thrown to the wind. He was no Englishman who dressed in dinner clothes in the jungle. He sat naked at the billboard of an oasis with beer flowing in its water-holes . . . He wanted illusion.

So on it continued . . . They went through the rehearsal always waiting for the real thing, repeating the memorized words and gestures with a lovely sincerity. There was always some reason why the first night never came. Sometimes they forgot the words and then there was panic in their eyes and lips not knowing what to say. It almost became reality when the backdrop sprouted leaves and flowers but quickly wilted when they found their old well-worn script. In the beginning they were the only two actors but little by little other parts crept in, and sometimes there were stand-ins of themselves. Once they heard them rehearsing behind the door and through the keyhole watched their doubles in white painted masks mimicking them, leaving them dumb with terror. And occasionally false actors appeared and said they had been sent by the director and they lured them into other strange scenes that were not part of the act.

And then there were days they suddenly discovered they were reciting alone, saying words to a scarecrow actor when the wind suddenly lifted the clothes to show the handle of a broom and the words flew out like crows that flapped their wings and landed with laughing echoes – repeating inside masked holes of eyes and mouth.

Finally they were told the play would never be given and they could forget their lines but they were too much a part of them, so they repeated the same old phrases until they stripped themselves like old publicity billboards, leaving papier mâché masks rotting in the sink and the unfinished monologues parroting in an empty room.

The frost came early that year blighting the artificial roses on the sill, blowing paper petals into tired pink mouths that withered on the ground . . .

THIRTY THREE : CROSSING THE BORDER

And that last day she saw it reflected again . . . She had cleaned the house – all the cigaret butts, the crumbs and grease; she'd washed the bedspread which only looked more faded and scrubbed the stained rug. She had bought a bunch of roses and put them on the mantelpiece next to their island photo . . . It had been raining heavily all day. Then she heard him stumbling at the door and he came in. He was so drunk he could hardly stand. The rain outside had a sound of crushed tissue paper. He had on his army olive slicker and Vivian's green crocheted hat which she'd finally finished. Water was running down his hair and beard like the bronze masks under fountains.

– Where's the bee . . . err . . . ? – he stuttered.

– My God – she cried.

He fell on the bed, water running in little pools to the floor.

– Take off your coat, you're soaking the bed.

– Don't tell me what to do. I want a beer. Who the hell do you think you are? My company commander . . . a fucking princess? You always think you're better than anybody else . . . don't you? – he sneered.

It was then blind fury welled up inside her. She felt now she had crossed the border like in *Lost Horizon* and there was no way back. She was leaving her oasis or mirage. She was a hundred and fifty years old, skin hanging, her eyes bloodshot. She grabbed him by the raincoat. It ripped along the back with a screech. She tore off his green soaking hat, the ends of the wool unraveled like bits of seaweed. He looked at her stunned. She grabbed him with a strength she didn't know she had and pushed him against the wall. He slid down and she placed him back again, tearing at his beard.

– Get out . . . Get out – she screamed – I can't stand it . . . I can't take any more . . .

He stood there idiotically.

– This is the end, I can't take this life anymore . . . or you. All you do is drink . . . drink . . . It's not a life, I'm drowning with you, I'm going crazy . . . Get out . . . Get out . . . Saliva drooled down her mouth, her hair fell in heavy strands over her face. She was shaking, screaming and crying.

Suddenly he came to himself, he had turned very white. She had crossed the borderline of her illusions. She was getting older and older, her teeth were pointed her hands were claws.

– Fuck you . . . Fuck you – he cried, and tore off the ripped raincoat – Okay, you son of a bitch . . . I'm going . . . but don't go sniveling around like you usually do to get me back again or I'll spit in your face . . . It's over . . . You hear. It's over and I'm fucking well going but don't ever . . . ever . . . try to see me again.

He stumbled out toward the door, threw it open and without a look backward slammed it so hard the hall mirror cracked.

His torn raincoat lay like a frog skin in a pool of water. She kicked it, her foot caught in a pocket and out fell a pack of crushed cigarets, his key and a green candy. The unraveled hat lay like a pile of seaweed.

She fell on the bed crying convulsively, stuffing the pillow in her mouth. Outside the rain beat like sticks against the window.

THIRTY FOUR :
THE SEALING OF THE LIGHT

The door had shut and a coffin keyhole sealed the light. There was no need of a key now to lock the door. The closing bang rattled the windows scaring the nested rats and the gloom of evening shadows filled the room settling like mourning covers over the empty bed. The clock ticked. Breath went on. The heart beat. She would have thought that when the door shut everything would have stopped. There had been a death in the house with no body, only the weight of dead emotion lay heavy on the heart.

Should she light candles, incense and read *The Tibetan Book of The Dead* over him . . .?

"You will one day enter another womb, but make thy selection of the womb according to this best teaching . . ." Like the Boddhavistas who burn out their vices in a great conflagration, she saw this long passion burn out in an evening . . . Monks smoldering in a combustion of oily rags leaving ashed bones, black skin and teeth . . . and she saw the charred unconsumed remains spread around her in an ugly circle. It was like drowning seeing the past years in quick flicker images flashing before her eyes, squeezed into a few seconds.

And the days were split apart – the iron grille closing on the cemetery at six. The sound of an amputated hand clapping . . . The nausea of unbalanced thoughts swinging from desperate waves. Burnt landscapes compressed into coal.

Abandoned keys left from forgotten doors.

The leaves outside the window clung to the branches like dry frozen birds and the wind blew open a window onto an unfurnished room. The newly-bought roses wilted in five dead minutes. Another corpse piled up but there was still breath in the body, the funeral was premature, the flowers had already faded. The petals were dying and falling and dying and falling while the last agonized breath escaped from the creature's mouth, until finally this time the body lay rigid. The candles burning and dripping, burning and dripping in their slow sealing tears of wax.

Once he had said . . . "If I go, I'll smash every fucking thing in the house . . . the windows, the lamps, the mirrors . . ." Everything that reflected him and her, everything that gave off light he'd break. She belonged to him and without him she didn't exist. What he couldn't understand was her rejection of him. Because of her own fear of rejection – did she reject them before they did her? It was like a wound with a foreign body in it, build a wall around the stranger. She lay in a glass coffin with a piece of poisoned Adamic apple stuck in her throat, and only the right prince could wake her up. She had need of a hero, a prince, while he would rather be a frog, and an ordinary one at that. He ate out of her plate, drank out of her glass, wiped his dirty feet on her clean sheets, followed her around, and only left her to go out and get drunk and then come back and rant and rave about "this fucked-up world". She rejected him so he could grow outside her, not inside. She threw him against himself, against the wall of her reproach, where he would have to break open and accept her not as an appendage to himself but as a separate entity.

The whole system was built upon some masculine symbol of power and force and she sat in this closed tower letting down her golden hair for who in God's name to climb up.

And she thought . . . Wake up, Cinderella, it's after twelve o'clock and the prince isn't coming. He's turned into a pumpkin and you're no fucking princess in a dress of shining illusion but a poor scullery maid left holding a bag of ashes.

She had always imagined their affair to have been composed of rare pearls arranged in a special order on a gold thread of heightened experiences – each pearl a different iridescent color, from rainbow lights to smoky gray. Every bead arranged carefully on the thread, landmarks placed and cataloged. She could see the pearls gleaming and reflecting, small mirrors representing a special event; but when the thread snapped brutally, torn apart, the pearls scattered all over and there was no way to put them back in order, to remember which pearl belonged next to which. There they lay separated, cut-off, their iridescent skins peeling, fading, now looking like cooked fish eyes. Not only was there no order, but the pearls she had thought were real were false, and little by little her colored shiny experiences in memory turned into dark negatives . . . no longer fit to be developed . . . a few of the pearls she hid away in her little gold souvenir box.

After he had gone, it was no longer a love, it was now like being possessed. Psychic mirages rose in front of her screened onto an unconscious horizon projected in the crystal ball of space . . . she saw him everywhere. She had just missed him . . . A man in an olive raincoat . . . pouring rain . . . her heart beating . . . his wet hair dripping like a faun . . . She ran and slipped on the wet street. It was certainly a new raincoat replacing the old one he'd left on the floor, but he'd disappeared behind bars of rain . . . Or she saw his face in a diving mask pressed against a bus window that was blotted out by a flashbulb of sun . . . There across the metro tracks, a man in green corduroy going through a door and then the train vanishing down a black tunnel . . . or in a movie house a dark form that might be his, till the lights went on . . . or at home listening for his knock on the shutters in the early dawn as his drunken footsteps stumbled throughout the couryard . . . phantoms that rose like smoke from the fireplace or in the mist behind the window.

Once she was sure it was him. At dusk a group of traveling players were walking across the street, one in a white mask with just his build, bowed to her and then he put his arm around a girl in a white satin dress. His white mask was mocking. A boy playing the flute followed them. They turned a corner, the masked figure waved and they were gone.

But it was a love now that had become a drug . . . She was an addict. It was in her blood. Every image she thought she saw of him was a fix. She saw his face in the Chinese Lotus Restaurant, both their faces reflecting under water on the polished formica table – when she opened the steaming tea pot their eyes spilled together till the waiter separated them into different cups.

She went down into underground sewers to wallow in all the last dregs that remained. She wanted to scream, her movements were jerky like some puppet with a crazed master. Only the sight of him could restore her – How she wanted him. No matter if dead drunk beside her . . . snoring . . . smiling. She felt delirium tremens, hallucinations coming over her. Let him crawl over her like white snakes, scaly lizards, slimy frogs all sucking at her. But when the crisis passed, she saw cracked mirrors, the stained sheets, the heavy odor of beer that still hung over the room. She cleaned, washed, tidied everything to forget, to be reasonable.

It was no good. Would she go through it all over again? She didn't know. She put her long hair in a bun. Then one day she cut it off. She saw her tresses laying on the floor – shorn – and she remembered on the Island when one afternoon they had passed a herd of sheep being shorn – bleating forlornly, and he had picked up a handful of fleece . . . warm and golden in the sunlight . . .

She wore black sweaters and skirts, no make-up, her skin was white and translucent, her lips bloodless . . . dark possum rings circled her eyes. Any man that looked at her made her shiver. What was this riddle that to become herself, she had to deny herself, this craving for him to tear herself in two, this ambiguity again – the masked self . . . The changeling who in reverse turned from a land creature into an aquatic being, something pre-evolutionary that escaped her completely. She was chained to a desolate rock like Andromeda – to be suddenly swallowed by a monster who came out of the deep and would pull her down into the unconscious after all her efforts to remain lucid and stay on land.

On the way to give English lessons she passed by the Canal St Martin on the bus. Sea gulls flew over the water and then flapped, out of place, over the cars and streets nearby. At the edge of the canal was a small house with a worn sign: *SECOURS AUX NOYÉES*. The windows were screened so one couldn't see in. But each time she passed she saw the same scenario . . . A drowned woman dragged up with a rope from the canal. She was naked . . . her body greenish covered with scum, she was laid out on a black and white tiled floor, water gushing out of her mouth into a round drain in the middle of the floor . . . her pale eyes opened to the ceiling – And outside an old toothless man in a large black-brimmed hat was staring at her through the screened window . . .

Sometimes panic would seize her and she wanted to fly and leave everything behind her, running down the street, suddenly seeing his mocking face in store windows, hot breath behind her neck.

She continued her life, statue-like, numb, as if she were made out of granite. Everything outside had a heavy opaque look about it. When she passed the Seine the water seemed to be layer after layer of moss-colored marble where if someone were to fall in they would be caught and entombed in a heavy glass coffin.

For Halloween, Vivian gave a costume party. She wore a black mask and stayed for an hour in a corner talking to no one, anonymous – feeling without an identity. Adrienne stared at the threads of wool tangled in a corner and thought of what someone had told her of an old women's home where they were given threads of wool to knit and every night the nurse took the knitting apart and each day they were given back their same Penelopian wool to begin again.

Then one night she went to the Snowflake. She sat at the bar, the white satin walls glowing pink under the red lanterns. There was a dark-haired guy in a black turtleneck sweater. He offered her drinks. She got high and went home with him. Before the cracked mirror she saw herself split in two – half in shadow, half in light, staring at each other – two strangers who'd just met with a wig of darkness covering her in a lonely street where a silhouette in a doorway opened in a keyhole of lust and a stranger held up a mirror to an impostor he'd never met.

And she felt like those gray women with their legs stretched out in a tunnel of secrecy, hiding behind doors or in unlit closets waiting like empty bins for the masked coalman to ignite them with burning coals, warming their cold barren wombs . . .

She had a dream that night that she was in bed when a strange purple light dimly lit the room. She looked up and standing at the end of her bed was a figure in black gauze tights covering the whole body – even the head like a silk stocking bandit – the black silk flattening the features. She couldn't make out the face. His penis showed through the black gauze and over it in a black gloved hand he was squeezing a green fetus-like creature. She woke up trembling. After this one night stand she felt emptier than ever.

THIRTY FIVE :   PARADOX

Time went on and spring came, but bringing no new buds inside her. One evening she ran out quickly to do some last minute shopping not bothering to lock the door. Afterwards she went to their usual café for a few minutes. The moon glowed pale reddish, a bruise in the sky. The three muses were holding onto each other dreamily. Across the way a small black and white bitch went yelping down the street followed by two mongrels snapping at each other. She went back home and put some salad in the sink to wash it, when she thought she saw a worm on one of the leaves. She needed her glasses, she was nearsighted. Suddenly she realized she'd left her purse on the café table. She rushed back to the café. It was gone. Someone had taken it.

She went back to the house, shattered and fell on the bed completely annihilated. Why was that? When she remembered some Freudian interpretations of a purse. The purse was her cunt. She often dreamed of purses, large ones, small ones, ones that didn't go with her outfit. What was in her purse . . .? Her make-up . . . no new face to put on . . . a picture of her and Arthur, the picture was overexposed. A cracked mirror ... her eyeglasses . . . her sunglasses . . . a Kotex tampon . . . a folding umbrella . . . was that a masculine sex symbol she carried around with her? . . . a passport . . . a woman tries to prove she exists with no identity papers . . . her address book . . . no communication outside . . . her change purse, not much money in it and her key . . . but luckily there was

Arthur's old key left in the torn raincoat. But now the door was open to any stranger who wanted to come in. She felt weird, far away.

She went into the bathroom and ran very hot water in her tiny so-called yogi bathtub. She was adrift. She felt as if she had fallen into the Bermuda Triangle like William's brother. In this one moment she had left her purse with her identity and slipped out of time. The bathroom mirror misted, she saw herself as foam and flu. There she was suspended, zonked out – bongo – and she had left everything behind her. Could she exist without a passport, glasses, photos, make-up, mirrors? Was there somewhere else where she could acquire a new identity? Did she need to belong to an ethnic . . . state . . . cult . . . religious . . . political . . . sexual category? Could she exist somewhere without a preconceived image?

Could you love someone without a face, love someone without a nationality? Was one only conditioned to love images like on television that bombarded the brain? Were there smiles without lips? On just the obscene teeth? (Or expressions without eyelids?) Only a globed eye, unchanging, without the expressive creases of a lid – a cut-off head on the mantelpiece – for those who had no identity were dragged in for dissection.

Once a man had picked up a prostitute, when they arrived at her room she removed her wig, false teeth, her wooden leg, falsies and threw them all into a drawer. The man stood there stupefied. She called out . . . Well, what the hell are you waiting for? He stammered . . . I don't know whether to jump into the bed or into the drawer . . .? But what is the choice?

How much belongs to us and what do we need as standard equipment to belong? A friend's boyfriend had died of a heart attack some time ago and had been cremated. Her friend had gone to Pèrc Lachaise for the ceremony where she watched the life-sized coffin go down the chute to be burned and later she saw this tiny urn holding his ashes, not more than the quantity of a few burnt out cigarets. She couldn't realize what had happened to him . . . It was a leap into the absurd . . . the mind was not capable of solving this paradox. Here you are . . . then you're not . . . like a magician's disappearing act inside the box. Lift the curtain and he's gone. Of course it's all a trick – there must be a logical answer somewhere.

And in love did one receive some sort of enlightenment that only lasted the time of a flash bulb and to repeat the picture did one need again and again a new flash?

Now she would have to re-live her exile from him, for he was also in exile, not in his proper skin, he was neither fish nor fowl. He was not yet made for dry land. Yet the love she had for him was her agony. It ate into her flesh. It was a hair shirt that scratched her night and day because she could not accept him as he was. But one day he would come back to her. He would be wearing a white suit, his hair shining in the sunlight, his blue-green eyes open to their full focus with an enigmatic smile at the corners of his lips and he'd come to her, arms outstretched, announcing . . . Here I am . . . I've changed . . . and she'd go to meet him in a gold dress saying . . . Not only you, but I also have changed, but . . . then . . . then . . . would they still be able to recognize one another?

However, it was not for now. He could only come back to her changed into fire and light crawled out from his watery element. He was the Messianic future.

But there was another solution that frightened her, of accepting the burden of him – accepting every degradation that he could inflict on her and suffering it gladly as a martyr – that was what made her shudder, to what Christian agonies might she not be capable of suffering for him – yet not ready for Christ.

For this rejection went on from generation to generation, "Why have you forsaken me?" . . . IS THERE REALLY ANYBODY OUT THERE . . . And this rejection was a cross made to be carried on each one's back until it was finally shouldered into a redemption.

THIRTY SIX : GHOST TOWN

Then little by little they began tearing down the end of the street where the market started. The towers took over. The shop doors were walled up with gray brick and plaster and like in the *Telltale Heart* one could imagine the echoes of footsteps and heartbeats locked in behind the cemented walls. Windows painted an opaque white seemed to be eyeballs gone blind. The Arab cafe closed down . . . faint sounds of camel bells tinkled behind the back door. The Hôtel des Meuses closed down. Only the three stone muses continued to hold on to each other desperately. Once in a while a pigeon sat on their heads. Till one morning when she looked for the three muses there was an empty hole. They had disappeared. In the night someone had cut them out of their niche and carried them away.

In unwalled doorways *clochards* lay down to sleep on yesterday's newspapers. Cats meowed and crawled under the wood slats of empty lots where old ladies left bloody papers with chicken gizzards. Squatters moved into the deserted buildings and painted yellow sunflowers on the walls – smells of their hash and incense floated through the alleys. In the late evening shrill flute notes wailed through the closed windows.

But the towers were spreading out like great cancerous prostate growths. They erected into the sky ejaculating sick sperm clouds that dribbled away into drops.

Once in a deserted doorway lit by the late tarnishing sun, she'd seen the shadow of a man – a lock of his reddish blonde hair sprouting in a crescent moon – tender horn of a young animal. She had caught only a glimpse of him and he was gone – disappearing into a thicket of traffic.

At night the streets were veiled over into a ghost town. Sometimes a light shone out of a crack. Torn posters hung down like authentic pop paintings. In the deserted buildings rooms jawed open showing black cavities. And the Sheldon Tower glowed brilliantly at night, its pink candied lights shining out from aluminum paper frosting – a great birthday cake celebrating all the rose-colored dreams of childhood. The expectations that would come with a touch of the wand. Wishes wrapped up in plastic, fresh and new . . . never used, then maybe used one time and abandoned. Below were the melted, used up houses, their windows black holes where the birthday candles had burned through to the crust and left burnt dough . . . one dimensional houses of stale cardboard left for stage decorations where the wishes were now all gone.

THIRTY SEVEN : TOWARD THE SHORE

And as for him, he had gone back to the States, to California – but what had happened was that her rejection had not turned him into a prince. He seemed to lose his sense of balance; he drank continuously and one drunken night after a fight he threw his false teeth over a bridge into the water. They sank slowly, as inconsequential as being dumped down a toilet. He now sucked in on his gums and lisped when he talked. After a bad fight he went to prison and then spent time in detoxication – halfway homes – once escaping with the green striped pajamas, which he wore for a week.

At night he slept in the open laundromats on piles of dirty sheets. The machines turning twenty-four hours a day churned continuous soap suds. One night as he was lying there, he watched the frothing suds and he saw pale cherry blossoms dropping into light green soup . . . The last thing he heard as he was falling asleep was the sound of water bubbling and bubbling and he dreamed he was swimming in the ocean with his green flippers when suddenly they fell off – waves began rising and falling and his flippers floated out on the foam. Struggling and gasping for breath, he turned toward the beach kicking desperately now with his own bare feet . . . trying to make it to the other shore . . .